ADVENTURES IN SERENDIPITY

Discovery & Healing

M. Erin Earlson

Table of Contents

Chapter 1

There comes a time in every single woman's life when her friends decide she needs to date. Mothers usually start in early, but friends hold out until you are approaching thirty, or they are themselves happily paired off. I'm 29 years old, and my best friend, who is single herself, has decided I need to be fixed up on blind dates. I know she has good intentions, but she isn't the one trapped for hours.

Why do I keep doing this to myself? I let Jess convince me I need to be more social. Accept a blind date from one of her minions and find myself locked in the never-ending litany of "How great am I?" for hours and hours. I could be home reading, running, doing yoga, hell, sorting my socks would be more fun than listening to this guy drone on about himself anymore. I don't need a man in my life right now; I'm content. Well, having a dance partner occasionally would be nice, but I've got male friends for that, right? Seriously, I've completely tuned this poor man out, and he is not even aware of it. This constitutes torture, plain and simple. I'm NOT doing this again, no matter how much she nags, bribes, or begs.

Laying my napkin on the edge of the table, I scoot back my chair and stand up to make another unnecessary trip to the ladies' room. This will make the third trip, and he probably thinks I have issues. He's STILL talking. I don't even bother with manners. I just grab my clutch and walk to the bathroom. When I get out of sight but close to the restrooms, I pull out my phone and text Jess. Knowing she will read my text with the sarcasm intended, I fire off, "If you don't get me out of this disaster called a blind date, I'll do something horrible to your shoes…ALL OF THEM."

Her immediate response comes through, "Anderson Elizabeth Sullivan! I'm shocked at your callousness. Gary isn't that bad. Give him a chance." I can hear her laughing at me. We know each other too well.

I snort and shoot back, "He hasn't shut up about himself in almost 2 hours. TWO HOURS, Jessica Jane. I'd rather be at the gynecologist for 2 hours than go back to that table. GET ME OUT OF HERE NOW."

Jess sends me a laughing emoji and then a facepalm emoji before she relents and texts back, "Fine. Give me 5 minutes, and I'll call with a vet emergency. But you totally owe me."

I send her back, "I don't owe you a single thing but retribution for this disaster," followed by the scowling emoji. Then I smile and send her the facepalm back.

Stowing my phone in my clutch, I turn back to the table with a cringe. I can handle five more minutes without losing my mind. Right? It's five minutes. I slide back into my seat and reach for my napkin as Gary lets out a loud sigh and says, "I thought you ghosted me as the last girl did. Where was I?"

I smile benignly and resume my expression of polite interest. I don't even last two minutes before I start imagining teaching this guy a little something about me, well, about women anyway. "Hey, Gary. Gary. GARY! Stop talking." He may or may not stop talking, but I would continue.

"Listen to me. Lean in, and listen closely because this may very well save your life one day. You have not stopped talking for two solid hours. TWO HOURS GARY. I've heard more about you and your life and how fabulous you are at your IT job than I got out of my last boyfriend in 6 months. You've got to stop talking so much and, for the love of all that is holy, try having a two-way conversation with a woman, and she won't ghost your sorry ass next time. Did you get that? Stop talking about yourself so much and try asking about the female who is unlucky enough to be your dinner partner. I'm not normally so blunt or so rude, but honey, you really need some dating help, or you'll continue to make the female population consider switching sides just to avoid guys like you. Now, I'm leaving money for half of the dinner, but I'm leaving by myself. Best of luck, and I hope you listened to what I just managed to say in under 90 seconds." I can't help but smile at the thought of losing a tirade like that on him, but sadly, I just can't do it. Instead, I take out some cash and pass it over to him with a smile.

"Gary, this has been….an evening, but I've got an early appointment tomorrow, so I need to go. Here's some cash for dinner. All the best in the future!" I grab my clutch again and head for the door and freedom, just as Jess calls me with the fake emergency. Grinning, I look back to see Gary still sitting there, looking like a carp. I answer Jess with, "Too late, I managed my escape on my own. Poor Gary is sitting alone at the table, looking confused."

Hearing a big sigh through the phone, I can't help but defend myself, "I don't care, Jess. He was a complete dud, and you know it— no more setups. I can't believe I put on heels and Spanx for this. Totally not worth it."

"Why don't you meet me at Gallagher's? I've got a really awesome opportunity for both of us."

"Swear to me it doesn't involve men, and I'll consider meeting you. I need a drink after all that mess, but I was not prolonging my torture by ordering one after dinner."

"No men, I swear. Well, except for Uncle Rick, but he's old and happily married. Plus, you like him."

"On my way, but you're buying my drink. You haven't gotten out of trouble for this disaster of a date. Thank goodness I insisted on driving myself."

***

Gallagher's is a trendy Irish pub not far from our townhouse. We both like being in a trendy area where we can walk to just about anything, and Atlanta has a lot of options, with more popping up every day. I opted to drive home and park, then walk the two blocks instead of trying to find parking. Knowing Jess as I do, I know she'll have my drink waiting when I get there. Noting the patio is crowded, I open the heavy oak door to enter the lively watering hole owned by a genuine Irishman and his brother. I really like it, and it's a favored place for Jess and me to meet up with friends, grab drinks or dinner. The atmosphere caters to an eclectic mix of old and young, single and families. I am never disappointed by an evening at Gallagher's. Smiling at Cassidy, the hostess on duty tonight, I point to Jess, who is already ensconced at a bar table with two drinks. Waving at a few friends and at Phil, tonight's bartender, I plunk down my clutch and give Jess the mock glare she deserves.

"Do you even know me? I mean, Gabbing Gary, for Pete's sake? I don't deserve this, Jess." I give her a side hug and then sit down myself.

"I suck. I deserve to be beaten, covered with locusts and boiled in something," she says without an ounce of remorse and a huge smile.

"Diva," I laugh. "What am I drinking to erase the memory of the last 2 hours?"

"Phil has a new drink he's debuting tonight, so I said we would play guinea pig."

I interrupt and ask, "Haven't I suffered enough? I was guinea pig with Gabbing Gary too!"

Taking a large drink from her martini glass, Jess says, "You'll like this, I promise. It tastes like our last trip to the beach."

I take a sip and have to agree Phil has a hit with this one. "What is he calling this? Because I need to know when I order my second and your…third."

"Fourth. I'm celebrating. Phil's Pleasure Island."

"Corny but cute. Now, tell me what Uncle Rick has dangled in front of you."

"Us, actually. He wants both of us."

Jessica's Uncle Rick is a well-known television producer in Los Angeles who seems to have the magical touch for long-running series. I have no idea what he could need a trauma doctor and a veterinarian for, but I'm game to listen. As far as I know, Jess hasn't seen him in a couple of years, but her family is tight, so I'm betting they talk or email frequently. Jess signals Phil for another round, and I must smile. She rarely has a night off like this and even more rarely drinks more than one cocktail.

"No work tomorrow?" I ask as Phil drops our order. I added an order of loaded fries because I can see having to guide Jess home in the future if I don't get her some food to soak up the alcohol. Flashbacks of our college days remind me it's been too long since she cut loose. Makes me wonder what prompted this trip down the cocktail lane. I know Jess will tell me all, so I sit back, sipping my lovely cocktail and wait. As I scan the bar, I see several people we know from around the area and a couple of newcomers. Plus, one young family with the cutest little boy who is obviously beyond tired. Momma looks stressed, and Dad looks like he could use about 12 hours of sleep. Little man is having none of that as he keeps tossing toys and silverware with abandon.

"Nope," Jess states with chagrin. "I sort of got into it with the attending today, and my chief resident put me off the schedule for a couple of days to cool off. I'm fine, but the attending was being a first-class bitch who thinks she is the first woman to ever study medicine. Please. Step out of your Prada's and come down where the real work is done for a reality check. Prissy bitch."

"Wow, you got suspended from school!"

"I did not. My CR knows the attending was" ticking off fingers now, Jess continues, "wrong with her diagnosis, being a haughty know-it-all bitch, and finally, not listening to her patient. I just stepped up for the patient and called her sorry ass out before she looked like more of a fool."

"Ohhhkkkkkk. So, Clarence, he's your Chief Resident, right? He had your back?"

"Yep. Like always. It's just 48 hours off, so I'm grateful. It's been a few weeks since I had that much time off."

"Ok, since you've had a rough day, I'll hall pass you on Gabbing Gary for now but listen closely. NO MORE BLIND DATES. I'll get my own dates the old-fashioned way, k?" Making her look at me, I see that glint of laughter that tells me she understands but also that she's not going to stop trying. "Am I so awful I can't get my own dates?"

"You know as well as I do that all you have to do is look around this bar, make eye contact one time, and you'd have a guy hot-footing it over to our table to talk to you. THAT is not your problem. Your problem is you never take the time to try it, and if you do it by accident, you blow them off. You avoid anything close to a relationship and have since…well, you know."

"Since we are not talking about it, tell me, what does Rick want with us? Yes, I'm changing the subject," I say as I brush my mahogany hair back over my shoulder. My hair is longer than I've worn it in several years, which normally doesn't bother me, but tonight, I wish I had a hair band to put it up in a ponytail. Wearing my hair down went with the dress I picked out for tonight's date, and I didn't think about going in to change when I got home to park.

"Oh yeah! That's right. Ok, so you know Uncle Rick is shooting the second season of this series, right? I told you about it. Hot guys, strong women, historical fiction kind of thing. You wouldn't watch it with me, but that's your loss."

"You know I'm not a huge tv person, and to commit to a weekly thing with my travel schedule is impossible. Moving on."

"So, they use a lot of local people as well as bringing in people from LA and such for the production team. He wants to have an on-site medical team to handle simple triage stuff but also basic illnesses and such so they can avoid the downtime of having to go somewhere or wait for someone to come out. Simple enough, right? He also told me he has a lot of animals being used this year, and they're using the same guy to provide them all as last year. But, he wants someone who knows animals and animal care to basically protect the production company's interests. He remembered you went to vet school and asked if you might know someone who would be mobile. Of course, I told him about Doc on a Walk, and he said you were always too smart. He wants us to fill these two spots for a six-month time, possibly up to 10 months," taking a breath and a drink, she smiles at the server who drops off our loaded fries. "I'm all in, but I want you to go with me. Think of it as a fantastic adventure. We haven't had one since…"

"Since the last one," I laugh. We seem to always have adventures, but that is the best part of having a best friend. Shared experiences and adventures are what knit our lives together with so much color. "It does sound interesting, but I have to say, he could totally use local people and save money."

"Nope. We get paid scale just as they would, so it's a wash there. The only other expense is housing, and they have an entire apartment building reserved for people who work for the production. Bam! Next objection? I'm prepared for all of them, of course."

"What about the work I have booked already for the next 8 months?"

"He's ok with you taking off for those as long as you don't book any more during the time we are contracted. I sneaked a peek at your calendar, and there are only two things committed right now. You've got six or seven tentatives and a ton on your waiting list. You also said you were thinking about bringing on an intern or maybe even hiring another vet. You can't keep up with all the requests you get, plus all of your volunteer work around here."

"When?"

"Three weeks from yesterday. I got slammed in the Emergency Department last night and was wiped when I got home, so I didn't wake you up to talk. One of your bookings is during a two-week break they have anyway, so that's fate!"

Looking at how excited Jess is and seeing how she seems really keen on doing this, I state the obvious. "What will happen with your contract with the hospital? I know it's almost over, but you've been offered an extension, right?"

"I don't think that is where I am meant to be. All those uppity doctors seem more focused on billing than they are on getting to know their patients. I need to find a place that's focused on humans and not on the dollars. I've already declined the extension and have 2 weeks left. That gives me a week of sleep before our next adventure starts. Big bonus, we'd be doing this together!"

"Aren't you sick of me? We've lived together, mostly, since we were 14. I would imagine you could have this adventure without me and be perfectly fine. You're like a bright light no matter where you go. You attract people and fun in spades."

Jess reaches out and clasps my hands in hers, smiling sweetly and flashing the dimples she despises but uses like weapons, "but you are my best friend, the sister of my heart, and I want you to do this with me."

Squeezing her hands tightly, I smile. We've been through a lot together. Friends, since we were four years old, we've seen more lows than I want to remember, and this could be a fun trip. Jess and her family took me in when my parents were killed in a car accident that left me in the hospital for months at age 14. Our parents were the best of friends, plus they are as much family to me as my own parents would have been. Jess has always had my back, and I know she always will, even if she gets a little bullish about it. I glance down as I get a bit misty-eyed, thinking of how grateful I am for Jess and her family. Looking back up again, I squeeze tight to her hands and say, "What the hell? Let's do it!"

"Great! Uncle Rick is sending the contracts tonight because I know you! I know you like the back of my hand, and I wanted to do this so much that you just had to do it with me."

"You are cut off, Jessica Jane. You aren't making a lot of sense. Time to head for home."

***

Chapter 2

For me, Saturday mornings in Atlanta are usually filled with volunteering at one of several local animal non-profits. This one is no different. I stretched as I got out of my old SUV and headed around to the back entrance of Paws & Claws Animal Rescue. Noticing the drop-off pens had dogs in them, I walked over to take a quick look. One looks like a pit mix, and one looks like a husky mix, but both are on the skinny side and have "the look" of an abandoned animal. I get so angry when I see an animal that is just abandoned, but I've had to learn to bury that anger and focus on what I can control.

"Hi, babies. You guys are new and scared, I know, but I promise you'll be ok here, and I am going to take care of you!"

"Hey, Andi. I was just coming to see what we got overnight," says my friend and Paws & Claws director Gretchen Durant.

"Good morning, Gretchen."

"Morning. Looks like a couple of young ones. Skinny but no visible signs of mistreatment or neglect. I was late getting here, or they'd already be inside and being eval'd."

"Let's get them in, and I'll start with them. Any issues I need to address before I tackle these guys?"

"Not a thing. Two classes from Atlanta Technical College were here this week, and I'm really pleased with their work. Several have said they want to volunteer at least once or twice a month. Thanks for the hook-up."

"Great. What about the Georgia Tech program students? Do I need to follow up?"

"I'm working out a schedule with them, so all is well there too."

"Then let's deal with these boys, and then I'll just do a quick random check while I play."

"Whatever you want, Doc. Do you want them bathed first? I can smell the pair of them from here. Plus, we've got a couple of high school students volunteering this morning. One is exceptionally prissy and thinks she's too good for … wait for it…. menial tasks like bathing and grooming," Gretchen drawls with a dramatic roll of her eyes. "Why do these kids 'volunteer' when they have no desire to actually do anything more than talk to each other, text on their phones and hide from the work? Or do they want to snuggle the kittens and puppies but not clean up the crap?"

I grin and shrug, "Maybe their parents don't make them clean up after themselves? I know they need volunteer hours to put on their college admission applications. Those two definitely need to bathe these boys but let me make sure they are safe and sound first."

After an examination, some snuggle time and a bit of play, the stinky twins are sent off with the high school girls for a nice bath. Gretchen and I share a look that says we have a bet on who comes out with the most water and soap. From the happy looks on the dogs' faces, I'm going to bet they are in on our little joke too. They both have sweet temperaments, but they are still puppies.

Grinning, I head out to check on the latest crop of kittens that always turn up by the dozen during this time of year. There are only about two dozen right now, and only four are bottled-fed. Checking the littles out, I can't help but snuggle a little solid grey baby who is tinier than the others. I wasn't sure she was going to make it last week, but she's a scrappy little thing. She's gained a half ounce, so I'm feeling good that she'll get there. She's Gretchen's project for the moment; she swears she isn't keeping Tiny, but I'm pretty sure she will. As I put her back into her cage with her siblings, Gretchen comes in with a huge grin.

"Remember that actor guy I told you wanted to take a tour of the facility when he's in town?"

"No, but you know my mind is always on the animals, not necessarily on the business side. He'd definitely qualify as the business side in my brain," I say with a cheeky grin. Gretchen knows how much I love Paws & Claws, but she also knows I'm not getting pulled into the business side. That's her part.

"Well, I may not have told you, but that's not the point. I decided he's an actor who wants a tour, so let's throw caution to the wind and send him an invitation to the gala as well as a VIP tour."

"We have a VIP tour?"

"No, but for the exposure and potential donation, I'll create one," she states with a laugh. "Who knows, maybe it will start a trend. Anyway, his assistant just emailed back that he's coming!"

"Glad to hear it. Remind me when the gala is?"

"You are kidding, right? Six short days from today. Thank you again for the event planner. I'd be even more crazed than I am now. You sent back a confirmation. So did Jessica. Don't back out on me. I need friendly faces." Gretchen looked stressed, so I immediately handed her a kitten and reassured her.

"We'll be there. Don't worry."

"Good. Now, help me figure out what a VIP tour consists of so I don't look like an idiot."

Laughing, we linked arms and went to the front of the facility to take a look from a stranger's point of view. Two hours later, I got back in my SUV and headed home. Feeling confident Gretchen has everything under control and will wow the fancy actor until he leaves with an animal or less money than he had when he arrived, I spent the rest of my Saturday doing laundry and cleaning the condo.

Chapter 3

The following week was spent working on the books for Doc on a Walk and taking a hard look to decide if hiring another vet was my best option and can I swing full or part-time. I've got a waiting list of clinics and facilities that want my services, but I am not able to commit to their requests. After a long meeting with my accountant, I decided it was time to take the plunge and add one more vet on a trial basis. Full-time would be better, but right now, I have to put a toe in the water, so to speak, before I dive in.

A business that started as a pipe dream to allow me the ability to travel and still help animals has now grown into a real benefit to clinics and facilities around the US. If I were honest with myself, I'd admit this business kept me from having to put down roots. Since the accident changed my life so drastically, I've struggled to stay in one place. I love to visit new places and meet new people, but after a bit, I'm ready to move on. Jess tells me I am avoiding deep relationships by not staying around long. She also tells me I'm strange because I'm a vet that doesn't have a pet of my own. I am a bit cocky when I point out how quickly Doc on a Walk has become successful, and I'm really excited to tell her about hiring someone, even on a trial basis.

I know my old professors at UGA will help me find a recent graduate who has itchy feet like I do. I can't be the only one who does not see settling into a clinic and a 5-6 day a week job as ideal at our age. Feeling confident, I sit back at my desk and smile. This means I have to work fast, but if I do, I'll be clear about the production job with Jess. I'll still have to cover a couple of the jobs, but my new employee will cover the rest, and we can bring on a few more of the facilities on the waitlist.

"Where are you? Helloooooooooooo?" Jess yells at the top of her lungs.

"Office," I respond as she comes barreling up the stairs like a runaway train.

"Do you have your dress? Shoes? Jewelry?"

Rolling my eyes, I lock my laptop and stand, stretching up and then leaning down to touch the floor. Jessica loves any opportunity to dress up 'fancy', as she calls it. I am not a huge fan, but I can handle it. I'm definitely not a girly girl, but I'm no slouch, either. Easing into the down dog position, I look up at her and smile benignly.

"What do I need that for? The dogs and cats don't care what I'm wearing as long as I have treats."

"Oh, puhleeze. If it were anything but one of your charities, I'd believe you, but Paws & Claws guarantees you will be there and dressed nicely. Dazzling donors and animals alike. There will be animals, right?"

"Yes, Gretchen will have about a dozen dogs and cats dressed in their finest available for adoption."

"Dressed? Seriously? But you hate clothes on dogs and cats. How did you get on board with that?"

"Males are wearing bow ties, and females are wearing jeweled collars or collars with a flower. No suits, dresses, etc. because that is asinine," glancing out the window, I laugh and point, "I give you exhibit A, Francine and her poor pet Sasha," I put air quotes around "pet" and roll my eyes. Francine is one of our neighbors who has a chihuahua that she dresses up. Francine likes to think of herself as a real-life Elle from Legally Blonde, except she's not hunting for a law degree but a husband. Her poor dog has issues, as many chihuahuas do, but the outfits make her worse, in my opinion.

Jessica snorts and asks me what I'm wearing as she heads to her room with what looks like a dress bag and possibly three pair of shoes. Girlfriend loves her shoes despite wearing athletic shoes for most of her week for work.

"Black sheath with the rhinestone collar. Comfy shoes. Chandeliers."

"Hell no, are you wearing comfy shoes? You will not make that outfit look like old lady Betty goes to the theater," pronounced thee-ah-tah. "You'll wear the patent Louboutin's or the strappy Prada's you bought last year, or I'll drag you out tonight to get some new ones."

"I refuse to wear new shoes. The Prada's will work. They aren't killers, and they look good."

Jess sticks her head out of her room, wiggling her eyebrows and says, "And your legs look hot."

"Smooches to my bestie! Are we carpooling ourselves or ordering a car service or Uber?"

"Gala means car service. It's my turn to pay."

I take a deep breath and tell Jess, "I'm hiring a vet for Doc on a Walk on a trial basis."

"Oh Emmm Gheeee!!!" rushing at me, she hugs me tight, "We're celebrating this tomorrow night too! Our next adventure is around the corner, and your business is growing. So proud of you."

I hug her back and smile. Life is good.

***

Flourish was voted Atlanta's best event venue a few years ago and has been in the headlines consistently with weddings, corporate events, and galas for those who want every detail perfectly executed. The event planner I suggested to Gretchen nailed it with this venue. Hosting the event on a Friday evening may have seemed odd to some, but it saved a lot and let the venue host a wedding over the weekend.

The car pulled up to the Porte-Cochere, and I had to grin. This is on point. Guests are going to feel like they are walking the red carpet in Hollywood. The valets come to help us out of the car and give us both an arm to the open-air courtyard. Smiling our thanks, I lean over to Jess and say, "Car service was the right call."

Jessica immediately sees people she knows, so we split up. We're typically each other's plus one for events like this, so we have a system that allows us to roam freely and mingle. I immediately go to the animal set up near the middle of the courtyard. The volunteers look great in their button-down, embroidered black shirts and black pants. They are meant to remain in the background of the animals as much as possible. Dogs are happily sitting on leashes and panting as though to say they are having a great time. Volunteer pockets are stuffed with treats designed to keep behavior in check and create happy dogs. Directly across the way, the cats are showcased on high-top tables, with each volunteer holding a thin leash. If the dogs look happy, the cats look utterly unimpressed. I grin as I watch a cute 5-year-old Siamese disdainfully lift a paw and begin washing his face. His bow tie slips but is quickly corrected by the high school student assigned as his handler. Knowing I'd much rather stay here with the animals than socialize, I grit my teeth and turn to find Gretchen. I know she's got to be wound up tighter than an eight-day clock at this point. Spotting her talking animatedly with a couple dressed suavely, I head in her direction, smiling at those I know and greeting a few friends.

"Andi, you look stunning. The dogs are so cute, and I can't get over how well the cats are behaving! I was nervous about this part of the event, but you were right. It's a hit! The bow ties especially. All of the cats have been reserved for adoption, and all but two of the dogs. The other two are likely being reserved now if I can read Missy right. She's looking a bit ragged but is smiling. I'm rambling, aren't I?"

"Relax, Gretchen. You look great, the venue is perfect, the animals are perfect, and tonight will be perfect too. Take a deep breath and find yourself a cocktail. You need to relax."

"I can't relax until this is over. Oh my gosh, the assistant is here. That means Mr. Miller is arriving soon. I've got to make sure I don't pass out. Have you seen him? He's beyond gorgeous. I almost swallowed my teeth this morning when he came for the VIP tour. Thanks for helping with creating that, by the way. It was a hit." Gretchen looked as though she was going to have a stroke or hyperventilate, so I quickly grabbed her left hand and, with my right, reached for a glass of champagne on the tray of a passing server. Handing it to her, I sternly say, "Drink."

"Only a quick swallow. I want to make sure Mr. Miller arrives smoothly."

"That's his assistant's job, Gretch. Your job is to smile and rake in the money. Dinner starts in a half hour?"

"No," glancing at her watch, she startles and says, "Good Lord! It starts in 15 minutes. I need to go move your and Jessica's names to the table with Mr. Miller."

"Stop right there. You will leave us where we are. I told you I would sit with the junior senator to make sure he knows about the upcoming bill to make animal cruelty a felony. I want to make sure he's on our side. I don't need to spend the night tuning out another overinflated ego. Remember Gabbing Gary, the blind date I told you about? I'm not up for that tonight. Jess has promised to woo the table of baseball players and their wives, so leave her alone too. You get to enjoy the gorgeous guy all to yourself."

Without another word, Gretchen took off heading for the assistant she spotted, and I looked for the junior senator. Clutching the unwanted glass of champagne, I decided to indulge and have a sip. I spotted the senator and his new wife near one of the dogs and headed over. Perhaps they were in the market for a pet as newlyweds; they might be a decent couple for one of our pups. Feeling a tingling awareness go down my spine, I turned to see Gretchen shaking hands with a man who just arrived. I couldn't see his face but assumed he must be the famous Mr. Miller. Turning away, I can't help but wonder why I got that feeling. Just then, Archie, the lab mix, decided to raise a ruckus, so I headed over to help the wide-eyed teenager calm him down. He's such a fun boy but has too much energy to be contained for so long. Just a few more minutes, and they all would be loaded up and returned to Paws & Claws.

***

Hours later, I get a call from Gretchen, who is ecstatic about the money raised at the event. It exceeded our estimations, and everyone had a great time. Add to that, we got some press from the senator, the professional athletes and the unexpected actor attending, and all the animals showcased were adopted. Gretchen kept apologizing for not introducing Mr. Miller to me, and I kept telling her it didn't matter. I was there for the animals and her.

"He asked about you, not by name, because he didn't know who you are, but he definitely watched you A LOT. Asked for an introduction twice, but we couldn't catch you. Those heels are sky high, and yet you still move like a gazelle. How do you do it?"

Her comment gave me a moment of unease; why would this man be so keen to be introduced to me? No one knows I'm the financing behind the non-profit or tonight's event. I don't want it publicized, and Gretchen respects that.

"Relax, Andi. He saw a woman he thought attractive and asked me who you were. I told him you were one of our patronesses and a veterinarian. He hoped to meet you, but whenever we moved toward you, someone came up and wanted a photo with him. I didn't realize how well-known he is until now. Great for us since he made a very tidy donation and promised to send us some items for use in a silent auction. I'm hoping the press about his being in attendance draws in more interest to the shelter or at least the website."

"I'm glad he enjoyed himself." Dismissing the man who I believe is responsible for those tingles, I felt down my spine more than once. "More important, the junior senator is behind the bill all the way and is already vocal about it. It seems he and his new wife are animal lovers and donate to ASPCA as well as the World Wildlife Fund and

Atlanta Zoo. Jess told me several baseball wives want to start a volunteer group to come out at least monthly, and the players talked about setting up an adoption area at the stadium for home game days. Not sure that will work but have fun exploring it."

"You are amazing. Jessica is amazing. I am so blessed to have you in my life and backing Paws & Claws!"

"Hush. You are rambling because your brain has clicked off due to exhaustion. Go to sleep, and don't get up early tomorrow. You earned the late morning. I'll be in touch if there is anything you need to know about at P&C tomorrow."

"Goodnight, Andi and thanks again for all you do!" Gretchen disconnects, and I smile and murmur, "Thanks, Mom and Dad, for leaving me the means to do it."

Sometimes it feels like they are here with me, and I know they would be proud. Other times, I miss them so strongly I ache with it. Sighing, I shake off the melancholy and remind myself of all the good things we accomplished tonight. That's what matters.

***

Chapter 4

Across town, in the comfort of an Atlanta hotel suite, Sean Miller glances at his phone as it rings. Knowing the time difference, he answers immediately, worried something is wrong. "Mum, what's wrong?"

"You've finally met her, haven't you?"

"Who, Mum?"

"The one I told you about. The woman who is your soul mate, the one I dreamt of all those years ago. I had another dream last night that told me you met her."

"I don't think I have, Mother. But thanks again for trying to run my love life from thousands of miles away." Smiling but still a touch sarcastic, I shake my head and run my hand through my hair, grasping my neck.

"Sean Alain Miller, you listen to me. Your grandmother had these dreams, and her grandmother and her grandmother and so on, so far back in our family history, there aren't records of it. If I tell you I know something, I know it. Bank on it. Write it down. Remember it. I told you when you were mixed up with that hussy Gabriella, and I'll say it again. You had not met the woman you are destined to be with them, and I was right. Now I'm telling you, I think you've met her."

"I'm in Atlanta, Georgia. I'm pretty sure the woman of my dreams isn't here."

"Not your dreams, you daft boy. She's the woman I know is your match, your soul mate. She's not very tall, but she's beautiful inside and out. You'll know it when you see her."

"Can you give me a bit more than that to go on? I see so many people; I may pass her by and not even know it."

"Don't be snarky, son. Not to worry, you'll know it. Something will tell you immediately." Smug satisfaction is rolling off my mother's tongue now, and I'm too tired to take offense to it. Rubbing my hand over my eyes I remember the beauty I saw at the gala tonight and how elusive she seemed to be when the lady from Paws & Claws tried to catch her for an introduction. She definitely caught my eye, but that's it.

"Hate to bust your bubble, Mother but no such luck. Maybe tomorrow when I catch the flight back. Maybe she's the pilot bringing me home. Maybe she's a good British girl going home after a holiday in America. Who knows what tomorrow brings, right?"

Ignoring me, she says, "I wonder if you've just been in the same area but haven't met yet. I'll need to see what my dreams bring me next. Anyway, you're coming home tomorrow, then? I thought you had business in New York before you came home?" My mother can keep a calendar in her mind like a general directing her troops. My family never needed one of those corkboards in the kitchen to keep us all straight while growing up. My mother's brain kept it all in order and never confused a date or an activity. Hard to do with five children running around, not to mention my father's travel for work, but she did it.

"I canceled New York so I could get a few more days with you and Dad before work starts back in a couple of weeks. I'll see you tomorrow, late in the evening, ok?"

"Sounds good, dear. Get some rest. I love you."

"Love you too, Mum. Hug Dad for me." After ending the call, I decided against checking social media. I'm tired, and I know Instagram and Twitter will pull me in for at least an hour or two. Tossing the phone on the bed, I walk to the windows overlooking the area known as Buckhead and can't help but picture that woman again. I'm pretty sure my mother is messing with my mind, so I turn away and opt for a shower and some mindless television viewing. No dream woman for me here.

Chapter 5

I was barely out of the shower when Jess barreled into my room and threw herself on my bed. The neatly made bed was now a shamble of tossed pillows and disgusted female if Jess's face was any indication. Walking to my closet, I open the door and disappear in to decide on the outfit for the day. We're packing and prepping the condo for being gone for an extended period. Not much for me to do, but Jess has plants everywhere that are going to our parent's house, so they live. I've got a perpetual brown thumb with plants, but thankfully I have a touch with animals.

"Spill it," I order as I pull on yoga pants and a long T-shirt.

"Mom called and wants us to come to dinner at the club tonight. This is our last night here, and I was kind of hoping we could hang with friends at Gallagher's, ya know? I do not want to eat at the flipping country club with the plastic minions. It's become unbearable lately."

I laugh out loud and remind her, "It's only unbearable because you tossed Scott Kramer back into the sea of eligible men that skulk around the club. Now your mother has been looking for a replacement, and the other bachelors see you as a target of opportunity."

"Bitch," she mumbles into my comforter, "Why do I love you?"

"Because I am brutally honest with you at all times and have no qualms telling you your ass looks fat in those sweats," I reply drolly as I yank on her faded, old navy blue sweats.

"Scott Kramer can kiss my behind."

I interrupt with a quip, "He'd love to, but you won't play nice."

"He's a self-righteous prig with a stick up his ass the size of a Georgia pine. He actually thought - and said," she emphasized, "that

I only went to medical school to land a doctor, not to actually become one."

"He's an ass, but you didn't need to publicly call him one. He can't help being stupid with no more sense than a goose. Now he's bad-mouthing you to his cronies, and you are likely going to tell him off again, which will embarrass your mother…..again. Why not suggest we eat somewhere else? Meet in between so we can do both – dinner with the 'rents and hang with our peeps at Gallagher's. Win. Win."

"THAT's why I love you. Because you're so smart and canny, you always come up with the best solutions. And my ass indeed looks fat in sweats; it is supposed to look fat in sweats, or I would resist working out."

Swatting Jess on her butt, I say, "Your logic is as warped as old wood. Get out of my room," pointing, "after you fix my bed. I've got to finish packing. Are you sure I can't bring scrubs to wear? That's what I wear for work every other place I work."

"Uncle Rick said they aren't formal there, and the vet he had to use in the past wore jeans. Besides, it's colder there than it is here, so your thin scrubs won't keep you warm. I refuse to treat a person who knowingly got sick because of pure stubbornness. T minus 28 hours until Adventure TV Series begins!"

***

My suggestion had merit and was accepted. We meet up with Jessica's parents, my former guardians and the closest thing I have to parents in my life now, in between our condo and their house. Hugging them both tight, I hear Mom sniff a bit. Pulling back, I look closely at her and see the same love in her eyes I saw when I woke up after the horrible accident that killed my parents. She was a rock for me during the weeks and months that followed, and I can never repay her for that. If I ever voiced that thought, I know those eyes would quickly fire up, and she would tear a strip out of me for it, but I still wish I could find a way to repay her and Pop for taking me in and blending me into their family. They didn't have to do it, but they loved my parents as much as I did. They had all four been in college together and married so close to each other. It's always been the four adults in all the photographs and memories until we kids came along. Two for Mom and Pop and then just me for my parents. Vacations, holidays, Halloween, and more summer bar-b-ques than I can remember until that drunk driver ripped away my parents.

Mom must have sensed where my mind was going because she squeezed me tight again and said, "I'd kill for your hair, you know. And we aren't talking murder here; we're talking premeditated murder."

My eyes widened at that, and I started laughing so hard I had to let her go and bend a bit. "What the heck is that mess? You've been watching too many crime shows on tv. Besides, your hair is gorgeous as always and just the right amount of curl, unlike Corkscrew Candy over here." I always love poking fun at Jessica's hair. She says she hates it because it can be a living nightmare, but it fits her personality and physique so well that I know she's happy with it.

"Corkscrew Candy? You are so rude, Anderson." Jessica touches her hair and gives me a haughty look. "At least my hair doesn't resemble a horse's tail."

"Let's not go there for the thousandth time, girls." Pop patiently says as he holds his arm out for Mom to take. "I'd much rather go have a great glass of wine and hear more about what Rick has in store for the pair of you in the UK."

Several hours later, we hugged them goodbye promising to call, text and email frequently. Another few hours were spent laughing and hanging out with friends; we call it a day. We've got a mid-day flight the next day and a night in New York before the seven-hour flight to London. We haven't been to London since we graduated high school and went on our European tour as a family, so we've decided to spend a few days there before taking the train to Scotland. I have to admit I'm a little excited about the trip now that it is only a few hours away.

***

24

Chapter 6

"We're finally here! I'm so excited I can barely speak!" Jessica was bouncing up and down in her seat across from me on the train. The train ride was entertaining, and I'm glad we opted for this way versus a flight straight into Glasgow. Jessica may think she can barely speak, but honestly, she hasn't stopped talking for the last 4 hours, and I can't help but laugh. I'm excited also, but I'm more subdued. Between the two of us, I'm the laid-back, quiet one, and she's the firecracker. It's always been that way and will always be.

"I hope we have time to check out a few museums and such while we are here. There is so much history in this area."

"Oh my gosh, if I go into one more museum, I may turn into a relic. Let's have some fun! Go on pub crawls and meet hot Scottish guys. I may even snag myself one to keep."

"Snag or Shag?" I say with a cheeky grin and batting eyelashes.

"Bad girl. Such a bad girl, Andi. But who knows? Maybe both. Ok, the train has stopped, and Adventure TV Series has officially begun." Jess stands up, stretches and then turns to me and says with wiggling eyebrows, "Let's go to a local pub and scout out the scenery."

"We haven't even made it to our flat yet, much less unpacked. Remind me to thank Uncle Rick for letting us live together." I roll my eyes after saying that, but she knows I mean it.

Laughing, Jess says, "He assumed we would want to live together since we live together now. I think he believes we are 'together' in a different way, wink wink." If you know Jess, you know that is so far from the truth. Me, I'm the one who could easily qualify as a nun, but Jess, she's the typical contemporary career woman. I wouldn't think either one of us was lesbian, but who knows what Rick thinks.

"Well," I say as we slowly disembark, "he saves on housing anyway, and our routine doesn't change."

***

We get to our flat and open the door to be somewhat underwhelmed. Tiny is an understatement, but it's quaint and appears clean, so we both toss our luggage in and take the short tour. The living area is small and boasts a love seat, an upholstered chair that looks like it came out of someone's attic, and a sturdy coffee table. Across the way is a modern flat-screen television and DVD player. One small window with an unremarkable view leads the way to an open dining area that has a bistro table and two chairs. The kitchen is galley style and barely big enough for the both of us to stand in together. I laughed when I realized it was impossible for both of us to be side by side if the refrigerator door was open. That appliance is about 1/3 the size of the stainless one in our condo in Atlanta, but it's not like either one of us cooks much. A two-burner stovetop and a tiny microwave that may be able to cook a bag of popcorn are sitting next to a Keurig, so we're both happy on that front. Coffee is the elixir of life for both of us, so having a coffee maker is critical. Noticing the washing machine is in the kitchen, we both look at each other and shrug.

Moving down the short hallway, we find a bathroom that is smaller than each of our walk-in closets. Looking at each other, we laugh because this apartment reminds both of us of the dorm we lived in for the first year at UGA. Cramped was an understatement. At least this bathroom has a tub reaching out. I push back the curtain to note it is much smaller than the bathtubs at home. So small, I doubt either of us will be soaking away any aches and pains we may get. The last door opens to a small room complete with another window and two twin beds. Between the two beds is a chifforobe that looks antique but sturdy. The other side of the room has a door to a closet the size of a phone booth, a dresser with eight drawers, and another flat-screen television.

"Storage space is going to be a problem since you brought your entire closet with you," I quip in a teasing voice. "How do you want to divide up this situation? Each of us gets 4 drawers in the dresser and a closet. The chifforobe looks like it might be a bit larger than the closet. You can take that, and I'll take the closet. Sound good?"

"Sure. Let's head to the pub."

Jessica is practically vibrating with energy, so I give in. "Fine, but I'm only going for one drink. I'd like to get settled and unpacked tonight."

The closest pub was less than a block away and an easy walk through the mist and fog. If I were alone here, I might be a bit spooked, but Jessica has always been like the sun. She shines bright wherever she is, no matter her surroundings. As we approach the front door of Charlie's, a door that looks as old as the entire country, I smile and hear cheers. Just like home, there has got to be some sort of sport on the television.

"Jess, do try to leave a few hearts intact tonight. We will be here for a while, so pace yourself." With that said and a wink, I swing back the heavy door and gesture for Jess to precede me into the chaos. Conversations didn't stop, but the volume of voices definitely dimmed considerably as Jessica unwrapped her scarf from her hair and shrugged out of her coat.

I've spent over half my life in very close proximity to my best friend and have never understood her ability to stun a room just by walking in a door. I smile at her and wink again while whispering, "Same thing, different country."

Twin dimples appear, and she explodes with laughter, answering with her usual, "Damn straight, my sister!"

A quick look around shows more than one curious face until Jess turns, smiles that 1000-watt smile and says, "Hi y'all!"

More than one man immediately rises to come forward to meet her. I say her because I slide back to take off my coat and try to disappear into the dark walnut walls. I'm not a fan of crowds and prefer to avoid the limelight. Jess is the light and the laughter, whereas I'm the more shadowed, hidden kind. Some may say she's a glutton for always taking the limelight, but I know better. We fit together perfectly without the worry that one will get upset or hurt feelings. It really started after the accident. People would stare at me and whisper until Jess began to make her grand entrances to distract them from me. I love her for that, and it suits both of our personalities perfectly. She is an extrovert, and while I do not consider myself an introvert, I definitely do not need people around me. Solitude is often my friend.

I slide over to the gorgeous, old solid wood bar and find a stool in the corner. The perfect spot to keep an eye on her and to be entertained by her. I take a slow glance around the pub and can't help but smile. It is a postcard-perfect. It isn't large, maybe ten booths and ten tables plus the tiniest of stages and a postage stamp dance floor of cracked parquet. It smells exactly as an old pub should smell; smoke from a fire, faintly of spirits (I'm willing to bet money it's the whisky the Scots are so fond of), fried food and a touch of cologne. Not altogether unpleasant but different from home. There's something to the scent that speaks of age or history that most places I've been to in the US do not have. It sounds odd to say that age or history has a smell, but step into any Catholic Church, and you'll know exactly what I'm talking about. There are a few similarities to places I've been at home but more similarities to the pubs we visited in London recently and on our previous trip to Europe. This place has a very old-world feel as if it has been here since time began.

"Care for a wee dram, lass?" asked the bearded bartender in an accent so thick I had to cock my head and almost close my eyes to untangle the words. He smiled and repeated the question a bit slower. I blushed and smiled, declined the whisky and asked for a vodka cranberry.

"Not a whisky drinker, eh?" he asked as he reached for a lowball glass.

"No, I generally stick to clear liquors when I drink," I replied with a smile.

Cocking his head a bit and grinning, he says, "Surprised you didn't order a more fruity drink then."

I laughed and told him I enjoy fruity drinks well enough when on vacation or at the beach but have expanded my palate somewhat as I've matured. "I feel like Scotland requires a bit more than a fruity cocktail."

We both share a grin and a laugh. He wipes the bar with a towel that he slings over his shoulder and says, "My name's Charlie. Welcome to Scotland."

"Thanks. My name is Andi."

"Do you have a vodka you prefer?"

"Titos or any craft vodka, if you have it. Honestly, I am willing to bet you don't have it. The places we visited in London didn't, so I had to drink whatever premium vodka you use."

"Come from London, huh? Are you on a tour? "

"My friend and I just came up after a couple of days in London," I gesture toward Jessica, who has barely made it more than half the distance from the door to the bar.

Charlie looks that direction as he slid the lowball over to me, and his expression didn't really change, but I noticed his gaze sharpened as it landed on Jessica. ''Well then, what brings you to our quiet part of the world if not a tour?"

"Ironically, a short-term work assignment.''

"What is it you do, Andi? I'm guessing you are American by the accent. What part of America do you hail from?"

"You ask a lot of questions, Charlie."

He laughs and has the grace to look sheepish as he says, "Two beautiful American women walk into my pub, and it makes me want to know why and how long I can hope they'll stay."

I laugh out loud as Jess breaks free from her admirers to plop down next to me on a barstool. "Gimme your drink, bestie. I'm parched!"

"Get your own, hussy," I say playfully with a swat of my hand, grabbing my drink.

We both crack up as lifelong friends do with a shared joke. I swivel to introduce her to Charlie to discover his expression is now shocked. "Charlie, this is my best friend and the sister of my heart, Jessica. Jess, this is Charlie. He thinks we're beautiful Americans and asks a lot of questions."

"Hey there, handsome Charlie. It's a pleasure to meet you."

"Believe me, miss, the pleasure is all mine," he replies with a touch of gruffness. I mentally raise my eyebrows, then smile and turn to my drink. Another Jessica conquest signed, sealed and delivered. Sneaking a glance at Jess, I'm a bit surprised to see her blushing and playing with a bar napkin Charlie just put in front of her. The pair of them have locked eyes and don't yet realize the silence is stretching. After a moment or so, I ask Jess what she's in the mood to drink tonight.

"I'm frozen solid and need to thaw out. Can I get something like an Irish coffee or tea with a shot of something good?" she asks Charlie with a sweet smile that only throws one dimple at him.

"Getting tired?" I ask.

Part of the reason we opted for a few days in London was to adjust to the time difference, but today had been a long one for both of us.

"Yes, hit me when I'm down. I'm one and done, just like you are tonight," she sighs, and her shoulders drop. I know she was really hoping to get a taste of the nightlife tonight.

Charlie brought back a steaming mug and then asked Jess how she liked her tea. Not too tired to be flirty, Jess replied, "Like my men. Strong but sweet."

I almost choked, and Jess's face went beet red. Charlie laughed and gave her the sugar, the tea and a shot of whisky to add as she wanted. Jess sipped the shot, grimaced and downed it instead of pouring some into the tea. She then went back to stirring sugar in her tea. Charlie laughed and said he thought she wanted the whisky IN the tea.

"I did, but decided I get it over with quickly so I could enjoy the tea and the atmosphere," she stated with a wink as she turned to me.

We both shifted ninety degrees to look around the pub. Most were back to their tables and the sporting events on the liberally sprinkled flat-screen televisions, but a few were hovering hopefully nearby. Noticing their interest but dismissing it, Jess turns back to the bar and her tea with a sigh, wrapping her hands around it. Several moments later, we were both feeling relaxed, so I decided to turn the tables on Charlie a bit. ''Charlie," I call out, "is this your place? I can't help but think it is based on the name." The pub's name is Charlie's Place.

"It is," he says with a proud smile. "Been in my family for over 120 years."

"Wait, what? One hundred and twenty years? Are you a vampire?" Jess sputters with a laugh.

"My family has owned and operated this pub for 120 years, and we always have a Charlie here. My father was the previous Charlie and his father before."

Jessica looks thoughtful and says, "So you are a third or fourth?"

"No, we don't have the same name, just Charles somewhere in the mix. I am Charles David, whereas my father was Martin Charles, and my grandfather was Oliver Martin Charles. Follow?"

"Wow, that is pretty cool," Jess exclaims.

Visibly impressed, I say, "That's amazing. What a wonderful connection to your family, your history and your country."

"Thank you, ladies. I hope you'll be frequent visitors while you are here on your short-term work assignment. What was that again? I didn't catch your answer."

"You didn't catch it because I didn't give it. I imagine we will be frequent visitors. We're here for several months, right Jess?" I nudge her since she's been staring at Charlie.

"What? Yes, it could be up to 10 months, Uncle Rick said." Jess delicately suppresses a yawn.

"Time to go, Jessie. Charlie, how much do we owe you?" I ask, reaching for my purse and wallet.

"Not a pound, my beauties. Not a pound."

"Sugar, we always pay for our own drinks. No man,"

"Or woman," chimes in Jess.

"Pays for our bar bill. I am rigid on this point, so please give me a tab; thank you very much." My voice had hardened a bit, and I knew I sounded like a witch, but that lesson was learned when Jess and I were barely old enough to drink. Never let anyone you do not know to buy your drinks.

Looking somewhat concerned, Charlie said, "My sincere apologies, ladies. I didna mean to give offense, only to welcome you to Scotland."

"Charlie, I'll tell you the story sometime, but please know we aren't offended or mean to be ungrateful," Jess says smoothly.

"No worries, the charge is 3 pounds and a wish for you to come back anytime to share that story."

As we paid and left, I felt that same tingling of awareness down my spine that I did at the Paws & Claws gala. It's such an odd feeling and new to me that I turn back around to see what may be causing it. I see no one and feel like an idiot. Nearing the coat rack by the door, we grab our coats and scarves.

"Jess, I sounded like an ass, didn't I?" I ask as I wrap my red scarf around my neck.

"A bit but…" she breaks off abruptly, looking behind me, eyes widening briefly, then continues, "You just sounded like you didn't mean to take no for an answer."

"I'm a bit embarrassed," I admit sheepishly.

"You'll forget about it after a good night's sleep, and I'll explain it all to the hunky Scot bartender on my next trip in here."

As we turned to leave, that tingle came back, and I turned again to check behind me. Charlie and another man were leaning over the bar talking, but no one else had moved or appeared to even notice us leaving. Nothing strange. "I am tired. Let's go get unpacked and go to bed."

I didn't notice the man talking to Charlie slowly turned and watched us leave with a stunned expression on his face.

****

Chapter 7

I'm always filled with a combination of excitement and fear on the first day at a new clinic or assignment. My work is set up in such a way that I am on the move constantly and rarely in the same place for more than ninety days. I noticed, during my internships, there was an opportunity to be a mobile vet of sorts, filling in for the vacationing or ill, allowing small clinic owner-operators to take a break without disrupting the care given to their patients, adding an extra set of hands during busy times and always offering extra hands during disaster recovery. During each successive internship and in conversations with professors, etc., I began to see my niche would be this specific market. My parents left me more than comfortable, so it's not about the money. As a matter of fact, I often end up donating my fees if the need is real. I never would have imagined my word-of-mouth niche business would become so popular. I turn down almost as many as I accept. I've finally accepted that it is time to expand, and with help from the same professors who helped me perfect my business plan, I hired a recent graduate with a yen to travel and see the US before deciding where he wants to settle. Now I must take on more of the business side, which makes me grimace a bit. Doc on a Walk was born to fill a need for animal caregivers, but it's also filled a need I never really knew I had—the need for challenge and adventure with the added caveat of being temporary for me. No roots mean no deep ties and no relationships that cause pain when they end.

Today begins another adventure, one I've never experienced before. I've been contracted to be the equivalent of an on-call veterinarian for a television production company. I'm not sure I even know what I'm supposed to do on a day-to-day basis, but since their locally contracted vet had a heart attack and I had just finished my last assignment, plus Jess was hired at the same time, I was up for the adventure. Timing is everything.

"You're up very early. Who are you, and what have you done with my BFF?"

Jess is startled in the tiny kitchen and spins around. She's still in pajamas with wild hair and sleepy eyes. "No matter how long I know you, nor how much I love you, I will always hate you for being a morning person, Anderson Elizabeth. Let me have my coffee."

Laughing, I push her out of the way and stick a pod in the Keurig. Sliding the cup under the machine, I press the button to start it. The little machine makes a few grunts and groans before the liquid slowly streams out into the cup. The delicious smell of coffee fills the air, and Jess rubs her hands over her face and smiles.

"There she is. I'm starting to see signs of life in there." Laughing, I hand her the cup. During her time in medical school and as a resident, she developed a habit of drinking it strong and black. I'm still a milk and sugar girl, but Jess, she goes for the hard stuff. That makes me realize we didn't get any milk or sugar. We got lucky with the K pods being here.

"Enjoy your diesel fuel. I've got to go find a convenience store or grocery store so I can get a few essentials. You know, milk and sugar."

"I'll come with. Rick isn't supposed to pick us up until 10 am, so we've got a couple of hours to scope out some groceries."

///

The meeting with Jess's uncle goes well, and he gives us a tour of the production facility and surrounding areas. He gives me the name of a driver to take me to where the animals are housed and tells me he will be there within the next hour. Shooting is scheduled for the late afternoon/evening, so I'm not really needed until the end of the day. Ben, my driver for the day, Rand, I head over to a nearby farm the production company leases shortly after lunch to check out the accommodations for the horses, goats, and sheep that are used.

Ben is a wonderful older gentleman who is happy to answer the myriad of questions I have about the landscape, the culture and the production. He pulls into the farm and drives up to a rather impressive barn with a thatched roof but otherwise could belong on any working farm in the US. It's freshly painted and even has some flowers planted in half barrels along a walkway leading from a parking area. Ben tells me the family that owns the farm had initially intended to sell it because no one in the family has worked with animals since the patriarch passed a few years ago. The production company found the property and negotiated a lease that benefited the family and allowed the use of the property until the show concluded. The farmhouse is rented to one of the production crew from the US, who brings his family. It sits about two hundred yards from the barn and is not involved in the day-to-day with the animals.

Rick shows up just as Ben concludes his tour of the farm and a very old cemetery closer to the original homestead site. The history in the area is so rich and rooted; it really amazes me. There was one gravestone that could barely be distinguished but read 1697. Unreal. The land feels so; I don't know, old and yet still strong and vital. It's difficult to put into words the feelings this area keeps bringing up in me.

"Did Ben give you the nickel tour?" Rick asks with a smile. "You're looking slightly overwhelmed."

"No, I'm just," I pause, sweeping my arm out, "in awe of this place. It's amazing."

"That it is, Andi, that it is." Ben tips his hat as he says this, then bids us farewell. "I've got another run to make before lunchtime. I'll be back for you later, miss."

"Thank you, Ben."

Rick and I walk toward the barn, and the familiar smells of animals, hay, and earth assault my senses. The shaded barn is cool and quiet, and the animals housed within are dozing happily. Rick introduces me to the horses as we pass each stall. The horse has a name plaque on each stall door, and when the name is called, the big head swings toward us in curiosity. First up is a roan named Betty, who is dainty and has a white star almost directly over her left eye. We quickly make friends and move down to the next stall, where a very large Friesian with a regal manner and a gorgeous dappled gray coat.

"Rock?" I ask, quirking a brow at Rick. "Because he looks like a rock?"

Rick chuckles, "It could be, but I'd say because he has the attention span of a rock. He's forever causing us to reshoot a scene because he mentally wanders off, and his feet follow."

"Well, I think you're a handsome boy, Rock."

Across the aisle are two more stalls, but only one is occupied. A very pretty white Andalusian mare named Thistle occupies the space. She looks down her nose at us and keeps her distance, but I'll win her over soon enough. The last stall has a nameplate that states the occupant is Zeus.

"Where is this boy?" I ask Rick. "I assume he's huge due to the name."

"You are correct. I'm not sure where he's at right now, but you can't miss that big beast."

We walk past what is obviously a feed-and-tack room on the right and an office on the left. The other end of the barn houses two larger stalls with three horses each. There are three mares named Heather, Bluebell and Primrose. The opposite side has three geldings named Bog, Moss and Dwarf.

"Tell me, Dwarf is the huge Clydesdale in the corner." I laugh and point to the chestnut horse with hooves the size of dinner plates.

"You'd be right. All these horses are named after Scottish flowers. Lester Reid, the owner of the horses, cows and goats, let his wife name them when he bought them at auction five years ago. She has a thing for flowers."

"When will I meet Mr. Reid?"

"He's due to be here shortly to prep for shooting this afternoon."

We walk back out of the barn as Rick tells me about how they use the other animals. The horses are obvious, but the cows and goats were unexpected. As we step into the sunshine, I see a battered truck coming down the drive pulling a stock trailer.

"Here's Lester now," Rick says as he waves.

Lester Reid parks the truck and trailer, gets out and walks to Rick. Rick extends a hand to shake as he greets the man, then turns to introduce me.

"Dr. Anderson Sullivan, I'd like to introduce you to Mr. Lester Reid. Lester owns the animals you are going to be taking care of for us. Lester, Dr. Sullivan is a vet we've brought over from the US. She's your go-to for anything concerning your animals at no cost to you. Doc McInerney is recovering, but we want to make sure we've got all our bases covered during shooting this season. She can handle everything from nutrition to diagnostics and even smaller surgical procedures. Anything major will require the vet hospital across town."

Instead of shaking my offered hand, Lester sweeps his gaze up and down, then says, "I've got to get the horses fed before shooting today."

My first impression of Mr. Reid is that he is a rude, gruff man who has rounded middle age and begun to show it. He's about 4 inches taller than me and wears a wool cap that may conceal thinning hair. His lack of acknowledgement of my hand or the information Rick shared with him about my role here irritates me, but I brush it off because I'm not sure he was advised of me coming to Scotland. Knowing how bristly I can be when caught off guard, I shrug and smile at Rick.

///

As the afternoon shooting sets up, I spend some time watching Mr. Reid. He takes the horses out to the stable yard, where the actors will be shooting several scenes with no issues. Something about the man doesn't sit right with me, especially when I notice several of the horses shy away from him when he comes near. I make a mental note to keep an eye on him and thoroughly check each animal over the next day or two.

I turn around to look for Jess or Rick to make sure I get out of the way. I see them near a group of lights and head in that direction until I hear the trainer swear and a horse break loose. Turning, I see the horse knock over the trainer and bolt through the stable yard to the open doors. Not thinking, I run to another horse, mount quickly and take off after the escapee. Quickly adjusting to the saddle, I head toward the runaway animal. Catching up to the gelding, I continue to match the horse's pace for another 100 or so feet before reaching out to catch the reins and slow both horses down to a walk. Looking around, I see I'm not as far from the stable as I thought, so I take the time to dismount and soothe the animal, a large black gelding with a glint in his eye. The horse tosses his head and tries to rear, but I'm not messing with him and quickly get control. Using a soft voice, I soothe the animal until he relaxes and stops tossing his head. Seeing Mr. Reid approach on another horse, I remount and turn to return.

"He's fine. No harm done," I say as he reins his horse sharply to a halt.

"No harm done? That fool animal almost cost me my job here! He knocked me over and almost caused the others to unseat the bloody actors!" He tries to reach for the gelding, who quickly rears and shies away.

"I'll take him back. He's on edge right now. Let me soothe him out a bit before he has to go to work, okay?"

Scowling at me, Lester mumbles something unintelligible under his breath and finally shakes his head and says, "Fine, but hurry up. We're behind now."

Seeing the crowd has moved to the stable yard gates, I realize why Lester acquiesced so quickly.

"What's his name?"

"Zeus, but if he keeps it up, the glue will be his name, the bastard."

Knowing I have a short reprieve, I move forward with the gelding and ride smoothly back to the stable. Taking a few moments to dismount at the other side of the crowd, I rub down my mount and whisper praise before turning to the gelding. I continue to whisper to the animal, who has dropped his head to my chest as I rub his neck. I can feel him relax under my hands, and I slowly move to his side, continuing the massage as I go.

"Handsome boys always want to show off, don't you?" I croon to the big black gelding.

"Is that what he was doing? Showing off?" comes the deep voice of a man behind me.

I turn to the man while still stroking Zeus along the shoulder and jolt. He looks familiar to me. I realize this is the man I saw at the bar last night talking to Charlie, the bartender, when I left. At closer inspection, he was even more impressive than before—tall, at least 6'2 or 3", with bright blue eyes, the faintest of laugh lines at the edges and a slight tilt. He had a strong jaw with a hint of stubble and a very nice set of lips that rounded out his exceptional face very nicely. Thick hair that appeared light brown or dark blonde but had many sun-streaked highlights and worn a bit longer than is fashionable currently.

Determined not to let how awkward I felt show, I raised an eyebrow in question and asked, "May I help you?"

"Probably more than I can help you," replied the sexy stranger with a twinkle in his bright blue eyes. "You had no fear of jumping on that horse and taking off after Zeus, did you? My name is Sean, and I'm smitten." Offering his hand to her, the man smiles warmly.

"I'm not afraid of horses and was in a position to catch this guy quick enough," I reply as I extend my hand and grasp his, "and I'm not sure if you're charming or just full of it." Warmth surrounds my hand, and I feel a jolt through my hand up my arm. Eyes widening, I quickly remove my hand from his and focus my attention back on the horse.

Sean lets out a deep laugh and says, "Full of it, huh? Haven't heard that one in a while. Let's go with charming, shall we? Do I get the pleasure of your name? Or are you just Horse Whisperer?"

"Now charming, just slide over to just plain corny," I say with a smile.

The director shouts for them all to get into position, so I give Zeus one more vigorous rub and whisper, "Be a good boy, and you'll get a reward when I come to see you later." Handing the reins off to someone I saw earlier in the stable, I turn to leave when I realize I never gave the man my name. Turning back around to tell Sean, whom I have dubbed "bar guy," my name, I look up to see him settling into Zeus's saddle, grinning down at me with a wink and a cheeky smile. Deciding he's too arrogant for my taste, I turn back around to leave and hear him taunt me with, "Not giving me your name, huh? I'll find out before we wrap up tonight, I promise."

//

There were no more incidents with the horses during the filming that afternoon or evening despite an unexpected rain shower. I decide I am not so keen on the rain here in Scotland. Atlanta sees more than its fair share of rain, but there is always a warmth to it that seems to be lacking from the rain here. The dampness is cold and will chill you to the bone. I watched Lester Reid and the grooms he employs rub down the horses, get them settled for the night and feed them. Slowly approaching Lester, I ask if there is anything I can do to help him or if any of the animals have any illness or concerns I can look at for him.

"Leave off, woman. I can take care of my own animals and don't need the likes of you butting your head in where it isn't wanted."

"Mr. Reid, as you were informed earlier, I've been hired by the production company to be here for the animals at no cost to you. Why not take advantage of that while you have it available?" I say as neutrally as possible, forcing a smile. I think again there is something about this man that does not sit right with me, and I can't put my finger on it.

"Well, I don't need you," Lester growls over his shoulder as he leaves the barn.

Walking over to where Zeus is kept, I have to admit the man has seen the horses settled very nicely for the night. Zeus stops munching and walks over to stick his head out and bump my shoulder. Knowing I've made a fast friend in him, I reach up and rub his ears and forehead. "I promised you a treat if you behaved during your work, didn't I? I have to get some tomorrow since I'm fresh out of them now. Tomorrow, big guy. I promise. Go back to your dinner, and I'll see you tomorrow."

As I walk out of the barn, I see the rain has drifted away, leaving the sky painted with oranges and reds as the sun descends. My first full day of what Jess had named "our TV adventure" is ending, and I wonder how her day has gone. Looking around, I see the driver, Ben, that brought me over to the farm, waiting by his car. I walk over and ask if he's also my ride back. He confirms he is and asks if I'm ready to go back to the flat. Having stashed my supplies in the tiny office in the barn, I just have to grab my small backpack before I get into the front seat. The ride back is just long enough for me to realize how pleasantly tired I am despite spending most of my day doing nothing but watching and listening. The production assistants and assistant directors were all wonderfully informative today, and I learned a lot. Now I want to download with Jess over a hot meal and a glass or two of wine. The ride is peaceful, with little conversation; I think my driver understands I'm tired. Thanking him for the ride, I get out of the car and head up to our flat. Based on the music I hear when I unlock the door, Jess is already home.

Chapter 8

"Hey! I'm feeling domestic, so I cooked." Jess said with a wink and blowing a curl out of her face. She's definitely got me curious, but there isn't enough space for me to get too far into the kitchen since the fridge door is open. Glancing over the door, I see vegetables cut and lettuce torn, so I'm going to say we are definitely having a salad. Noting the two burners are not on and no pots are visible in the sink, I have to ask, "What exactly did you cook?"

Laughing, Jess says, "OK, I didn't cook so much as I took all those yummy veggies we bought this morning out and chopped them up for a super salad. If you want to add meat, we can tear up some of the lunch meat. Otherwise, we can eat anytime."

"Sounds great. Let me grab a quick shower and change. 15 minutes?"

"Perfect."

///

Sitting in the pub later that same evening with Jess, I can't help but laugh at Jess's observations of one of the actors, who she thinks is a hypochondriac already. "Seriously, this woman will be in to see me daily; I am willing to be money on it. You know what you know, and I know this!"

I nod my head, then turn serious when I look at Jess. "The guy, Lester Reid, who owns the animals. I can't put my finger on it, but I don't get a good vibe from that guy. He's…."

"Slimy? Smarmy? Schmarmy?" says Jess as she tips back her martini and winks at Charlie, the same bartender as last night.

"Yes, all of that and then some."

"I wish I could have seen everyone's faces when you jumped on that horse and went after Zeus! I bet you raised some eyebrows for sure." With laughing eyes, Jess once again glanced at the bartender and winked.

I grin and realize there is another heart about to be lost to my best friend. No man stands a chance when Jess shoots those eyes, that smile and winks at them. They fall like rain.

"Probably, but I didn't notice. I didn't want him to hurt himself tearing out of there like that. I just reacted. It's not like I tossed some actor into the mud to get to his horse and take off. No one was mounted when it happened."

"And after your adventure, you blew off a hot guy. You totally dissed him and didn't give him your name. Harsh, Anderson. Harsh." Jess swats at my arm playfully while delivering the scold.

"I'm not here for a hot guy, as you put it." I say with a frown, "I'm here to take responsibility for the health and well-being of the animals employed for the series. Some of us can be in a place and not attract men like flies to sugar."

Jess gives me a hug grin and dramatically states, "As Shakespeare once said, 'Some are born great, some achieve greatness, and others have greatness thrust upon them.' I am great at attracting them, just don't keep 'em! And you may not be here for a hot guy, Andi, but you are the one who described him as such, my dear."

Laughing, I turned toward her just as the door opened, and Sean, the "the bar guy" walked in. He looked up and straight into my eyes. It seemed like everything faded until Jess bumped my arm. Breaking eye contact, I look at Jess and quietly say, "Speak of the devil, and he appears. If you turn around and look, I will knock you off that barstool."

Jess snorts and leans into me, saying, "I can see in the mirror, you idiot. Which one is "the bar guy" anyway?"

"Tall, darkish hair, fabulous arms."

"The one on the left?" Jess said as she straightened, eyes widening.

"Yep, that's the cheeky, charming flirt."

"Umm, Andi, my dear. You need to get out more."

I turn to Jess with a question in my eyes and a quirked eyebrow; she laughs, shakes her head and turns back to Charlie.

"What?"

"You'll find out soon enough."

\\\\   ////

I walk out of the ladies' bathroom straight into a very hard body. Before I could bounce off, strong hands cupped my elbows and said, "Steady there" in the most delicious husky voice.

"Sorry, I wasn't paying attention," I mumble as I regain my balance and look up. Once again, I'm locking eyes with Sean, the "bar guy".

"Hello there, Andy. That's an interesting name, by the way," he murmurs as he slides his hands from my elbows to my hands, taking them both in his.

"It's actually Anderson. Most people call me Andi with an i." I state tartly as I tug my hands-free. "How did you find out my name?"

"My spies are everywhere. Come, let me buy you a drink and tell me how you got that unusual name."

"Thank you, but no. I don't let strange men buy me drinks." I slide past the narrow hall and go back to my stool at the bar. Glancing back, I see Sean staring at me with a look very close to shock on his face then he shrugs and turns to go down the hall.

Jess leans forward and asks, "What was that all about?"

"What? Me nearly plowing the man over, or him knowing my name?"

"He knows your name? Interesting. It's only been a few hours, and already he's been blown off by you and managed to find out your name anyway. Very interesting. What else did he say?"

Rolling my eyes at her, I reply, "He wanted me to have a drink with him and tell him how I got my name."

Laughing, Jess shook her head and said, "Twice. You've dissed the man twice. And you don't even know."

"Know what?"

"Nope. Not saying another word. I'm ordering another drink and talking to this super hunky man."

"Ok, I'm out. I want to go check on a couple of the dogs from my last clinic."

"You work too hard."

"Blah blah blah, nothing new there. You say that all the time, and what do I say?"

"Pot meet kettle. Yeah, yeah. Get out of here and hurry if you don't want to talk to the hottie again because he's looking over this way like he wants to approach."

I grab my coat without looking over at Sean, "See you at home." This time when I felt the tingling at the base of my neck, I didn't turn around. I am well aware now that it means I am the recipient of a very intense gaze. I'm not sure if I like what that feeling means or not; pushing the thought and that odd feeling of awareness away, I head back to the flat.

\\\\\\\

Chapter 9

I pass the next several days working at the stable office without seeing the bar guy/actor Sean. I find myself tense at the thought of seeing him again, and I'm not sure why. After the first day passed with no sighting of him at the stable, I started digging into why the sight of him had me so tied up. The interaction at the stable and again at the pub had my adrenalin pumping in a way I hadn't felt in a long time—years, in fact. The more I thought about how those few brief interactions made me feel, the more I realized it was how I felt when I first met Justin but stronger, more intense. Was this really the same way I felt about Justin when I first met him? The thought makes me more uncomfortable than I was willing to admit.

Realizing this made me stop in my tracks just outside of Zeus's stall. He stuck his massive head out and bumped my shoulder. Lost in my own thoughts, I absentmindedly reached out to stroke his head and reached in my pocket for the dried apple treats I keep now. He keeps repeatedly bumping my shoulder and rubbing his head up and down my back.

These realizations are definitely unexpected and not something I want to deal with right now, or ever if I'm being honest. I don't ever want to feel like I did when I lost him. I wouldn't survive it again. I have to steer clear of this man at all costs. Resolving to stay away from him and any other man, I refocused on Zeus and gave him the attention he was demanding. Stepping into the stall with him, I gave him solid currying and noticed again he seemed off. I can't put my finger on it, but I feel that something is up. Deciding to draw blood and see if there was an underlying issue, I reached the stall door just as Lester Reid walked by and stopped mid-stride.

"Get out of there," he yells. "You've no business being in that stall with him."

Taken back by the anger in Lester's voice as well as his aggressive body language, I calmly exit the stall and latch it before responding to him. "Lester, you know I'm a vet. I don't understand why you have an issue with me being around your animals. The production company is paying me to make sure your animals are in prime condition, and it isn't costing you a dime. What's the problem?"

"You don't need to be in my business. I don't care who you work for; you need to steer clear of my animals."

Leaning against the tall door, I repeat through clenched teeth, "Seriously, what is your deal with me? Is it because I'm a woman? American? A vet?"

"Just stay out of my business."

"I can't do that; it's my job. Your animal's welfare is what I'm paid to ensure. If you have nothing to hide, you should have no problem with me looking after them."

"Women got no business getting into any man's affairs. We run the show; you just sit on the side and complain." He mumbled as he swiped a hand across his mouth and nose. I suddenly became aware of his glassy-eyed stare and unsteady posture, which caused me to take an involuntary step back away from him.

"I beg your pardon?"

"You're probably just like my wife. She always put her nose in where it didn't belong, nagging me about money and complaining if I did anything. I gave her a good home and food and a nice life, and she does nothing but nag me about going to see the races. All you women are just the same. If it's not just how you want it, you up and leave. Nothing but trouble."

"That has nothing to do with me or the job I am here to do. I hope everything works out for you, but we need to come to some kind of understanding. Can you and I agree on what I am here to do so we can get along better? I want good things for your animals, not to hurt them or your livelihood. Ok?"

"Just leave me and my animals alone." Slurring the words, he turns to leave the stable.

I'm concerned he will get into his truck and try to drive, but I notice he goes in the opposite direction. With a sigh of relief, I pat Zeus one more time, check on Rock and the others, and head out to leave for the day. I realize there is more going on with Lester than I know, and it is not about me, or at least not just about me. Wondering what to do, I ponder talking to Rick. I don't want to broadcast this man's private business around, but maybe Rick will have some insight into how I can make the working relationship better. I don't want to spend the next eight and a half or nine months fighting the man to let me do my job.

Deciding this is my best option at this point, I take my phone out and send Rick a quick text asking if I can have some time when he is free. He immediately responds that he will be at Charlie's tonight and to talk there. I hesitate but text back that I'll be there. I have avoided the pub and the possibility of seeing Sean, but I need to speak to Rick. I know he's busy during the day, so this may be my only opportunity for a while.

///

Chapter 10

Charlie's Pub on Thursday nights is a very popular karaoke spot with the production crew and locals. The pub is packed, and sports on television are muted as, one by one, people take the stage to belt out their favorite tunes. Charlie apparently has theme nights twice a month, and this one is pop night. Jess and I show up as one of the key grips performing a very bad Bruno Mars version of 24k Magic.

Jess and I look at each other and laugh. Karaoke was and is one of our favorite things to do, as cheesy and corny as it may sound. For Jess, it's natural. For me, it takes a bit of liquid courage and some good song choices. When we were in grad school and later in our respective medical schools, karaoke was a way for a group of us to blow off steam and be silly. Finding this at what has become our new regular hang-out spot is a perfect coincidence.

Jess immediately grabs a songbook and finds a spot at the bar. I notice Rick at a booth and head over to him. He's with one of the other producers/writers, and they are relaxed, so I am comfortable approaching him.

"Hi, Rick." Turning to his companion, I offer my hand and introduce myself, "I'm Andi, the vet on hand."

"Good to meet you, Andi. My name is Ezra Markowitz; I was around your first day and admire your equestrian abilities." He says with a smile and nods as he slides out of the booth. "I'm heading up to put in my song requests. Will you be singing tonight?"

"Possibly," I say, "after a couple of drinks and some scoping out the competition."

He leans down to say, "I'm awful. Can't hold a tune in a bucket with a lid and a handle, but it's too much fun making these folks laugh."

Laughing, I sit and watch him walk to the small table near the stage. Turning back to Rick, I smile again, but my serious tone belies the gesture, "This is business related. Are you sure you want to talk now? It can wait."

"Now is fine."

"I'm curious if you know any stories about Lester Reid and what is going on with him. He took an instant dislike to me, and I've not been able to overcome it or find out what the source is. I may have stumbled on it today, but I'm still not sure."

Sitting up straighter and leaning in, Rick asks, "What did you stumble on?"

"Nothing bad; he just went off about women and his wife. Seems like she left him or something along those lines."

"Was he drunk?" he asked quickly.

"I don't know if he was drunk, but he seemed like he had been drinking. He didn't get into his truck while I was there. He is adamant about my not being around his animals and has no hesitation in telling me so despite being told numerous times what I am here to do and that there is no charge to him."

Sighing deeply, Rick rubs his hands along the back of his neck as if to ease the tension there. Looking at me, he speaks in a grave voice, "At the end of last season's shooting schedule, his wife came to see me. She was concerned because she thought we had cut back his contract and wanted to ask if she could do anything to get it back. The thing is, we had the same contract for the entire season and didn't change it. He told his wife the contract was cut because he lost a lot of money at the horse races. He is a gambler, and he doesn't think he has a problem. I was able to piece together, with help from his wife, that he lost a lot and gambled more to try to gain it back. His losses got so bad she issued him an ultimatum asking him to either get help for his gambling addiction or she was leaving."

"Whoa. That's a lot to take in. I'm guessing she left."

"She left after the shooting had ended. A few weeks later, her car got repossessed for non-payment, and she was finished with him. I heard this from several friends here. She's moved away to live with their son and daughter-in-law. The thing is, part of the reason I brought you in was because I'm concerned for the animals. They don't look as…robust, for lack of a better phrase, as they did last year. They are dull, I guess and starting to look skinny. I'm not sure he's taking care of them like he used to."

"They are being groomed and fed well, from what I have seen. There is something going on with Zeus, but I can't get Lester to let me give him a full exam with blood work."

"The vet we used last year is an old friend of the Reid family, and I wasn't sure he would be upfront with me. The medical incident just gave me an excuse to bring in an outside opinion. I guess you being a female, have poked at that wound as well." Pausing, Rick looked down at his clasped hands and then back up at me, "I'll speak with him again. I want you to keep an eye on him, Andi. I know he's been drinking a lot more since his wife left. The house was foreclosed, and all he has left is the property where he keeps the animals when we are not using them. He lives above the barn in a small apartment. I don't know if he is getting help for the gambling or not, but I can tell you, he's stopped coming here after Charlie banned him for a week for getting drunk and causing a brawl. Watch out and let me know if you feel the slightest bit uncomfortable. I mean it."

"Ok. Thanks, Rick. I'm going to do a full exam on all the horses but keep my interaction with them limited to first thing in the morning. He doesn't get to the farm until mid-day right now, so I can do what I need to without pushing him too much."

"I meant it when I said let me know if you feel even a twinge of unease."

"I promise," as I turn my head, I see Jess get up for her turn at the karaoke mike. Turning to Rick, I ask, "Have you heard your niece sing before?"

Shaking his head, he opens his mouth to respond just as Jess belts out, "This girl is on fire!"

I laugh at the shock on his face and get up to head to the bar. I'm in search of liquid courage because I know my time is coming up. Charlie nods at me and quirks an eyebrow. I nod, and moments later, I have a vodka cranberry in my hands as I feel that tingle of awareness at the back of my neck again. I refuse to turn around but instead, flip the pages of the book until I find the song Jess and I performed at a fundraiser night a few years ago. I fill out the slip of paper and nudge it to Jessica when she saunters back. She looks at it, smiles and says, "Oh, yeah!"

I can still feel Sean's gaze on me as Jess turns in our song choice and comes back to her seat. My fingers are clumsy as I pick up my drink and chug half of it in one swallow. Having a best friend for the majority of your life means you have someone who knows you as well as you know yourself. Jess reaches across the table and touches my arm, "Slow down, or you'll end up on your face before our song. Is Sean making you nervous?"

"A little. He stares at me."

"Hon, that man looks at you like you're dessert. I'm kind of jealous. Have you figured it out yet?"

"What? You keep making these quizzical references, and I'm obviously missing something. What is it?"

"I'll tell you at home tonight if you don't figure it out before then. Who is the guy singing so badly I hear dogs howling?"

I look over and laugh; it's the producer/writer I introduced myself to earlier tonight. "Ezra is his name, and he freely admits he can't hold a tune in a bucket."

"He's right. Thank goodness it's over."

Next up is a woman I've never met before singing Adele's hit Hello. She does a pretty good job of it, but what's interesting is she's staring at Sean the whole time she's singing. I can't help but wonder if they're together but tell myself it's a good thing if they are, even as I hope they aren't. He's not looking at her. He's walked by me twice now but has not spoken to me. Each time, that sense of awareness gets stronger, and I get clumsier. I dropped my glass but thankfully didn't spill any of it. Jess shot me a quizzical look but patted my knee under the table.

Following Adele, we got to hear a fellow American guy with a solid voice who did justice to Justin Timberlake's Can't Stop the Feeling. He was good enough to get most of us up on our feet and singing along. That song is just too much fun. It also reminded me I haven't been keeping up with my cardio since coming here. It's time to find a gym. Two more rounds of drinks, and it's our turn to put on our show. I stand up, take my hair down out of the ponytail, shake it out with my hands and walk to the stage behind Jessica. She's flashing grins and dimples to all, and I'm just relaxed enough to smile, too, but I avoid looking at Sean. The music starts, and we blow their minds with our Sit Still Look Pretty singing and dance. No one knows we practiced this one for weeks for a charity karaoke fundraiser at the country club. We won and have the ugly trophy to show for it. Once again, we killed it. The applause validated our victory.

I lead the way back to our table to discover fresh drinks waiting and Sean sitting there. He's leaned back in his chair with an amused expression on his face. Jess grabs our drinks, hands me mine, and toasts our performance with a "Just like last time; we nailed it." We touch glasses and drink, but I can't take my eyes off Sean. He stands and pulls out our chairs, "ladies, you deserve to sit after that performance. Well done, by the way. Since that isn't the first time you've done this, would you do me the honor of sharing the story?"

"Karaoke is a fun activity we've indulged in for years. There was a fundraiser for the local children's hospital at my parent's country club a couple years back." Jess looked over at me in shared memory and laughed, "We decided we would go big or go home when someone paid for us to sing and we did. We went big and went home the winners."

"Paid for you to sing?" he asked in a deep voice that gave me goosebumps. The accent is glorious, but that timbre of his voice just kills me.

Trying to drag me into the conversation, Jessica looked at me to answer, so I replied, "You don't sign yourself up to compete; someone else pays for you to sing, almost like setting you up to look ridiculous. The whole night is a big musical comedy to see who can have the worst performance. Well, it was until we changed the game."

Jessica smiled slyly and said, "The song choice was mine, and it fit that crowd of straight-laced, overachieving starched shirts to a T. Add in the dance routine, and we were set. It's a serious competition now with very few bad performances. We still blew their minds, and it was fantastic." Another toast and clink of glasses before we settled back to watch the next performer, the woman who sang Adele, was back. This round, she sang Send My Love and again stared at Sean the entire time she sang. He wasn't paying attention to her, so I couldn't help but say, "Um, is that your girlfriend?"

"Who?"

"Adele up there, singing."

"Who, ah, Lizette. No, she's one of the regulars, I think; I'm not sure. Definitely not my girlfriend or anything remotely close to that." Returning his gaze to me, he appears to dismiss her. "I'm more interested in learning about your name and why you wouldn't let me buy you a drink the other night."

Jessica gets up, excuses herself and quietly heads to the stage to drop another song in the bucket. She glances back, smiles and doesn't come back to the table but instead goes to the bar to flirt with Charlie. I look down at my drink and mentally tell myself to find my gumption. This is just a conversation with a guy. Nothing more. Looking up, I find him smiling at me, and he says, "decided to talk to me, did you?"

"Sure." I stammer, blushing. "My name is a tradition in my family, a Southern tradition, really. The first daughter is given her mother's maiden name as either her first or middle name. Most use it as a middle name, but my mother's family went with first names. Anderson was her maiden name. Elizabeth was my father's mother's middle name."

"I like it; it's as unique and as lovely as you are."

"Thank you."

"Now, I seemed to hit a nerve when I offered to buy you a drink. There is no way I am the first to make that offer, so there is a reason it affected you that way."

"You're very perceptive, aren't you?" I ask as I drum my fingers on the tabletop. Reaching over, he touches my hand, covering my fingers to quiet them. That zing of awareness travels up my arm again at his touch.

"I'd like to think so." Slowly moving his fingers across mine, he says, "Tell me."

I slide my hand away and grab my drink, taking a sip before I respond, "When Jess and I were in college, we were at a bar with a group of friends. We were celebrating one of our friends getting engaged. It was loud and packed, but we were having a blast and didn't care. Twenty-two-year-old girls don't really think much about safety when they are in a pack of almost ten. A group of guys started sending drinks to our table, and we didn't bat an eye; we just drank up. Three rounds later, a couple of my friends started to feel really bad. Jess and I had slowed down drinking because we volunteered to be the responsible ones that night. You know, make sure everyone gets home with credit cards, IDs, phones, and hold hair back on the way if necessary."

I stop and stare over toward Jessica, who is chatting up Charlie like it's a full-time job and the bar is empty. Charlie doesn't seem to mind much by the smile on his face. I must have stayed zoned out like that for a couple of minutes before I felt Sean's hand on mine again. Turning back to face him, I continued, "Tessa and Korryn were the worst; they were so dizzy they could barely stand up. Becca and Shelby were also saying they felt odd. They said it wasn't a drunk feeling. That will sober you up pretty quickly. Jess and I had enough sense to get one of the bouncers to help us get a cab. Ten girls piled in a minivan and went to the Emergency Room. All four girls tested positive for a date rape drug." Looking up into his eyes, I saw the disgust there before it changed to empathy as he took my hand in both of his.

"That was disgraceful. Your friends were lucky."

"Exactly. That lesson was easy compared to how some girls learn it. We don't let men buy us drinks unless we are dating them. Even then, we are careful." I slowly start to pull my hand away, but he doesn't release it.

"I'm glad nothing happened to you or your friends. Thank you for telling me. I apologize for bringing up the bad memories now. How can I bring the good mood back?"

"Tell me about yourself. What do you do? Where are you from?" I tugged my hand again and was able to free it. Rubbing both of my hands together to get rid of the tingling sensation, I dropped them to my lap before glancing up at him. He seemed genuinely surprised by my questions. "Why did my questions surprise you?"

He looked down almost as if embarrassed and said, "You caught me off guard. Most women already know the answer to those questions. Some actually tell me things about myself as if to show off how much they know."

Raising my eyebrows, I can't help but chuckle and say with raised eyebrows, "Wow."

Laughing, he says, "I did sound a bit egotistical, didn't I? That's not how I meant to sound. I'm an actor, as you may have guessed. I've done a lot of small things and a few minor parts in films until this series. It increased dramatically in popularity, and suddenly I couldn't turn around without someone snapping a photo or asking for an autograph." A self-deprecating smile appeared on his lips as he looked back at me and said, "It's been a while since a woman didn't automatically know who I am. You're the first in a long time. I know that makes me sound like an egomaniac, but I actually like that you don't already know about me."

Not knowing what to say to that, I turn toward the stage as I hear Jessica laugh. Turning slightly toward her, I reach for my drink and take a sip. The music starts, and I can't help but laugh; Meghan Trainor's No comes out loud and clear. Jess is going to have a ball with this one. Looking at Sean, I see he recognizes the song as well, and I see the laughter start in his eyes before I hear it. He really is astonishingly good-looking. Turning back to the stage, I enjoy watching Jessica sing one of our favorite Zumba songs adding in a couple of the moves as well. We have so much fun at karaoke, and it's been too long. "I'm glad we found this place," I said off-handedly.

"I'm glad you did too. I noticed you the first night you came in. Your laugh caught my attention, but before I could get my brain to tell my legs to move, you were leaving. Charlie had little information about you, but I was hoping you would be back. You can't imagine how thrilled I was to see you the very next day. Jumping on that horse and then brushing me off just as easily."

"I mortally wounded your ego, didn't I?" I asked playfully with a flirty smile and side-eye glance, feeling a bit alcohol brave.

Laughing again, Sean gravely says, "Yes, it was almost the end for me."

"Yet here you are, or rather, there you were that night, trying again right in this very bar."

"Catching you, you mean. Bounced right off me and would have landed on the floor if I hadn't caught hold of you."

I raised my eyebrows again while holding back a snort of laughter, noting the playful tone in his voice; I glibly replied, "If you weren't built like a rock wall, I wouldn't have bounced off you."

Hearing his roar of laughter made my smile widen. This man was fun to be around and didn't appear to take himself too seriously. Pushing my hair back over my shoulder, I leaned forward and asked again, "Are you going to tell me more about yourself, or do I need to ask Google?"

"I've a better idea. How about I answer a question for each question you answer for me? How is that for a fair bargain?"

At first thought, I started to shake my head but then changed my mind and said, "Deal. I go first."

Just as I started to ask my first question, Jessica came over and said, "We're signed up for the next song. Get ready. I'm in a Meghan Trainor mood." Flashing another grin, she heads back to her spot at the end of the bar where Charlie is hanging out.

"She's like a tidal wave, isn't she?" Sean remarks with a laugh.

"At times. But she's the best friend I'll ever have."

"I wonder what song you'll be singing?"

"Meghan Trainor, plus me means… as this is Andi speaking it's either Lips are Movin' or All About that Bass. We've done those before and had fun with it." I down the rest of my drink in one gulp and start to stand up.

"You up for this?" Sean asks quietly.

I laugh and head over to Jess at the bar. He has no idea what he's in store for when Jessica and I go all in for karaoke. Jess has a fresh drink for me and is ready for a toast. Touching glasses and drinking, I ask what we are singing. Jess gets a shrewd look on her face, flutters her eyelashes and says, "Dear Future Husband."

I immediately think of Charlie and bust out laughing. If she's trying to scare Charlie a bit, this one will definitely freak him out. I'm laughing so hard I am tearing up and starting to gasp for air as we are called up. I take another drink and refuse to look at her. As the music starts, I think I have enough control over myself to get through, but I know I can't look at Jess during the entire song, or I'll lose it and fall off the stage laughing.

After the laughter and applause stopped, I grabbed my drink and felt comfortable enough to head back to the table where Sean sat. Lizette is there when I walk up, so I turn around and start to walk back to the bar. I get one step before my hand is caught in a warm, strong grip, and I'm turned back.

"Where are you going? You owe me a question," Sean asks as he draws me to the table. Seating me to his right, he introduces us. "Lizette, meet Andi; she's the production's veterinarian. Andi, this is Lizette; she's one of our regular actors."

I reply that I'm pleased to meet her and shake her hand, which is barely offered and quickly withdrawn. She doesn't speak and sends me a very nasty look. I bite my cheek to keep from grinning. She is clearly not happy that I'm now included at the table.

"I don't owe you a question; you actually asked two before I left, so you owe me two," I mention. Watching him replay our conversation in his head, he looks at me in question. "You asked me what song we might be singing and if I was up for it. Two distinct questions." My expression shows my satisfaction, and I'm feeling a bit victorious.

"Touché. The song choice was rather funny. Is your friend giving anyone a message?"

I let out a laugh and said, "I thought the same thing! She must be playing cat and mouse with a certain someone and wants to see if she can freak him out a bit. She's such a professional flirt."

Lizette chimes in, "I don't see what the problem is, saying something with a song. You can speak your heart through the song when you are too afraid to say it in words."

I turned away toward the stage and couldn't contain the eye roll. Ezra hopped up on stage, and I started to clap. He will make us all cringe but is guaranteed to also make us laugh. His performance also gives me a reason to turn away from Lizette. The two of us sitting with Sean make me uncomfortable, especially when Lizette obviously has her sights firmly locked on him and views me as public enemy number one.

Ezra's rendition of a Journey classic was not as bad as I anticipated. Journey songs are classic karaoke songs. As another guy I don't know takes his turn and tries to croon a Bruno Mars song, I look at Sean and ask, "You aren't going to highlight your vocal abilities?"

"I can't. I am not allowed to put myself in situations that can allow for negative publicity, and my singing is definitely cause for that."

Seeing an opportunity, Lizette reaches out to touch Sean's arm and purrs, "Your voice is amazing; I bet you sing very well."

Drawing his arm away, Sean's lips barely lift as he replies, "Not even as good as Ezra but thank you." He turns to me, leans in toward me as he stands and says quietly in my ear, "My turn now, but I'm saving my next question until another time when it's less crowded." With a wink to me, he straightens, turns to both of us and says, "Ladies, I'm going to take off. Enjoy the rest of your evening."

"Goodnight, Sean. See you on set tomorrow!" replied Lizette with a bright smile and hopeful eyes.

"Goodnight," I say and refocus on the stage. Feeling Lizette's eyes boring into my head, I turn to see her glaring at me. I wrinkle my brow, raise an eyebrow and start to speak, but she cuts me off.

"You really shouldn't barge into private conversations like you did. Sean and I are actors and deserve our privacy."

I'm a bit surprised, but then, not really, given how focused Lizette has been on Sean all evening. I smile at her and reply in a quiet tone as I also rise to leave the table, "Retract the claws, honey, because I'm not going play with you." With that, I get up and walk over to Jessica's perch at the bar, dismissing Lizette from my mind.

Jess and I sang a few more of our favorite karaoke tunes before we called it a night. Once we get back to our flat, I catch her up on Lizette and her comment. With her usual sweeping arm movement to indicate clearing the field, Jess brushes her off as a waste of time and zeroes in on Sean.

"Tell me about your time with the hottie," she says, waggling her eyebrows. "He seemed like he was pretty intensely focused on you while you were talking. And I saw him holding your hand a couple of times. Dish, Andi. I want the details."

I shrug and tell her, "I told him why we buy our own drinks. We had some banter and all, but it's nothing major. As for the hand-holding, I think he's just a toucher by nature. No big deal."

Looking at me with shrewd, knowing eyes, "You like him, don't you?" Jessica asks as she flops down on our little sofa. She's guzzling a bottle of water, and looks like she's about three minutes from falling asleep. I know this inquisition won't last long, but I'm reluctant to get into this topic before I examine it alone.

"I don't know him. But will admit that he is extraordinarily good-looking and gives me the tingles."

Jess smiles a sleepy but satisfied smile and says, "You'd have to be dead not to acknowledge how hot he is, and I think he could give my granny tingles. But I'm off to bed now. We'll chat more in the morning. 'Night."

Chapter 11

I've always been a morning person. Some of my best problem-solving happens as I watch the sunrise. Mornings are also my usual workout time since I rarely know what time my day ends when I'm dealing with animals. All those months after the accident, I lay in the hospital watching the sunrise; I wondered if I would get the chance to run again. There were even more months of physical therapy, and then slowly, I was able to run again. It's a pleasure I don't take lightly, or for granted, that's for sure. I also enjoy the solitude of a run as much as I occasionally enjoy the company.

As I pulled my hair up in a ponytail and grabbed the armband for my phone, I walked out, noticing that Jess was already by the door. She was bleary-eyed, but she was dressed for a run. I stopped short and was shocked. "I must be dreaming. Is that Jessica Jane up before the last possible moment? And dressed to exercise?"

I got a lovely finger wave to accompany the tongue stuck out. We both laughed, and she said, "I want to hear more about last night now that you've had a chance to dissect it and overanalyze things. With my schedule today, the only way to do that is to go on your run with you."

"I didn't tell you I was running this morning."

Rolling her eyes and grinning, "Please, you mentioned being winded at karaoke Thursday night. I know you as well as I know myself, so I translated that into going for a run. Plus, I know you puzzle out all of your concerns and such while you run. And this is the first day we've had off since we started, not that you need that as a reason to run." She finishes with a flourish of hands and a happy smile.

"Aren't you feeling proud of yourself?" I say as I hug her. "I do not overanalyze things at night. I wait until I'm on my second or third mile."

"Shush, no multiple miles. That's torture for me. You know, I only run when chasing a shoe sale or being chased by rabid animals. Let's keep it to a mile. Especially since we don't know where to go."

"Sorry, I already mapped out my route, and it takes us from here to a lovely park with a short trail. Round trip is about 5.5 miles. Don't ask me about kilometers, I can't calculate that yet."

"Good Lord! Five and a half miles? I think I need to find a scooter. Or a bicycle. I can't run that far," Jess says with a bit of a whine. I know she's only being silly because she runs more than I do; she just runs on a treadmill whenever she can fit it in.

"Let's go. I'm excited to see the trail. It says it has a couple of pretty garden areas with a lot of flowers."

We walk for a couple of blocks to warm up, then stretch and start a leisurely jog. As muscles warm up and we find a good stride that works for both of us, I know it's only a matter of time before she asks about Sean.

"What have you come up with after sleeping on it?" she asks as we enter the park.

Pausing to look at the signage to make sure we are headed in the right direction, we head left on the trail, which is wide enough for a small car and very well maintained. We have not had a lot of spare time so far to check out the local area, which makes this run equally entertaining. This park being so close to the flat is a bonus if we like the run. It will be a recurring one for me, I suspect, but I plan to find a gym, also.

"I think he is a nice guy, and I'm the new kid on the block, so to speak. His interest in me will fade."

"Did you finally figure out who he is?"

"Not really. Well, I guess I did because I googled him. I mean, he seemed so shocked that I didn't know who he was or anything that I felt like I had to look him up," feeling a bit ridiculous and knowing under my slight sheen of sweat was a very rosy blush, I ask, "Right?"

"So, you do know who he is and how crazy famous he is since the show became popular last year."

"I guess so. It's just so strange. He seems normal. He's actually really charming."

"You DO like him."

"Jess, come on. I met the guy six days ago. I don't know him at all. But I could like him if I got to know him, which I don't think will happen. He's busy; I'm busy; we're working and not here for that sort of thing."

"Evasion, dismissal. Andi, get to know the guy if you want to. He seems like he is pursuing you, so why not get to know him? If nothing else, it'll make a great story to tell our friends after this is over and we're back in Atlanta. He might be a fun guy to hang out with."

We reach the first garden and stop for a minute. Both of us are breathing harder than we normally would, which makes me ask, "What's the elevation here? We are worse off than we think or higher than home."

"I'd say it's us and not the elevation. When was your last run?"

Mentally going over my last several weeks, I realize it was almost a month ago. "Whew, too long. Almost a month. Definitely me and not the atmosphere here."

"Same."

We both turn as we hear another runner approaching. I almost tripped while standing completely still because Sean came around the corner with earbuds in and a phone strapped to his very impressive bicep. He glanced up and lost his stride. Stumbling a couple of steps, he came to a halt near us, bent over and told us, "You startled me; I didn't expect to round the corner and run into a pair of lovely ladies this early on the weekend."

Jessica looked over at me with an evil little twinkle in her eye but not saying anything. She glanced away at the garden, leaving me to respond. "We're out for a run ourselves."

"How far are you planning to go? I wouldn't mind the company." Stretching his arms over his head, he looks at both of us in askance.

Still no response from Jessica, so I am bound by manners to respond despite feeling like I'm blushing like a 12-year-old girl. "The route from our flat and around here is 5.5 miles."

"5.5 miles, let me think what that is in kilometers. I'm not good with math, but I think it's a bit less than 9 kilometers. Mind if I join you?"

"I actually don't think I can make it that far. I feel better knowing Anderson has someone she knows to run with, so I'm going to turn back now," Pipes Jessica as she turns back toward the park entrance.

"Now you speak up," I mutter. She gives me a huge grin as she slowly jogs away.

"I didn't mean to run her off," Sean says.

"You didn't. She's not a morning person, but she does run, so don't believe that flimsy 'I can't make it that far" baloney she threw out. She wants to crawl back in bed and go back to sleep, I bet."

"Ok, so it's you and me and the trail. You ready?" he asks me with a wink and a slight one-sided smile.

"Sure," I say and take off at a slow pace and steadily build up to my usual pace. He's a lot taller than I am, so he adjusts his stride to mine, and we run for several minutes without speaking. I'm hyper-aware of him next to me, but I also enjoy the fact that neither one of us seems to feel the need to speak. It's nice to run and not talk, especially since I feel like I'd say something stupid or corny. Who am

I right now? Geez. I'm a 29-year-old highly educated animal doctor, for goodness sake. Why is a guy making me feel like a silly schoolgirl? Still running at a nice pace, I suddenly notice we have a third runner with us. I can't believe I was so focused I missed when the dog joined us. Going strictly by looks, I say our runner is a Border Collie. Traditional black and white coat with longer hair, one flopped ear and a slightly curved tail. Definitely, solid Border Collie features on this one, but you never know for sure by looks alone.

"Friend of yours?" I ask Sean.

He doesn't break stride when he glances down and says, "Ah, you finally caught up, huh, Rab?" Looking over at me, he says, "This is Rab. He's my dog and sometimes my keeper; want to meet him?"

Slowing to a stop, we both pause and laugh as Rab runs further, then turn and look back at us. He barks as if to say, "Why did we stop?" then trots back to us. He walks to Sean's side, sits and looks up at him with the sharp brown eyes Border Collies are known for. Sean talks to him like he is human, and it makes me smile.

"This is my new friend Anderson. She knows all about the likes of you and your kind, so mind your manners. She's a vet, so if you misbehave, she'll take your balls off."

I burst out laughing and held my fist out to Rab. He sniffs and then offers me a paw to shake hands. "You're a clever one," I say as I shake his paw. Bending to pet his head and neck, he gives me a lick and then rolls over for a full belly rub.

"He has no shame, as you can see."

"He is a very handsome boy and smart too, aren't you, Rab? He looks like he's still got some growing to do. How old is he? About 1?"

"You know your business. He's just had his first birthday last month. I think he will get a bit thicker, but his parents were both about that tall, so I don't think he'll grow much more."

Rab issues three barks and starts running down the path. He stops about 10 yards ahead, turns, barks again and waits. Sean and I laugh and start jogging again.

"He's bossy, isn't he?" I say.

"Demanding and likes to get his own way," Sean grumbles as we catch up with Rab, but I hear the affection in his voice all the same. The three of us continue the jog down the trail. Fifteen minutes later, I realize we've made a full lap around the park and are back where we started. I stop suddenly, and Sean turns back, "Are you ok?"

"We've made the loop around the park. How did I miss the other garden?" I ask, baffled.

"It was just after Rab joined us. Want to make another lap and stop there for a while?"

"Sure."

When we get to the garden area, I notice this one has more trees and shaded areas. Rab flops down under a tree panting happily. Sean and I stretch a bit before we settle under the same tree. I sit with my legs straight out and lean over for a stretch. My muscles may protest the extra lap later, but for now, I feel good. Crossing my left leg over my right for a stretch, I notice Sean watching me. He's got a small smile on his face, and his face seems relaxed. Switching to the other side, I feel my cheeks heat up in a blush. The silly schoolgirl is back.

"I'm glad I ran into you," he says with a laugh. "Ran into you; I've a poor sense of humor."

I laugh lightly and reply, "It's been nice. Plus, it's nice to run with someone who isn't complaining. I love Jessica, but she prefers to run on a treadmill than outdoors. I'd rather be out here soaking up the fresh air and sunshine." Stretching my arms out and resettling my legs, I reach up for another long stretch.

"It's my turn for a question, I believe."

Chapter 12

ooking back at Sean, I see he's got a twinkle in his eyes and a bigger smile on his lips. "Ok, go for it."

"I've been able to learn a bit more about you and your friend, Jessica. Rick can't help but brag about his 'nieces' as he calls both of you. I know you aren't blood-related, but you and Jessica are closer than sisters. She is our new medic, and you are our new animal caretaker. Doctor and Veterinarian, respectively. My question is, how did you and Jessica become so close?"

I stare off into the garden for a few minutes, lost in my memories and thoughts as my mood takes a dip. Rab seems to pick up on my shift in energy and comes over to lay beside me and put his head on my thigh. Absently stroking the dog, I debate how much to share with Sean. My story is deep, painful and not something I share with many people.

"Can I change my question? I don't like the look I've put on your face. I didn't mean to make you sad."

"It's ok. It's a long story and sometimes painful for me to tell. I don't share it often."

"Then tell me where you went to school to be an animal doctor instead."

Smiling slightly and rubbing Rab's ears, I automatically respond, "UGA, University of Georgia." After a short pause, I start telling my story. "Jessica and I have been friends since before either of us can remember. Our parents were the best of friends, so it stands to reason we were basically family since birth. When I was 14, my parents and I were on our way home from a weekend trip when an 18-wheeler hit us head-on. The driver was two times past the legal drinking limit when he hit us. My parents were killed instantly, and I was trapped in the car for a couple of hours. My arm was broken, most of the bones in my face were broken, and my pelvis was broken. I spent months in the hospital. Had more surgeries than I want to count. Spent even more time in rehab, learning to walk again and strengthening my arm. The facial reconstruction took longer and was a slower process. My parents had a trust set up already because of an inheritance my grandmother left me, and they had already asked Jessica's parents to take care of me if something happened to them."

Sean reached out to me and took my hand, interlacing our fingers and squeezing gently. I closed my eyes, took a deep breath, let it out and continued. "From the moment my parents were killed, Jess and her parents were right by my side. They were there when I couldn't attend my parents' funeral because I was in the hospital. They were there when I had to be wheeled into the courtroom to testify against the man who did it and the company he worked for. They've been there for me during the lowest points, and I can't imagine my life without them. That's a lot for a 14-year-old to deal with and even more for a friend of one to deal with. But Jessica was there through it all. She was there when I was finally able to return to school after almost seven months. She was there when kids would whisper and talk and basically act like assholes because of my scars. She was there when that became a non-issue after the cosmetic surgery. She's just there. She's part of me. The sister of my heart, I call her."

"She sounds like the best of people, as do her parents." Squeezing my hand again, he raised our joined hands to his lips and gently pressed his lips to the back of mine. I'd been able to hold back the tears until that touch. Then one slipped down my cheek. I refused to let any more fall, so I sniffed and started to wipe away the tear, but I felt him reach out with his other hand and brush it away. "You are such a strong woman, Anderson Sullivan. I felt it when I met you, but I now have a glimpse at the depth of that strength."

Our eyes locked, and I started to feel a different kind of tension that was strange and exciting at the same time. Feeling unnerved, I broke eye contact and went on with my story. "Jess and I were joined at the hip throughout high school and college. We lived together when we went to grad school /medical school in Nashville and again when we came back to Georgia for more school. Jess was in residency, and I was in vet school. We've had a lot of great times to offset the hard times. Sometimes she's a hot mess, and more often, I am." I say with a laugh.

"I'd love to get to know her better; she is a true friend to you as well as a sister."

Rab chose that moment to roll over and demand a belly rub. Laughing, I obliged and asked my question, "How did you end up with this guy?"

"Ah, there's a good story. Last year when we were filming here, there were a couple of scenes that involved puppies. He and his litter were the stars of the set those days, for sure. I wasn't involved overly much, Shannon was in those scenes, but I was around. Puppies are so much fun to watch and play with. The energy, the clumsiness, their inquisitiveness melts the hearts of the hardest of men or women. His litter consisted of eleven total, and they were a handful. One or more were always sneaking off and getting into mischief and tugging at hems, barking their little barks at the wrong times. It was a bit of chaos, but everyone smiled when they were around. They were so chubby and fluffy." Sean was smiling with the memory of the time, and picturing it, made me smile in return.

"I was sitting off to the side on a rare break, eating some lunch, when I felt a weight on my boot. I looked down and saw this tiny ball of fur curled up with his head on my boot. No other pups in sight. He just wandered over, curled up and laid his head down to sleep. I reached down and picked him up. Since no one was looking for him, I set him in my lap and let him snooze. He snored if you can believe that. Little tiny thing was so cute, and when he snored, I laughed so loud it started him awake. He looked up at me, and the look in his eyes was a rebuke for waking him up!" reaching across me, he gave Rab a belly rub before he continued. "I took him back to the caretaker, who was looking more than a little weary and harassed. He had no idea the pup was missing."

"The next day, when I wasn't needed, I headed back to my trailer for a rest. This rascal followed me. I climbed into my trailer without knowing he was following; once I shut the door, he started howling. The sound was pitiful at best, but I still heard it and opened the door. There he sat. Looking up at me happily and proud of himself."

"You folded like a lawn chair, didn't you?" I asked with a grin.

"I'm not sure what that means, but I decided having a dog couldn't be too terribly hard to work into my schedule."

Pointing a finger at him, I laughed and said, "Lawn chair."

Sean pulled his phone from the armband and scrolled through his pictures until he found one of Rab as a pup. Showing me the picture, he said, "How can you say no to that? Look at him."

"Such a cute baby boy and fat, too," I say as I rub Rab's ears again. He opens an eye and gives me a reproachful look. "Did I offend you by saying you were a fat baby?" He sighs deeply, rolls over and gets up. With a long stretch, he looks at us as if to say, "Rest time is over; let's go!"

"I think he's ready to get going," I observe with a smile at the bright-eyed dog.

"He's been dragging me around since that day. The owner was happy to help me get him signed up for training classes and then later as a working dog, so he goes with me to most places now. He likes to fly."

"Spoiled, too," I say. Realizing our left hands are still interlaced; I pull my hand free as I stand up. "I think it's time I took off. I need to take care of some things."

"Have dinner with me, Andi," Sean asks as we start walking back toward the park entrance. "I've got more questions I want to ask you, and I'd enjoy spending more time with you."

My heart jumped, and I almost blurted out yes, but my brain caught up and made me hesitate. I do not want to give the impression I'm open to dating. Sean saw my hesitation and changed his request from dinner to meeting for drinks at Charlie's. I didn't want to say no; I had enjoyed our time together, but I still hesitated. If I say yes, will he think it's a date?

"Bring Jessica. As I said, I'd like to meet her again and get to know her as well. 9 o'clock work?" he persisted.

I sigh and say, "Sure, that would be nice." I know I'll drag Jess if she doesn't want to go. We reached the entrance to the park, and I turned toward the center of town. Sean halted and reached out to take my hand again, rubbing his thumb across my knuckles softly.

"Thank you for the run and the conversation. I enjoyed myself."

"As did I. I guess I'll see you tonight," I say and tug my hand free. Rab barks, and I squat down to give him another rub before I stand and leave.

I feel him watching me as I jog away. That tingling awareness that always seems to surface when he's looking at me. I think about it the entire jog back to the flat. It puzzles me and concerns me that I'm having a reaction so intense to someone I just met. I decide to talk to Jess but see from a note on the counter that she's had to run over to the production office to take a look at someone. I take a shower and get started on the laundry while I wait for her, which gives me more time to think.

///

A surprisingly short time later, I had a half-hour session of yoga thanks to my iPad, a shower, the laundry finished, and the flat cleaned.

Settling in with a glass of iced tea and my laptop, I cleared out my inbox just as Jessica returned.

"I was hoping you might be up for some exploring?" she asked. "I don't want to be cooped up when there is a new place to explore."

"Great minds. I was hoping to spend a few hours poking around the shops and getting a general layout of the city. Plus, I need some treats for the animals."

"Grab your stuff, and let's go."

Chapter 13

We spent the remainder of the afternoon exploring quaint shops and specialty stores in the City Centre while I caught her up on my morning with Sean. The architecture was beautiful and we discovered they have wall murals much like Nashville does. We had barely covered much when it was time to head back to our flat to clean up for our trip back to Charlie's. When I asked Jessica if she would like to go and spend some time getting to know Sean, she was all in because, as she cheekily informed me, she knows I like him.

I find that I am excited about the prospect of seeing Sean again. As we eat a quick bite at home and clean up, I am torn about my wardrobe for the evening. I am usually decisive about what I wear but I have been so casually dressed every time I have seen him, I keep thinking I need to dress up a bit more. Calling for Jess to come out of the bathroom, I gesture to the mess on my tiny bed, "Help me. I can't pick an outfit. What is wrong with me? This is not a date." Laughing, I collapse on her bed which is free of the variety of fabrics and colors currently covering every inch of my bed.

With a smug smile, she tells me, "Not a date, my butt. I'm willing to bet it doesn't matter what you wear but let's go with the dark skinny jeans, the white shimmery top with the tie on your hip and the keyhole in the back. Top it off with the black suede peep toe booties. Leave your hair down and dangles on your ears."

"I can't wear peep toes. I need a pedicure. How about your black booties with the leopard print on the heel?"

"Oooh, yeah. Those babies are fantastic and comfortable too."

"Thanks, Jess. I'm overthinking, aren't I?"

Coming over to give me a side hug, she says, "Sis, I'm just happy to see you excited about a man again. It's been too long. And yes, you are overthinking, but every girl needs help picking clothes for a date."

"It's not a date; you're coming."

"Whatever makes it easier for you. Now, get dressed; I am going to finish my face and decide which shoes I'm wearing to make Charlie drool."

"You like him, don't you?" I ask with a smug smile of my own. "You haven't been flirting with anyone else since the first night at the bar when we met him."

From the bathroom, I hear, "He's funny, gainfully employed, smart and good-looking. Add in the fantastic accent and what appears to be a fantastic body, and I'd have to be dead not to like him. He asked me out for tomorrow night, actually, but I haven't answered yet." I can see her face in the reflection of the mirror as she leans in to swipe on more mascara. She's smiling softly and taking more care with her makeup than either of us normally does. It's nice to see that softness about her.

"Let's go have a great Saturday night with a couple of handsome guys," I say when we're both back in the living room.

Just as we both grab jackets and purses, Jessica's phone rings, she looks down and then back up at me with a smile, "It's Dad."

"Hey, Dad! How's it going?" I say as she answers it on speaker.

"Hey, Dad! You just caught us. We're headed to the pub to pick up boys."

"Jessica Jane, you behave yourself. Andi, make her mind her manners." The gruff voice sounds stern, but you can hear the smile. He knows how we are and constantly tells us we are the reason he has gray hair at such a young age.

"I can only do so much, Dad," I say with a heavy dose of sarcasm.

Jess rolls her eyes and continues, "What's up? Where's Mom?"

"I haven't heard from you two in a while, and I asked your mother if she's read about any diplomatic issues cropping up with Scotland since you two arrived."

"Whatever, Dad. We've only been here a short time. Plus, you've got Uncle Rick as watchdog regardless of the fact we are almost thirty." Jessica has never had a problem giving sass to her parents. I've always been more reserved, always remembering what could have happened if they didn't take me into their family when my parents were killed.

"I still expect to hear from my daughters – both of them – at least once a week. We heard from you more when you lived 20 minutes away! Your mother misses you."

Knowing how he likes to use Mom as an excuse when it really comes down to him missing us, we both promise to call or email at least once a week.

"Andi, an old friend of mine from college, reached out a few days ago. His daughter is finishing vet school and needs to interview a vet for one of her final papers. When will you be back in the US for a bit? I'd love for you to be able to connect with her and tell her how you started Doc on a Walk."

Quickly pulling up my mental calendar, I respond easily, "I've got 2 back to back assignments in three weeks. Both are out west, but I can Skype or FaceTime with her anytime she needs. Just pass along my info."

"Thanks, pet. You're a delight, as always."

"And what am I, Daddy? Chopped liver?" Jess complains with a pout.

"Not at all. You're chopped steak, my dear. Now, get off the phone and go have fun but behave!" he admonishes.

"Love you, Dad," we chorus together.

"Love you both. Call your mother."

We disconnect, look at each other and burst out laughing. "Chopped steak?"

"Better than chopped liver, any day." I laugh.

Chapter 14

Nine o'clock on a Saturday night in Atlanta means the beginning of the evening for singles and couples. It appears no different here as we open the door to the pub again and get hit with a blast of laughter, music, voices and light. Taking off our coats, we hang them near the door and slowly make our way toward the bar. Charlie has customers two and three deep from the looks of it, but he looks up and catches Jessica's eyes. He motions toward the far side of the bar with his head and a bright smile. The man is smitten. I scan the room and don't see Sean; feeling a bit let down, I realize how much I was looking forward to seeing him again. I follow Jess to the far side of the bar, where Charlie has materialized. He gestures toward a spot further back down a short hall to a secluded booth with curtains partially drawn. I had not noticed this spot on any of our other trips here, but it gives a perfect view of almost the entire bar.

I notice Sean in the corner of the booth as we get to it. I can't stop the smile that spreads across my face. He quickly slides out of the booth and stands, reaching out to shake Jessica's hand and introduce himself. As they exchange greetings, he reaches for my hand as well but doesn't shake it. He just holds it until they fall silent. He turns to me, "Good evening, Andi. You, ladies, look amazing this evening." Gesturing me into the booth, he sits next to me and Jess on the opposite side. Charlie has returned to his post behind the bar with two other bartenders.

"It's very busy tonight, or is this a typical Saturday night here?" I ask.

"There's a match on tonight, and it's a good one, so many come to enjoy the company of others while they watch. It's more fun in a crowd." Sean explains. Seeing our puzzled looks, he goes on to explain, "A football match."

Both Jess and I turn to look at the television screens scattered around the bar and see what we call soccer being played. "Ah, soccer," I say. "I forget it's called football outside the US."

Sean laughs and tosses back, "American Football is not something you see here often. What would you ladies care to drink?"

I notice one of the servers has stopped by to get our drink order. My guess is that Charlie sent her back this way. I order a Greyhound, and Jess asks for a lemon drop. Sean sticks with the beer he already has on the table. The noise level is less intense in the booth, with the curtains loose.

"I never noticed this booth back here, but it's the perfect spot," I say a bit nervously. I want to fidget with my hands but refuse to show my nerves. The reality of sitting here next to Sean with Jess across the booth is somewhat daunting. I feel like a schoolgirl on a group date, and it makes me want to laugh. I chuckle under my breath and feel Sean turn to me.

"Something funny?" he asks quietly.

"Nothing really, just a random thought."

Turning to Jessica, Sean asks how she is enjoying her time here so far and does she have any plans to explore more of the area. The man is oozing charm and doesn't seem to have to work at it. Jessica, who is never shy with anyone, brightens and starts talking about our exploration this afternoon. Pretty soon, the three of us are comfortably talking about the different areas of town to visit. It's somewhat funny to realize that Sean doesn't know much about the area either, despite having spent almost a year here last year. A few things Jess and I had already researched to go and explore within an hour or so of the city are also places Sean expressed interest in seeing. The conversation turned to our choices of professions as the second round of drinks was delivered.

"Why medicine, Jessica? Is it okay if I call you Jessica? Or Jess? Or should I call you Dr. Elliott?" Sean said smoothly.

"Jess is fine, and I've always enjoyed helping people. I know Andi told you about her accident and all that she went through. That was a turning point for me. So many of those doctors could have easily blown past her without much conversation because she was a teenager, but they took the time to help her understand what was going on and why. That really helped all of us stay calm and in good spirits for the most part. Emergency medicine is important because it's often a critical time for a patient. Being able to help someone who is often in the worst possible moment of their life, that's what being a doctor is for me." Jessica smiles and takes another long drink. "I love it but appreciate the break right now."

"I was going to point out that the pace here is much slower than an emergency room. Thankfully, we don't have major accidents. Mostly hangovers, viruses and the occasional muscle strain."

I smirk and say, "That sounds like first-hand information there. Are those your ailments or a list of those you have heard about?"

Sean laughs, nudges me with an elbow and states very stoically, "I'm a professional; I would never have a hangover." He holds the expression for a beat or two, and then the laughter shows in his eyes and finally escapes his mouth. "I'll admit to a few hangovers and muscle strains. The work we do is often intense, and preparation may not be as long as we'd like. Many a night, I've gone home to sore muscles and ice packs. As for viruses, we got hit with a stomach one last year that almost took the entire cast and crew down for a week. It was not fun trying to stay on schedule when you feel like death on two feet."

"Viruses like that spread quickly and can really knock you down. I'm going to see what I can do to introduce some supplements to everyone to keep immune systems high and functioning at peak performance. Let's avoid that this year, at least as much as possible," Jess takes out her phone and quickly types in a reminder message.

"Anderson, why veterinary medicine?"

"I love animals. All and any. Doesn't matter. I can't stand to see one in pain or in a bad situation. I have to help." I shrug and finish with, "Plus, I generally get along better with animals than people."

Jess snorts a laugh and almost spills her drink when I kick her under the table, causing more laughter. "She really isn't a people person. She goes to a party and makes friends with the dog."

"There is nothing wrong with that," I say defensively but laugh along because it's true. I usually end up hanging with the pets when she drags me to some party. "What about you, Sean? How did you end up acting?"

Jessica pipes up that I refused to Google him even though she knows I did. I just did a very cursory search; I didn't get into stalker territory. I just had to see what was out there, and then I got overwhelmed because of the sheer volume of information, so I closed out and stopped looking.

Running his hand over his jaw, causing a slightly raspy sound that I refuse to admit does something to me, he says, "I was fascinated by movies and television when I was a kid. Not just the stories but the behind-the-scenes details as well. In high school, I was in the theater at school and in our local theater. It was great to be part of a production and see it come together. My parents were not so sure of it as a vocation but supported me regardless. It's a lot of work and not as glamorous as people make it out to be. I work 14-hour days more often than not and work sick, tired, hurt, etc."

"But you love it," Jess says.

"I wouldn't change my life for anything. I've been incredibly lucky with some of the roles I've been given and work hard to make sure I live up to expectations," he says with conviction. "Enough about me. Jessica, I want you to tell me something quirky about Andi."

"Quirky? Hmmm," Jess puts her hand to her chin and gives a comical impression of a thinker. I can't imagine what she'll say with a lifetime of ammunition stored in her brain, so I'm holding my breath.

"She hates for anyone to touch her computer screen. Refuses to rip wrapping paper on gifts. Oh, and she won't eat peanut butter and jelly with any jelly but grape."

Laughing, I shake my head. "You make me sound like a 15-year-old girl."

"I can go on if you'd like."

I say no at the same time; Sean says yes. We all laugh, but he leans toward her and says, "Tell me something else, something deeper and more thought-provoking."

Now I'm really nervous but don't stop her. She tips her head, studying him with serious eyes, then looks at me. I shrug and, with a sweep of my hand, give her permission to say whatever she wants. Jess looks at me and then at Sean and says, "She has a wicked temper when she's mad. Don't mess with her. It doesn't come out often, but when it does, stay far away."

Nodding, I accept this as fact. I keep my temper on a tight rein, but when it slips loose, it's not a pretty thing until I can calm down. That's part of the reason I started taking martial arts, to learn to control it. There were several times when I was in my late teens that it got away from me and scared me. Now I control it better.

"Duly noted. Anything I should avoid that triggers it?"

"Don't hurt animals or lie to her."

"I am equally fierce in protecting animals and believe lying is for cowards and cheaters. Not me or my style."

The conversation turns to a lighter vein, where we discuss favorite animals. I mention Rab to Jess, and Sean turns his phone over to show about a dozen or more photos of Rab. It's cute how he is such a dog dad and loves that pup. He talks about how he plans to have Rab as his plus one for an upcoming red-carpet event he is scheduled to attend. "He has a bow tie picked out already. It's red."

That makes my heart melt a little when I picture him with his dog on a red carpet. I look at Jess and see she's smiling a very knowing smile at me, and then I feel her nudge my leg under the table. She's not subtle.

"I got the idea from a gala fundraiser I attended in your part of the world. They had these rescue dogs and cats showcased as attendees arrived and walked down the corridor into the venue. It was fantastic. The woman who runs the non-profit told me almost all were adopted before I got there. I can't remember the name of the event, but the non-profit was."

"Paws & Claws," Jess and I say simultaneously.

"Yes, that's it. How did you know? Are you familiar with it?" he asks, looking between both of us.

I look over and decide since he donated, he gets the full story. "That's an animal rescue non-profit I started three years ago. Jess and I were both at the gala, and I can state with one hundred percent certainty that all animals were adopted by the end of the night. Not to mention, we exceeded our fundraising target by 35%; thank you for your contribution to that."

Seeming started, Sean turns in the booth and stares at me, "You were there? At the gala?"

"I was. Gretchen, the director who runs Paws & Claws, had me assigned to stick by a junior senator for the evening, so I didn't get to make the rounds."

His gaze seemed hazy, and I could tell his mind was far away. Wondering what he was thinking, I asked, "Did you enjoy the event?"

His gaze sharpened once again, and he said, "Yes, I did, but it would have been better if I had the chance to meet a certain beauty in a gorgeous black dress with a rhinestone collar and mahogany hair. I asked your director who you were, but she never told me your name.

She just said we would be meeting you as soon as she could catch you, which she never did. It WAS you! I saw you when I arrived from a distance but then never saw your face again, only the back side of you."

Eyes wide, I stammer, "You have a really good memory."

With a wink, he reaches for my hand and says, "A man never forgets a magnificently beautiful woman."

Knowing my cheeks are beet red; I look down at my drink before taking a quick sip. My stomach is in knots, and my hands are sweaty. This is unlike any situation I've ever been in, and I am at a total loss for words. Nudging Jess under the table, I hope she takes the hint and saves me.

"So, Sean, you supported Paws & Claws in Georgia. Do you often support animal rescue?" Jess asks with a smile that could blind.

"Actually, I have several I donate to, but I like to get my hands in whenever I can. The cast does a lot of travel to support the show, publicity at different conventions and the usual round of morning and entertainment shows. We try to spend a couple of hours volunteering at a non-profit and rotate who gets to select where we go. I've got several cast members who also have a passion for animals, so we get to meet a lot of wonderful animals and people. Sometimes we even get to volunteer at the local zoo."

Embarrassment and shyness gone, I lean toward him slightly and ask, "Where have you spent time? I may know some of the people or places."

The server drops off another round of drinks for the three of us as he tries to remember places he and his cast mates have volunteered at during the last year. He also shares several funny stories about mishaps and cheeky animals.

Charlie joined us a short while later, and conversation flowed as naturally as a stream through a meadow. The four of us traded stories from childhood antics, college days, and awkward stages we went through. We all laughed, and it seemed like we had known each other for much longer than the short time we'd been in this country. The bar noise slowly faded as the hour grew later, and people took their leave. Charlie occasionally checked on his crew to make sure he wasn't needed but spent most of the time with us. I can see he and Jess are getting along nicely and flirting constantly.

During one of the times, Charlie went to check on his team, and Jess visited the ladies' room. Sean slid his phone over to me and asked me to put my number in and text myself. Not the usual, 'Can I have your phone number' a girl normally gets but charming, like most things he seems to do. I texted myself a simple 'Hi' and slid the phone back to him. He smiled and turned it over. I noticed he hadn't been looking at his phone much since Jess and I arrived.

Jess returned to the table and asked if I was ready to head out. I wasn't, but I can tell when Jess is tired. She also seemed distracted despite the good time I knew she'd had this evening. I nod and nudge Sean so I can slide out of the booth. He was already sliding out and held a hand out to me to help me out.

"I'll take you back to your flat," Sean offers.

"No need," I respond. "The walk is short, and I don't think it's raining."

"It's almost 2 am. I would feel better if I gave you a lift."

Jess nods and tells Sean we're happy for the ride. Now I know something is up; she's usually the one who insists on leaving as we come. Another security protocol we have always kept. I also don't see Charlie as we head to where we hang our coats. Sean takes my coat and helps me put it on. I turn to thank him; I notice Charlie heading our way. Jess has her coat on and is reaching for the door when he calls out to her.

"Are we still on for dinner tomorrow night, Jessica?"

I notice she stiffens slightly before nodding her head. She turns her head slightly and gives Charlie a small smile before she opens the door. Catching her arm, I quietly ask her what is wrong. Just as quietly, she tells me Charlie kissed her outside the bathrooms.

Not sure why that has her so distracted, I say, "So?"

"Andi, I have never been kissed like that. I stopped thinking and forgot where I was. My brain still isn't functioning correctly."

"Ahhh, now I get it."

Looking at me with pleading eyes, she says, "Please don't poke at me right now. This is not what I need right now."

"You'll get your mind around it; just sleep on it." I hug her arm as we reach a sleek-looking black Audi A8. Sean opens the back door for Jess and then the passenger door for me. I can't help but smile at him and think he's such a gentleman.

"Nice car," I say with a smile. The interior of the sedan is gorgeous. The seat feels like it was made for me. "It's so quiet."

"Hybrid," he says. "I wanted to try one that looked nicer. I had a clunker a few years ago, and my friends kept making fun of me."

"I drive an old Ford Explorer. Whatever works for you where you are, right?"

"Exactly."

We reach our building quickly, as expected, but Sean doesn't get out. I am a bit surprised. Almost as if reading my mind, he says, "I would walk you to the door, but I don't want to seem too pushy."

I smile my thanks and reach out to touch his arm, "Thanks for the ride."

"Goodnight, Jess. Goodnight, Anderson," he says as we both start to leave the car. I almost didn't hear him say, "Sweetest dreams, Anderson."

Chapter 15

The next two weeks pass by in a blur of activity. Filming is fully underway, and there are times it seems grueling for the production team and actors. The weather can be terrible, but they keep right on going regardless of the rain, mud and chill. There were a couple of times the thunderstorms were so severe they upset the horses to the point we had to reschedule an entire day of shooting because I was concerned someone would get hurt. Rick and the other producers and directors agreed, and they shifted things around to give the animals the day off. I wasn't needed every day of filming since the animals were not used in every scene. The scenes are filmed out of sequence and grouped together to get the most work completed in each setting. It's really very interesting seeing how the bits and pieces are filmed, and then the final version is assembled weeks later.

When I was not needed to supervise the animals, I started a tour of trendy coffee shops as I was told the coffee scene is exceptional in the city. I found one I especially like, and I've spent a lot of my time there. With the exception of the second-floor open seating area, it is straight out of an episode of Friends. I find it a bit ironic that I find the company of others comforting when I'm not on-site or at the farm. It could be because the flat is so small, or it could be I'm enjoying soaking up the local culture. Either way, I spend many comfortable hours in the coffee shops of the city.

I have been able to handle all the business associated with Doc on a Walk and, in the afternoons, talked several times to my employee Noah. So far, he is enjoying the clinic he is working at and has a few clinics where he interned that are interested in coming on board as well. I feel good about him and the direction Doc on a Walk is headed.

I have a week before the two-week break in shooting, which coincides with my return to one of my favorite clinics in Idaho. It worked out nicely that I won't miss any shooting here while I'm working in Idaho. Rick understood there would be certain times I would be gone with work scheduled prior to contracting with the production company. I was able to cover several using Noah, but I kept this one for myself. The team at the Wilson Teton Animal Hospital are fantastic, and have become friends during the three times I've subbed there. They expanded a year ago and added two more vets due to the volume of business at surrounding ranches and with the local community. On this trip, I'm covering for the two new vets who fell in love and are getting married. I am invited to the wedding and then will lend a hand while they have a week's honeymoon—a bit of fun combined with a bit of work in a beautiful area of the US.

I've also found a comfortable rhythm of running and have picked up a membership at a local gym that offers martial arts. Sean has joined me for a couple of runs, but his schedule is often too brutal to allow for free time for runs. He will often send me random selfies and pictures during his day, which make me laugh and reminds me of what he does for a living. A few times, I've considered watching the first season of the show, but I'm afraid that will make me feel even more weird. I think we're developing a solid friendship one step at a time, so to speak. I still get those tingles when he is around, but I've convinced myself it's all one-sided and nothing that won't go away.

Sean doesn't push me to do more than hang out with him occasionally at Charlie's, go for runs, explore historical spots around the city and outskirts, or just be friends. A few days ago, Jessica and Charlie were out one night, and I decided to stay in, watch a movie and give myself a mani/pedi instead of being a third wheel. Just as I settle in with my two nail polish color choices of A Little Guilt Under the Kilt, Nessie Plays Hide & Sea-k and the remote, I get a text from Sean.

"Desperate to see you, open the door."

I text back, "I didn't hear a knock." Seconds later, the knock sounds. Laughing, I walk to the door and open it to find Sean with his phone in one hand and his other braced on the top of the door frame.

"Hello, beautiful. May we come in?" Looking down, I see Rab is with him, and both look wet. I suppose it's a good thing wet animals don't bother me because I step back and open the door wider, letting them both in. One shakes, the other does not. Shaking my own head, I walk to the little bathroom to grab towels for both.

"Hello to both of you. To what do I owe this treat?"

Sean takes the towel from me and dries off Rab before shedding his own coat and wiping his hair and neck. "It's bucketing down out there. Sorry for making puddles."

"No problem. I'm glad I decided to stay in if it's raining this bad."

"Rab and I were headed home and decided we needed to see you. So here we are. Barging in on your night."

Leaning down to give Rab a solid body rub, I grin at both of them and respond, "Well then, here I am."

Returning to the tiny sofa, I pick up the remote and inform them both, "I'm giving myself a mani/pedi and watching Friends reruns. If you are okay with that, mi casa es su casa, such that it is."

"You are a goddess. I know if I went home, I'd end up working, and I really want to just…be…for a while. Something I can't do around most people and don't want to do in a public setting."

"I completely understand. I think everyone needs that time to recharge. Get comfy. Does Rab need water?"

"He'll let us know if he needs anything." Glancing at the dog, he whispers, "Behave yourself." Rab acknowledges this with a pant and a wag of his tail. He then walks to the armchair and climbs up, curls around and lies down. "Sorry, he has no manners or boundaries."

Before he could make the dog get down, I told him, "It's not a big deal. I don't mind if he's on the furniture. I'm usually covered with pet hair, so finding it on the furniture is not a big deal."

We settled in to watch Friends season 2 episodes for a while. I'm ready to paint my toes but feel a bit uncomfortable about it. It seems really intimate to me to paint my toes with Sean sitting next to me. He picks up the bottles of OPI polish and reads the names. I immediately blush and stammer, "When in Rome, right?"

Laughing really hard, he holds up the red and says, "Definitely go with A Little Guilt Under the Kilt." Leaning over, I try to snatch the bottle, but he is bigger than I am, so his reach is definitely beyond mine. A short wrestling match ensues and ends with me being pinned on the floor, laughing as hard as he is.

"You've had some training in martial arts, haven't you?" he asks with a bit of surprise.

I'm a bit smug when I reply, "More than some. It's great cardio, not to mention the benefits of control and self-defense."

"Do you have a particular style you've studied?" he seems genuinely interested and not put off in the least. Some men do not like a woman who is accomplished in martial arts, so I tend not to bring it up.

"I've taken some classes in Krav Maga, Muay Thai, and Brazilian Ju Jitsu, but I'm a black belt in karate." I proudly say, raising my chin a bit. "Karate really helped after the accident. It helped me learn to control a lot of the emotions I was feeling and put them to better use. Plus, it was great for my physical rehabilitation."

"Remind me not to wrestle with you anymore," he says with laughter and a bit of awe in his tone. "I'd love to work out with you sometime. I'm probably not as good as you are, but I've done some Muay Thai and Ju Jitsu."

Feeling more than a bit relieved, I smile and say, "Sure, if you think you're up for it."

"Cheeky girl. But first, I need food. How do you feel about me ordering takeout? You can finish your pedicure while we wait. Sound good?"

"Go for it. Menus are in the first drawer in the kitchen. We don't cook much."

I'm over my shyness about painting my toenails, so I get started while he orders an enormous amount of Chinese food. Looking up, I ask how many people he is planning to feed. He just smiled and said he was hungry. Laughing, I start the next episode and finish my toes. The color looks good, and I always feel pretty after my toes are painted. Keeping your feet crammed in shoes and socks all day does not necessarily mean you have pretty feet. Jessica and I have always made sure we take care of our feet, given our jobs require us to spend a lot of time on them. I have the added bonus of occasionally getting stepped on by large animals, so foot care is important. Pretty toenails just make me feel girly and also give me an excuse to pamper my feet.

Two hours later, the food has been consumed, the pedicure completed, and the Friends marathon rolling along; we are sitting side by side with feet propped up on the small coffee table. I asked Sean if it was weird for him to watch television when he was on television. He said it's a bit odd sometimes to watch himself, and he's noticed he's getting more selective in what he watches. He told me with conviction ringing in his voice that there are certain shows he will watch no matter what. Friends is one of them.

There is an easiness between us, and we share personal information freely as well as laughs about favorite scenes or what we were doing when we first saw a particular episode. He really likes Matt LeBlanc's character Joey as much as I like Cortney Cox's Monica. Talking to him like this, sometimes I forget how he makes me feel things I haven't in a long time. I also forget who he is and really start to relax. He's a genuine guy and downright normal, which makes me cringe a little because of the unconscious stereotyping I've obviously bought into. Deciding my thoughts are too heavy for such a casual, relaxed night; I focus on the television just as Ross sees Monica and Chandler through the window of his apartment. His reaction makes me laugh, and I notice no reaction from Sean. Looking over, I notice he's fallen asleep.

Chapter 16

He looks so relaxed. That strong jaw holds no tension, and his mouth is relaxed and slightly curved. The man has the best eyelashes I've ever seen, and it's a crime; they are his and not mine. I sigh and realize I'm staring at him, then chuckle when I realize no one knows. He's so good-looking, and right now, I can look at him as much as I want without worrying about being seen by him or anyone else. I notice the slight bump on his nose and wonder what caused it. I can't picture him getting it from a fistfight.

Rab gets out of the chair, stretches and comes over to nudge my hand. I realized that he caught me staring at his human, but he didn't seem to mind. He's a good dog and obviously smart like his breed is known to be. He nudges my hand again, and I look back at him. He's got an expectant look in his eyes, so I ask if he needs to go outside. He doesn't make a sound but goes to the door and looks back at me. I guess I'm going to take him out.

Ten minutes later, we came back to my flat and dry off again. It's still raining but not as hard as it was. This country stays green simply by the sheer volume of rain it receives. Looking over as I dry off Rab, I see Sean has not moved at all. A quick check of the time shows me it's after midnight. I have tomorrow off, but I don't know if he does, so I opt to wake him up or rather, I get Rab to wake him up.

"Wake up, Sean, Rab," I say, and I point to the slumbering man who makes my tiny couch look like an oversize chair. Rab walks over and nudges Sean's hand like he did to me earlier. He actually gets Sean's hand on top of his head and then keeps lifting his head to move it. Sean slowly starts petting the dog but doesn't seem to be waking up. Rab obviously knows this routine because he then puts his front paws on Sean's chest and licks his face.

"Off, Rab," says a husky-voiced Sean. Blinking his eyes open slowly; I see confusion at first and then recognition as he realizes where he is and who is here. His eyes widen, and he sits up quickly. "I'm sorry, Andi. I can't believe I fell asleep."

"It's not a big deal. I don't have to work tomorrow, but I wasn't sure what you have to do. Rab seemed like he's a pro at waking you up." Smiling and petting the dog, I look at Sean and literally feel my heart clench. He's a bit rumpled, sleepy-eyed and utterly relaxed. Totally hot. Realizing I'm staring again and I've been caught, I feel my face heat up and turn away to clean up the few things left on the coffee table.

Sean grabs my hand as he stands up. Slowly pulling me toward him, he wraps his arms around me and hugs me. For such a large man, he isn't awkward or rough; instead, I'm held gently yet securely without feeling trapped. He rested his chin on the top of my head. The man gives me a good hug. I laugh, and he pulls back with a questioning expression.

"My hair is in a knot on top of my head. It has to be in your face."

"It's not, but if it were, I wouldn't mind," he says in that husky voice as he pulls in back in again and hugs me. He just hugs me. Not too hard and not too loose. I sound like Goldilocks and the Three Bears, which has me chuckling again. I'm nervous, I realize and hug him back. I hear his heartbeat under my ear, and the sound smooths me out and takes some of the nerves away. Giving in to the moment, I rest my head on his chest and just enjoy the comfort of being in a man's arms again. I haven't been held by anyone other than Pop or Jess's brother Paul since Justin was killed four years ago. I haven't wanted to be close to a man since then, but now, it seems right. That thought makes me nervous, but I push the thought away for now.

/////

Sean rests his head on top of Andi's head and holds her snugly against his chest. He can tell she's nervous around him, especially this close, so he just holds her and hugs her. No matter how badly he wants to kiss her, he holds off and absorbs the feeling of her in his arms. There are times like now when he sees how jumpy she gets and other times when she's flirty and relaxed. The contradiction makes it hard to know where he stands with her. He's been burned in the past but feels in his heart and knows in his mind that she is different. Flashing back to his conversation in Atlanta with his mother, he smiles wryly as he realizes she may have been right. He didn't meet Andi in Atlanta, but he did see her. His mother will likely gloat, but he'll keep that information to himself.

Giving her another tight squeeze, he kisses the top of her head gently and eases back. Looking down at her, he says, "I've got to get going. I'm not filming tomorrow but have a lot to go over with my assistant before next week. Thank you for letting me crash your night in. I haven't had the chance to just relax and unwind in a few months, and it feels great."

"You're very welcome," she says as she smiles shyly.

"If I can work it in, would you like to meet for a martial arts session at The Warehouse tomorrow late afternoon?"

"Sure. I need to start practicing more frequently and just joined a gym here but have only been once."

Sean smiles, squeezes her hands and says, "I'll text you tomorrow about class times. Good night, Andi."

Rab follows Sean out the door, then turns, gives a quiet bark, and walks out. Seeing Andi laugh at the dog, he smiles and, shaking his head, says, "Sometimes he acts like he is human and has manners."

Sunday was a relaxing day spent exploring with Jessica and then the MMA class with Sean. I know I'll be sore for a few days, but it's a good kind of soreness. It also reminds me I've been slacking off in my workout routine, and my body shows it. The pain will keep me going back until I'm back in shape, but seeing how impressed Sean was with my skill is additional motivation.

Chapter 17

The week starts out with another long Monday followed by a rainy Tuesday. Wednesday promises to have warmer temperatures and dry weather, so I head to the barn a bit early. There is a full day of shooting with the horses today, and I need to make sure everyone is ready to go after a long rest. Jess drops me off, and I immediately see a horse in a round pen being exercised, but something looks off. I quickly realize the horse is not responding well; in rare form, as usual, Lester uses the whip with so much force until he's beating the animal. I cannot abide an animal being mistreated under any circumstances. Seeing Lester bring that whip down on that animal with such fury you can hear it whistle through the air makes me lose my temper completely. I see red, and logic flees my head.

Not thinking, I stalk over, vault the fence and snatch the whip out of the man's hand. He's a stocky man about 3 inches taller than my 5'6", so I've got to look up at him when I tell him to leave the animal alone. Seeing how the horse is favoring his front leg, I throw the whip away and go to him. He's skittish and tries to rear up. Quickly grabbing the headstall, I softly speak to the gelding while looking him in the eye.

Behind me, Lester grabs the whip and, unbeknownst to me, pulls back his arm to hit me with the whip when someone bellows "STOP" nearby. Turning toward the shout, I see Lester swinging, so I release the horse, spin and kick out at the larger man. Catching him in the knee, he immediately falls, but the end of the whip slashes across my arm. Lester immediately starts yelling at me to get away from his property and mind my own business, which makes me lose the tenuous grip I'd started to have on my temper.

"Your treatment of this animal IS my business," I say with clenched teeth. My arm is stinging, and my temper has me barely able to keep from beating on Lester to see how he likes it, but I'm better than that. Breathing deeply, I close my eyes briefly to center myself and rein in my temper. The brief moment of calm I've managed to grab evaporates at Lester's next statement.

"He doesn't belong to you, so bugger off" roars Lester. "He needs some discipline before he will act right tonight."

"You will not use that whip on that animal again, so help me, God," I fire back at him. "He is obviously favoring his front leg. Let me see to him."

"I'm not letting some American woman touch my livelihood. He's fine. Just being stubborn." Lester reaches for the whip again, and I see the horse shy away and shuffle back.

Worried for the horse, I try again to calm and reason with the man. "Look, he's obviously favoring that front leg. I can look at it and see what the problem is right now. This is what I do and why I'm here. Please let me look at him."

Lester suddenly backed off and stared off to the side, where he noticed several people had gathered, several of the producers, a couple of the actors and the executive producer, along with a slew of others. Knowing he is being watched and not wanting to appear to be the problem, he quickly agrees to let me look at the animal. "Fine, look at him, but I'm tellin' ya, he is just being stubborn. He's been coddled the last few weeks and isn't acting right. Needs discipline."

Cautiously I turn my back on the man, not noticing or caring that the others are watching the scene; I walk back over to the horse who towers over me, tossing his head nervously.

Completely focused on the animal, I begin to speak softly again. "Hey, boy. Easy now. How's Rock today? Not feeling good? Let me give you a little rub down here. That's a good boy. You're such a big guy, aren't you? And strong too. Arrogant, aren't we? Hmmm, and a bit ticklish on the back of your ear. But you like that, don't you?" Circling the horse and petting him softly, I slowly make my way to his chest and head again. Rock dips his head and shoves my shoulder hard enough to knock me back a step, but I laugh softly and, crooning now, say, "I know you like me. They all do. I'll tell you what, you let me have a look at that leg, and I'll give you a long brushing and a surprise."

Slowly sliding my hand down his chest and foreleg, I squat down and gently feel around the entire leg and hoof. Feeling the heat in the hoof, I stand up and grasp the hoof, bringing it up to examine the bottom. Just as softly, I cluck and release the hoof. Returning to his head, I grasped his headstall and whispered, "Poor baby, I know exactly what's wrong, and we'll get you fixed right up."

Turning, I notice the crowd of people gathered around the round pen. Seeing Sean walk up, I nod once, then glance at Lester and say, "He's got an abscess in his hoof and will be down for at least a week. I can make a poultice for it and get him some relief, but he's not working tonight."

"He has to work tonight; I don't have enough horses to cover him being out. He'll be fine for the night shoot, and I'll fix him up tomorrow."
"No."

"You can't tell me no, lady. He's my animal. All of these animals are mine. My business. My livelihood. I decide what they can and can't do, not you." Lester is back to shouting again and no longer seems to care who hears him.

"Fine. Sell them to me right now. How much for the lot of them?"

Looking at me as if I've lost my mind, the burly trainer responds, "More than you've got, I guarantee that. Unless you want to pay another way."

"I strongly suggest you apologize to the lady for that remark, Reid." says a deep, clipped voice, "You're way out of line talking to her like that." Turning to the voice, I see that Sean has drawn closer.

"Mr. Miller, she's putting her nose where it doesn't belong. Surely you can see that?"

"Apologize to the lady. Now."

My anger over the situation with Lester bubbles over onto Sean in one searing look, and I say, "I've got this, Mr. Miller." I turn back to Lester, "So what is it? What's your price for the animals?"

"Are you serious?"

"Very. If you won't let me care for this horse, the likelihood of your other animals remaining healthy and sound is slim, so that they will need more care. If I'm going to put that much time and effort into them, I may as well own them. Plus, it keeps you from abusing any of them."

Lester stepped forward with clenched fists and a red face but was quickly blocked by Sean.

"Back off; I can handle this," I say quietly to Sean before raising my voice higher so Lester can hear me clearly. "Name the price, Lester, or I'm calling the local authorities."

Realizing he isn't going to get the opportunity to show this American woman how things are done here, he spits out, "Hundred thousand." Smirking because he thinks I'll turn tail and run at that ridiculous amount, he is shocked when I merely nod.

"Done. Get me the routing information for your bank by tomorrow, and I'll have the funds transferred. Now leave so I can treat this horse."

Staring in shock, Lester repeats, "That's a hundred thousand pounds."

Walking toward Rock, I turn my head and say, "I heard. Get me that banking information."

"Best be on your way, Lester. You've sold your animals for a nice price and can be a man of leisure now." Says Derek, one of the grooms, as he turns Lester toward the gate of the round pen. "Go on and tell the boys at the bar you'll be buying the next round."

Still shocked, Lester walks off, casting glances back at me the entire time. If I had been paying attention, I would have noticed he was seething with anger and already thinking about how he would get back at me.

Sean stands and watches as Lester gets in his truck and leaves with gravel flying behind him. Rubbing the back of his neck, he looks back at Andi and shakes his head. She thinks she's so tough, but she doesn't realize that man could have seriously hurt her if he had taken the notion. He is also a bit pissed that she wouldn't let him stand up for her. Martial arts background or not, Lester has about 100 pounds or more on Andi. His mind was spinning as he watched her crooning to the horse again as she walked him out of the round pen. She stopped long enough to pick up the whip, hand it to Derek, one of the grooms, and tell him, "Burn it."

Without a backward glance at him or any acknowledgement to the crowd of people, she took the horse back into the barn.

Looking over at the production team, Sean finds his assistant and motions her over. "Tell make-up. I'll be there in about 10 minutes. I need to check on something."

"Okay. We've got a few minutes. They're trying to figure out the horse situation since we are short one." Maureen is a fantastic assistant and always seems to know what is going on with the production crew, writers, directors, etc. She's also got her ear on the ground in town as much as is able in a city this size.

"See what you can find out about what Lester gets himself into today. I don't like how he was acting toward Dr. Sullivan."

"Sour old bastard," she says. "I'll bet he spends the rest of the day in the bar. I'll find out either way."

Sean turns toward the barn and enters quietly. He hears the softness of Andi's voice as she's working on the horse named Rock with Derek holding his head. The horse appears to be almost asleep, and I wonder if she's given him some sort of tranquilizer. As I get closer, Rock must hear me because he tenses, jerks his head and tries to pull away. I realize then he isn't drugged; he was lulled into a relaxed, passive state by Andi's voice. She's almost singing to him like a mother would sing a lullaby to her baby. I also realize she is not likely going to talk to me right now since her focus is on Rock and his hoof. I stand for a few moments, watching her very capable hands work quickly and efficiently on the horse. I am fascinated and want to know more about what her job entails and why she is so passionate about animals, but now is not the time.

She looks up just then, straight into my eyes and smiles at me, then turns back to Rock. That's it. I'm a goner. I step back and rub my hand across my chest, which is suddenly tight. A strange feeling and one I don't have time to think about, so I block it out and leave the barn. The next 9 hours go by at a fast pace, and despite being one horse down, we get everything filmed we needed with few adjustments. I think it worked out better in the long run.

/////

By the time I see all the animals after production wrapped for the day, I am more than ready to be done. I am still struggling with my temper and have moments where it flashes so hot and fierce I can almost feel the heat of it rolling off me. Lester was smart enough to send his banking information to me via one of the other grooms. I honestly think I might have laid into the man if he'd come back.

Jessica has called and texted several times today because word travels fast around here. She's been sending silly selfies all day to try to help me cool off. I laugh at them and even manage to send one or two back to her, but the anger is still simmering. I need a venting session and some alcohol to chill out. She's already at Charlie's when I'm finally finished and ready to leave, so I hitch a ride with one of the other Americans, a Texan named Drew, who is a wizard with lighting. He's always been nice to me and seems to appreciate having another American or two around.

When I get to Charlie's, I realize I didn't bother to go clean up or even change clothes. I'm not the cleanest, but neither am I as dirty as I have been before, so I head in and find Jess. She's in her usual corner of the bar with her head bent to Charlie's. It's fairly quiet as it is mid-week, but that works for me.

I sit down with a sigh, and before I can even acknowledge Jess or Charlie, he slides a drink my way. Reaching for it as my phone buzzes, I take a long drink before looking at my phone. It's Sean.

"I've got another hour before I can leave set. Want to talk when I'm free?"

I need to apologize to him for being such a harsh bitch today and prefer to do it face to face, so I text him back,

"I'm at Charlie's about to vent and drink. Meet here?"

"Grab the snug."

I finish my first drink quickly, smile and say, "You are a god among men, Charlie. I needed that several hours ago."

I head off to the ladies' room to clean up a bit before coming back and telling Jess and Charlie about Sean meeting us here later. Nothing else needs to be said; Charlie immediately goes to the hidden booth, wipes it down, and with a flourish of his bar towel, bows us into the bench seats.

I laughed for the first time today. Looking at Jess, I wink. He's a cutie, and I know she likes him. I finally got her to admit it. Jess waits until he delivers our next round before she says, "Okay, no witnesses, let it fly. Tell me all, and I'll compare it to the multiple stories I've already heard. Then we find Lester and beat him to a pulp with broccoli."

"Broccoli?" I ask. "What did the poor vegetable do to deserve that mistreatment?"

She laughs and says she has never been a fan of it. Only eats it under duress. I launch into the whole story noticing Charlie quickly joins us. He's heard about it also but doesn't comment. Jessica makes a few sounds but otherwise lets me get through the entire thing without interruption. She shows Charlie out of the booth, stands and says, "Let me see the arm." Her tone breaks no argument causing me to slide the long sleeve of my shirt up to show her my arm and the lovely welt that is now bruising colorfully. With her usual medical efficiency, she pokes, prods and generally annoys the wound until she's determined nothing is broken. Now that it's aching, I look over at Charlie and ask for a double.

While Charlie is mixing my drink, Jess sits next to me, side-hugs me and says, "We can totally go kick his ass if you want, with or without the broccoli, but from what I heard and what you just said, Sean was about to wade in and do it for you."

"I think he was the one who shouted at Lester, but I can't be sure. That red curtain had descended at that point, so I couldn't really do much but keep myself from completely losing my shit and getting physical with Lester."

"Let's not forget Sean putting himself in front of you and demanding that ass Lester apologize." She says with a wiggle of her eyebrows and a nudge in my side. "Such a knight in shining armor."

"Dear Lord, Jessica, give it a rest." I am sighing and laughing at the same time because now that my anger has receded and I can look at things objectively, Sean was exceptionally sweet. I knew at the time I was being harsh, but now I feel worse. Thankfully, I'd already planned to apologize to him. Speak of the devil, and he appears if the tingling at the base of my neck is any indication. Sean walked through the door and headed our way without acknowledging anyone else but Charlie.

Jess got up and moved to the other side of the booth in time for him to sit down heavily. He grabbed my hand and asked, "Are you okay? How's your arm? Did you have Jessica look at it?"

Looking at Jess for confirmation, she nods and says, "No break, no broken skin, just a welt and some lovely bruising. Possibly a bone bruise, but I'm thinking not."

The look on Sean's face would be frightening if I thought it was directed at me. He seems to go into himself for a moment, and I feel his struggle for control of his temper. Ironic, I think. I'm finally calming down, and he seems to be ramping up. I reach over and pat our joined hands before withdrawing mine, snapping him back to the present. "I'm fine. It's over, and I've got a nice bunch of animals I don't necessarily need."

Jess laughs and says, "I told you it was odd that a vet didn't have a pet. Now you have a few dozen."

"In a different country, too," I say with a shrug.

I see Sean hesitate then he says, "Are you really going to buy those animals?"

"Already did. Lester delivered his bank info via Liam this afternoon. I went online and set up the transfer. My accountant won't be happy with me, but I doubt he'll say anything. At least not yet. I emailed him."

Sean looks a bit surprised and says, "Um, I'm probably going to put my foot in it here, but that's a lot of money. Umm, are you okay with that?"

Jessica chokes on her drink and then decides to slide out and go visit Charlie at the bar. I can tell she's laughing. She knows how much money my parents left me. It's not something I usually tell people, but I feel like I need to tell Sean. I hinted at it when I told him about the accident, but now it's time to come clean.

"It's fine. Now it's my turn to feel awkward."

"Why?"

"Sean, I told you about the accident that killed my parents and the trial. What I didn't tell you was the obscene amount of money I was awarded. Pop's firm took care of the litigation and wouldn't take a fee which left me with a large amount of money. It's been sitting there, gaining value every day. I didn't touch it until after I got out of vet school. My grandmother created a trust for me for my college expenses, and it was more than generous enough to pay for school, so I didn't need the other money."

Looking at my hands, I added something that it took me years to admit to myself. "I also thought it was blood money and wouldn't touch it because it took my parents. Therapy helped me with that, and now I use the money for things that make me feel like I'm making a difference, like Paws & Claws. Buying those animals today kept them from being abused and me from physically assaulting Lester. I think that's a good use of funds."

Sean gave me a startled look, so I amended it to, "Okay, I wouldn't have become violent, but I thought about it. A LOT."

"Pardon me for this, but you're well off?" Sean asks with his eyebrows almost to his hairline.

"You bet, sugar." I smiled brightly, feeling better than I had all day because I was able to shock this charming, handsome man. "Now I'm convinced you only like me for my money." Looking over at Jess at the bar, I see she's watching with ill-concealed interest. I give her a big smile, and she bursts out laughing when Sean turns in that direction. He looks shell-shocked.

"Well, okay then." He stammers out as he takes a drink of his beer, "Hold on, that's not true." Taking pity on him, I stop laughing.

Sobering a bit, I reach out and lay my hand on top of Sean's, "I know; I need to apologize to you for how I behaved earlier today. I was lost in my temper and not thinking clearly. I shouldn't have bitten your head off when you were standing up for me. I'm only used to Jess being the bulldog. I'm sorry."

"You have nothing to be sorry for," he says quietly, flipping his hand over so we are palm to palm. "That jackass Lester is the one who still owes you an apology. I'm going to see that you get it, too."

"No. Please. Just leave it alone. He's been paid; the papers will be signed at the bank tomorrow in order for the funds to be released to him. He'll be out of my hair."

"I still don't like it. But I did enjoy the way you knocked him on his arse. You've got skills." He said, raising his glass in a small toast. "I will admit that seeing you in a temper made me remember what Jess told me about not pissing you off. I'll be taking that to heart. Your voice was like thunder. I was in the production trailer in a discussion when I heard it as plain as if I was standing next to you. 'You will not use that whip on that animal again, so help me God' – I think I felt the trailer shake."

Laughing at his description and attempt at my Southern accent, I primly replied, "I wasn't the one who roared out STOP like a lion. I believe that was you?"

"Yes, I couldn't stop myself. He was going to hit you with that whip. I still can't believe it. He should have been arrested for it."

"Your shout made me turn and block the worst of it. And sweeping his leg would have gotten me arrested along with him, I believe. Best that things ended as they did."

"I'm still not messing with you when you're in a temper. It has to be the red in your hair."

"You sure it isn't dyed?" I toss out as I turn to see Jess and Charlie walk back over. The talk turns to Thursday Night's Karaoke theme; this week, it's American Country. Jess and I grin at each other, and both look up our schedule for the next day. We need to have plenty of energy for tomorrow night. By the time we leave a few hours later, my mood and temper have smoothed out, and I know I'll sleep soundly. The extra drinks will ensure that I'm out the moment my head hits the pillow.

Chapter 18

Thursdays at Charlie's means karaoke night, and every other Thursday is a theme. This week is American Country which Jess and I discussed over breakfast. We didn't realize there was non-American Country music and decided to start looking into international artists to see what the sound was and who are the big artists. Many of the crew are as crazy about karaoke as Jess and I, so we talk about it and start a little friendly rivalry. The Texan, Drew, tells me he is all in for karaoke and asks how I am with duets. I laugh and tell him I'm in. We plan to pick a couple of good songs once we see the list. He's also hit up Jessica for a few duets. It should be a good night.

The day was light for filming, and the weather cooperated with little to no rain. I was able to baby Rock a bit and continue the treatment on the abscess. He'll be back to new in a few days and likely better than that since he doesn't have that horrid man beating on him. Rick stopped by as I was leaving the stall and casually asked me if things were settled. I know him well enough to read between the lines.

"Lester signed the papers at the bank earlier this morning. The money is transferred, and ownership of the animals is finalized. Do we need to sort out the details for the production company's use of them? Or we can just add an addendum to my contract. That might work out."

"Anderson, I do not like what that man did to you yesterday. Sean Miller wants his head on a pike for what he said, but I didn't hear it, and Sean wouldn't repeat it. Do we need to get legal involved?"

"No. He'll go away now that he's a comfortably wealthy man."

"Come to me immediately if something changes." Walking off, he turns back and says, "I'll get the legal team to add the addendum to your contract and cancel his. You will start getting the fees he was earning this week. No argument."

I smile serenely and say, "Yes, Uncle Rick."

"Get to work."

Jessica and I have been texting back and forth all day, making plans for karaoke. Sometimes I think we are so childish because we like this so much. Then I think we studied so hard for so long during college, grad school, vet and medical school that this was our time to be wild and free. Some students would drink too much and experiment with drugs and sex. We decided on karaoke since we weren't horrible singers. We just let off steam and have fun; this week has been a lot more intense for me, so I'm ready to let loose. We've agreed to finalize details over a dinner of takeout at our flat, and I finish up with a final walk through the barn. The goats are happily munching hay, the sheep are sleepily blinking at me, and the horses are working their way through their grain. All is right in the land of my animal friends.

Roxy, a lovely woman who works in Craft Services and has some developmental challenges, has been stopping by frequently to visit with the horses. I've heard from Liam that she was always run off by Lester Reid, so I make sure she knows she can visit with the horses as long as one of us is there. She likes to bring them carrots and apples, as she did today, and always giggles when they nip them from her hand.

"Roxy, it's time to go. Is your ride here, or can I take you home?" I ask as I approach.

She smiles at me as Rock snaps off a carrot she's holding in her fist. We both grin as he munches and makes a mess of the vegetable. He takes the last piece of it, and Roxy wipes her hands on her pants before she turns to me and smiles again.

"My sister is a princess. She's going to pick me up."

"She is? That must make you a princess too."

"No, only she is a princess because she said she found her prince. I'm just a girl."

"You are lovely. Is she here to pick you up?" I'm scanning the area but don't see any cars that don't belong to my team.

"I'm supposed to walk to the postbox and wait until the top of the hour."

"It's almost the top of the hour now. Would you like for me to walk with you?" I ask with a smile. She's as tall as I am, maybe an inch or so taller, and I would guess several years older, but she reminds me of a girl of ten or so. With such innocence and sweetness, I can't help but want to hug her.

She looks at her watch and then breaks into an awkward trot toward the drive. "I'll go now."

I watch as she makes it to the bend in the drive, and the trees block the view. Patrick is getting ready to leave, so I ask him to drive slowly and make sure she is picked up. I know he is fond of her, so he will probably wait at the end of the drive and chat with her until her sister picks her up.

Hearing a bark, I turn and find Rab at the entrance to the barn. He takes it upon himself to stop by and see me when Sean brings him to the farm when filming there. He will hang around for a while, mostly trying to get me to play with him or let him herd the goats or sheep. If I don't fall in line with his wishes, he'll either go find a spot for a nap or go back to Sean's trailer. Either way, he's a sweet dog who is too smart for his own good. I find myself talking to him like I would a human. Hazard of my job, I suppose, I talk to all animals.

"Hi, Rab. It's late for a visit. I'm getting ready to leave." I say as I squat down to give him a good rub and ruffle his ears.

"We're on our way out too. I was hoping you were still here." Sean says as he rounds the corner of the open door.

"I thought you had a couple more hours to go?"

"We had problems with a couple of the cameras, so we're done for tonight. Tomorrow will be longer, but it gives me some time off tonight. That's where you come in."

"Ummm, okay. What did you have in mind?"

"Dinner before karaoke at Charlie's." He says simply with a smile that could honestly melt the knees of a nun.

"Jess is picking up takeout for us. We're finalizing our karaoke plan. You could join us if you'd like."

Laughing, Sean shakes his head, "It's funny how serious you both are about something as silly as karaoke. I was hoping to spend a little time alone with you."

"It's serious business to us." I say, then cock my head to the side and before I overthink, "How about I call Jess and have her grab takeout for one, and I take you up on your offer? She and I can meet up later. Do I need to change before we go out?"

"I'm in the mood to cook, and we have time; how about we go to my place?."

"You cook?" I ask, a bit shocked and not a little unnerved by the idea of being along with him at his house.

"I do and fairly well, I'm told by my friends." He says a bit smugly.

Dramatically grabbing at my chest, I say, "Be still my heart, a man that cooks and does it well. When's the wedding?"

"Let's start with dinner first; then, we can pick out china patterns."

"Deal." I enjoyed the lighthearted banter and quickly texted Jess that I was ditching her, which I knew she would understand. She immediately replied with a thumbs up and kissy face emojis. I reply with a finger emoji and see her at Charlie's at 9. Turning to Sean, I say, "Do we need to stop and get food?"

"No, I keep the kitchen stocked. Let's go."

Chapter 19

I found myself very curious about where Sean lived and was surprised when he turned off the main highway to what looked to me like a Victorian home, complete with ornate moldings and woodwork. He had already told me he lived in an older, established neighborhood with large lots and walls around most of the homes. He said his lot was over an acre and had a wall around the entire perimeter. I teased him that it was obviously to keep the adorning throng at bay while he was home.

"Actually, no one seems to have found me yet. I bought the house in my sister's married name. My neighbor's all respect my privacy as I respect theirs; it works out nicely all around, I think."

"This big wall helps with that; I'd bet," I say as we drive up to the gates that slowly open. Looking over at him, I ask, "Did you have to push a button for that?"

He laughed and explained he has a very close friend who owns his own security business, so he has installed a system for the house that also included automatically linking the car to the gate. "As long as I am in this car, I don't have to enter a code to get the gates to open. I can also use my phone."

Impressed, I laugh and say, "I bet you can also arm and disarm the security system and turn your lights on in the house, right?"

"Yes. Brendon is a tech wizard, and I get to be his test dummy. It's great until there is a glitch, and the alarm starts blaring at 2 am. I almost killed him for that one, but he's gotten a lot better."

I could tell he really enjoyed the memory by the smile on his face and the laughter glowing in his eyes. He seems more relaxed right now than I've seen him in a while, and I comment on it. He reaches out and catches my hand, giving it a squeeze; he says, "Must be the company I'm keeping."

I know I'm blushing as I pull my hand away and look out the window at the lawn.

Pulling into a garage that looks like it is detached, he turns off the car, quickly jumps out and walks around to open my door. "Welcome to my home." He takes my hand again and leads me through a door into a glassed breezeway that leads to the main house. Opening the door, we walk into a mudroom that opens into the kitchen. I am momentarily stunned by the kitchen; I'm no great cook, but this kitchen is magnificent.

The room itself is large, with tall ceilings and a large sitting area off to one side. The island in the middle of the kitchen deserves its own zip code. Five bar stools line one side, and a solid white sink sits at one corner of the acre of "Marble?" I ask.

"Good eye. Yes."

The island and the lower cabinets are a dark smoky gray, and the upper cabinets are several shades lighter. The marble blends perfectly, as does the backsplash, which looks like a combination of glass, stone and tile. The farmhouse sink is large enough to bathe a big dog and overlooks the backyard, or garden as they call it here. There is a mixture of open cabinets and a glass front that offer plenty of storage. I wander around the kitchen, noting the six-burner stove that looked complicated enough to belong in a restaurant, the stainless steel refrigerator, the small wine cooler, the dishwasher and what I am guessing is a microwave tucked under the far end of the island. This kitchen would make Martha Stewart envious. It's lost on me because I'm not a good cook, but it would be a lot of fun to bake in here or host a party.

Sean has disappeared for a minute, and then I hear music. I look up to the recessed lighting and cock my head to the side. The music is coming from the lights, but I can't figure out how. Sean returns and notices my puzzled look at the ceiling.

"The recessed lights are also speakers; they run throughout the house so I can listen to whatever strikes me and not have to blast it. Another Brendan connection there. He's really amazing; I'll have to introduce you the next time he comes around. Now, would you like a tour, or do you want to go straight to dinner?"

"Let's eat first; then, you can show me around a bit before we head to Charlie's. Sound good?"

"Anything you want. I didn't think to ask if you are vegetarian, vegan or have any food allergies. Do you?"

"No allergies, and I do eat meat, but I'm not a fan of mushrooms. What can I help with? I'm not a good cook, but I know which end of a knife to use." I say with a big cheesy grin.

"You'll have a seat there and enjoy a glass of wine while I take care of the rest. I'm not making anything complicated, so we should be eating in no time." He turns to the massive side-by-side refrigerator, opens and starts grabbing fresh vegetables and chicken. Setting everything on the island, he grabs a bottle of Pinot Grigio and brings it over to me. "How does this look? I admit, I rely on my mother and my sisters for the wine, but I do know this goes with chicken." With a wink, he hands over the bottle for me to review. I shrug and say, "It looks good to me. I don't want too much, though. I missed lunch, and wine on an empty stomach gives me a horrible headache."

He pours me a half glass and himself a full, then heads back to the other side of the island to start washing the food. He seems very confident and comfortable in the kitchen, which I tell him. The conversation flows easily as he quickly chops, sautés, seasons and stirs our dinner. The smell is divine, and my stomach starts to make those embarrassingly loud noises. To distract him so he doesn't hear my stomach, I ask, "Where did you learn to cook like this?"

"My mum taught all of us to cook as well as clean up. I'll admit I hated learning about it, but now I enjoy it. It relaxes me and lets my mind wander. Not to mention, I can avoid a lot of heavy sauces and all the additives and garbage put into most foods now."

"How do you do it when you're so busy? Surely you are exhausted when you work 14 hours a day." I ask as I imagine how sad my culinary practice is most nights. Jess and I either eat takeout or keep it simple, like salads.

Sean walks over to his massive stainless steel side-by-side again, but this time opens the freezer to reveal a lot of small containers. "My family makes sure I'm fed well when I'm working."

"Do they live close?" I ask, thinking his family must descend at least once a month to stock that massive freezer with all those containers. "That's a pretty impressive number of dinners in there."

"My parents live outside of London. My sisters and my brother are scattered around here and there, but we always get together as often as possible. Sometimes once a month, but things have been a bit more crazy than usual. I haven't seen them in almost two months." Sean returns to the stove, gives the pan with the chicken and vegetables a shake, turns off the burner and takes the pan to the plates he set out.

With practiced ease, he tips the stir fry onto the plates. Turning back to the stove, he takes the saucepan with the rice and adds it to each plate. Grabbing both plates, he walks around the island to my side and places one in front of me. It smells divine, and my stomach makes itself known with a loud rumble. He is gracious and doesn't comment, which saves me from more embarrassment.

Sliding onto the bar stool next to me, he picks up his wine glass and turns to me with a toast, "To a lovely dinner with a lovelier companion."

Smiling, I raise my wine glass to his and drink. The wine is tart and tastes good. I set it aside and reached for my fork. My first bite proves he is as good a cook as I expected. The simple meal he invited me to tastes wonderful, and conversation slows as we both turn our attention to our food.

"Tell me more about your family," I ask. "You mentioned your parents, sisters and brother. Where did you grow up? How many sisters do you have?"

"My parents were both born in Ireland but moved to Liverpool after they married. My father is a semi-retired engineer, and my mother was a schoolteacher until last year. My father's company moved us around some; we lived in Manchester, Nottingham and Leicester before they decided to retire and open a B&B with my Aunt and Uncle. They are happily living outside Liverpool in a massive house catering to tourists and travelers."

He's smiling as he speaks of his parents, and I can see the affection and love on his face. Turning to me, he continues, "I have two older sisters and one younger sister. Frances Catherine is the oldest, five years older than me; Siobhan is next; she's three years older than me; then Aileen who is younger than me by two years. My brother, Keane, is the youngest, and he follows two years after Aileen."

"Five children. Your parents had a houseful!"

"It was crowded. The girls shared a room, and Keane and I shared a room. It certainly made for some memorable times." "You're the middle child. That makes you the peacekeeper, right?"

"My sisters wouldn't say that, but I have read that middle children are peacekeepers. I remember mediating a few rows in my days at home. The girls shared the larger room, but there were still three of them in one room, so it meant someone was always wanting privacy. It got so bad at one point my mother hung curtains to divide the room into thirds. They stayed that way for almost a year before the girls grew out of that nonsense."

"And you and Keane? Did you put a stripe down the middle of your room to divide it in half?"

Laughing, Sean glanced up, lost in thought for a moment, then replied, "No, but I did spend several summers at my grandparent's to get away from all of them."

"I can imagine it was chaotic with five children under ten years. I was an only child until I moved in with Jessica and her family. Things took a while to adjust to, but I never know if it was the circumstances or the chaos of having a brother and sister." I pick up my wine to take a sip and notice it's empty. Without thinking, I get up and move to where I see the glasses and make myself a glass of water. As I sit, I realize I may seem pushy, making myself at home in his kitchen. I feel my cheeks heat up as I glance over at Sean.

"Don't be embarrassed. I'm glad you feel at home here." He states smoothly, clearly interpreting my unease as well as my blush. Taking pity on me, he continues, "Dinners were the best for as long as I can remember. We always talked about our days, and if one of us had a problem, all of us helped come up with the solution. If one of us had a triumph, we all celebrated it. And the food, ah, the food was magnificent. My mum is a spectacular cook."

"Your mother isn't the only one; my compliments to the chef," I say with a satisfied smile as I rest my fork on my plate. I ate almost half the portion he gave me and considered eating more, but I knew it would make me miserable. I'm comfortably full now and more than content, but it tastes fantastic.

"It's just a simple stir fry. You could make it too."

I laugh and say, "I doubt that. You didn't have a strict recipe to follow, and that is my only hope. I can't toss in seasonings the way you did and expect any success."

"It's just practice. This is one of my go-to meals if I don't want to eat takeout or take the time to defrost something. It's quick, healthy and filling."

"You forgot, flavorful and amazing. Is it your go-to when you cook for women?" I could rip my own tongue out for saying that, and the blush returns in full force.

Sean smiles and says, "Thank you for the compliments on my cooking. And no, it's not my go-to. You're the first woman I've ever cooked for who was not a family member or cast mate. I sometimes have them over for dinner when things aren't too crazy. Now, would you like that tour of the house now?"

I check my watch and am happy to see we have time. "Yes." I can't keep from circling back to his statement that he's never cooked for a woman before. It is odd, but I feel a bit excited about that. Pushing that feeling away, I tell myself we are strictly friends as I gather my dishes and follow him around the island to the sink. He takes my dishes, puts them down and gestures for me to precede him.

We walk out of the kitchen into a large living room dominated by the sectional I saw when I arrived. The pillows are large and soft, and the cushions are overstuffed but not hard. I'd love to sink into it; the perfect spot to lounge and read a book. I say as much before turning to the fireplace, which dominates the wall opposite the sectional.

"Wow, that's a large television. It's the entire width of the fireplace mantle." Glancing over at him, I continued, "I thought you weren't a huge television watcher?"

"It's a man thing, I guess. I watch the occasional show or movie, but this is mostly for sports."

Deciding to tease him a bit, I point to the soft throw over the back of the sofa and say, "You cuddle up with that while watching sports?"

He laughs. "Siobhan is a decorator and took charge of the whole place when I bought it. Certain things were non-negotiable, she said. That is one of them. I don't think I've touched it since she put it there."

We move down a short hallway that leads to the main foyer and staircase. Going up, he shows me four large bedrooms, each decorated beautifully and each with a bathroom. I can see why his family comes to visit and tell him so. I also note that none of the rooms feels like it belongs to him.

"None of these rooms are yours," I say absentmindedly as we walk back down the stairs.

"How do you know that? Do you think I'm messy?" he says with a wink and a smile.

Without thinking, I blurt out, "Not one smelled like you do." I stop suddenly on the bottom step and wish the floor would open and swallow me. I feel my cheeks fire up as I look anywhere but at Sean. I have got to get hold of my brain and think before I speak, or I'll keep embarrassing myself.

He walks back to me, crowds in a bit closer than I'm used to, ducks his head down to align with my eyes and, in a husky voice, says, "Don't smell like me? Do I have a distinctive scent, then?"

I bite my lower lip and nod, unable to break the eye contact. He reaches up and very gently pulls my lip out from between my teeth and rubs his thumb across it. I change my mind and no longer want the ground to swallow me up. I get chill bumps and can't repress a shiver as he strokes my lip. Noticing his eyes have darkened, I drag my eyes away and quickly mumble, "It's not bad. You don't smell bad, I mean." Mortified, I silently wish I had better control over my mouth.

With a grunt, he drops his hand and gestures me down another hallway off the foyer. I am a bit concerned I've offended him in some way because he doesn't say anything. As we pass two doors in the hall, I rub my hands together nervously. Approaching the door at the end of the hall, he gestures for me to precede him and enter. I open the door and step into a master suite that I immediately recognize as his personal space. I stop just a step into the room and scan the area. He has a massive bed, a seating area by another fireplace, vaulted ceilings, acres of lush carpeting and three doors.

I feel him come up behind me and stop when he's barely touching my back. My neck tingles as he leans down to whisper in my ear, "Does this smell like me?" I have to lock my knees to keep from melting back into the man. He's so damn sexy; he makes my eyes cross. Especially when he talks in that low gravely voice.

Determined not to look like a schoolgirl and drop into a puddle at his feet, I stiffen my spine, step toward the first door and ask, "Bathroom? After seeing the other bathrooms, I've got high expectations for this one."

"Not that door, the far one." He says, and I think I hear what sounds like exasperation in his voice. Glancing back at him, I see he's turned away toward the window and has his hand at the back of his neck. He's probably ready to get me out of his private domain.

I quickly open the door to the bathroom and come to a complete stop. "Oh. My. God," I practically moan. This bathroom is beyond anything I've ever imagined. It seems long and narrow, with dark cabinets from floor to ceiling on one wall with two sinks built in but separated by more cabinets. At the end of the room is a nook that houses a soaking tub I would die for, surrounded by stacked stone and the same dark wood as the cabinets. I see heated towel racks near the tub, and as I walk toward it, I get another shock. To the right, after the cabinets, is another area which houses a small water closet for the toilet and a shower straight out of a fantasy. The shower shares a wall with the bathtub nook. It is a walk-in but has stone walls halfway up and glass to the ceiling. There are body jets and a rain head that make me think of long showers after hard days. I blush profusely as I immediately imagine a naked Sean under that rain head.

Turning to Sean, I know my expression is still shocked and likely beet red when I say, "Can I have your bathroom, please?"

He laughs and tells me it would be hard to pack in my suitcase. I tell him I need pictures and plans so I can recreate this bathroom in my future home. Then a thought strikes me if the bathroom is this nice, the closet must be amazing as well. Turning to him, I widen my eyes and say, "Please tell me the master closet compares to this remarkable bathroom. I'm a woman; these things are important to me. I need to know."

Gesturing me back out of the bathroom, he shows me to the door immediately next to it. There are about four feet or so between doors, so I guess this is the closet. Opening the door, I let out a sigh of pure feminine delight. If the bathroom was worthy of a moan, this is definitely sigh-worthy. The same dark wood is used in the built-ins, but it doesn't make the room appear small since there is a large window at one end and a lovely light fixture in the middle that provides light worthy of a make-up mirror. The built-ins make me want to weep with envy. There are shoe cubbies, dress hanging rods, short rods for shirts, pants, etc. and mirrors that slide out to reveal more hanging space. Down the center is an island that has so many small drawers I wonder what they could be used for. I imagine socks, lingerie, scarves, jewelry and more but refuse to invade his privacy by asking or, heaven forbid, looking at myself.

Looking at Sean with glazed eyes again, I say, "If you tell me that the third door is a laundry room, I may be forced to kill you so I can have your home all to myself."

Sean roars with laughter to the point he has to bend over and put his hands on his knees to stay upright. "I need to let my sister know your reaction. She took it as a personal mission to remodel this part of the house to be enviable. I told her I didn't plan on anyone seeing it, but she insisted. I'm glad I let her have her way now. She'll get a kick out of your reaction."

Straightening, he takes a deep breath and answers my question about the third door. "No, it's not a laundry room, but that's a good idea. Come see what it is. I think you'll be equally pleased, and I'll be on my guard in case you decide to try to take me out."

It's ridiculous to be so giddy about a bathroom and closet, but I am. Sometimes a girl just needs a good soak and to spend some time in a fantastic closet deciding what to wear. Smiling, I reach for the third door, wondering what other surprises can be waiting. It opens to reveal a short hallway with stairs leading down. Turning to Sean, I ask, "Do I need to be worried about you taking me out in the dungeon below?"

He laughs and says, "Maybe it's my secret playroom."

Laughing, I start to walk down the stairs and toss over my shoulder, "Do not go 50 Shades on me, Sean." I turn the corner at the bottom of the stairs and enter a gym that is both simple and impressive. "Wow. I really do need your house. Why do you go to the gym in town when you have this?"

"I like to spar with partners and also like to join classes occasionally because there is something about the competitive vibe that makes me push harder."

Nodding, I agree with that statement. I don't consider myself a very competitive person, but I do reach down and push myself to achieve more when I'm in a class. The gym has a wall of windows reflecting the darkness, which makes me check my watch. It's 8:30 pm already, and I promised Jess I'd meet her at 9. I realize I'm not ready to leave, but I've really enjoyed this time with Sean. I have been able to see a different side of him and like it a lot. We are becoming good friends, and sometimes I think I want more, but that makes me nervous, so I focus on the friendship.

"Are you ready to get your butt kicked at karaoke?" I ask as I walk back toward the stairs. Stopping me, he turns to another door and leads me up another flight of stairs which come out in the hall between the foyer and kitchen. While walking up, he tells me he won't be singing and plans to watch others get their butts kicked.

Chapter 20

Charlie's is packed by the time I get cleaned up and arrive. Some adventurous locals are singing 70's country songs with the enthusiasm of the original singers. Spotting Jess in the partially hidden snug, I start to make my way to her while Sean stops to greet several who have spotted him.

"Hey!" I say as I get to Jess.

She gives me a big, cheesy smile and says, "How was dinner? Did you have dessert?" Waggling her eyebrows suggestively, she follows that with, "Give me the details quick before the guys get over here."

"Dinner was great, but his bathroom and closet are beyond amazing. You'd positively die if you saw them. And he has a gym downstairs that is awesome."

Jess looks a bit surprised by my statements. "Um, you went to dinner at a sexy, hot guy's house and just told me about the food and his bathroom? Are you ok?"

Charlie walks up at that moment. He gives me a side hug and asks what I'm drinking tonight. Jess and I are in for the long haul tonight, so I go for hard cider. He leaves to get my drink, and Jess pokes at me again.

"Seriously, Anderson. Didn't you get any sexy time with him?"

"Jess, he and I are friends. Or we are starting to be friends. He doesn't look at me that way."

"Honey, you're either blind, stupid or scared. I'm not unpacking that tonight, though. But mark my words, Anderson, we will revisit this topic. Now, I've looked over the list of songs, and we are going to have a great time. Charlie said he's changing things up tonight, but

I'm not sure what that means. Doesn't matter; we've got great material to work with, so it's the Andi & Jess show tonight."

Glad to be given a reprieve from the inquisition, but knowing it would be coming around again, I let out a sigh and settled into the booth. Charlie brings my cider in the bottle. I told him no mug; I'm going straight up country and drinking from the bottle. It's a local hard cider, so I expect it will be a treat. My first sip proves the choice is a good one. Tart enough to give a bit of a bite but sweet enough to go down easy.

Charlie moves off to the microphone and quickly explains what he means by changing things up. "Welcome everyone to Country Karaoke Night at Charlie's! We're changing things up a bit tonight."

"Instead of the traditional format of turning in a song choice with your name, we're mixing it up and having you fill out separate slips for your name and your song. They will go in these two glass bowls, and we will choose one song and then choose singers based on if it's a single, duet, or group song. You won't know what you're singing or who you're singing with until you get up here. Get ready for some fun tonight! Take the next 10 minutes to get your drinks, fill out your songs and your performance cards."

"This is an unexpected turn," Jess says as she looks at me quizzically. "We've never participated with rules like this, but it could be fun. Unless we get paired with a super bad singer."

Shrugging, I say, "It'll still be fun anyway. You know there will be someone singing Delta Dawn and Fancy."

Those songs were constant repeats when we were in college. Between those and pretty much every Journey song, you could always count on some good and bad singers. Add in those who treat karaoke as if it's an audition for American Idol or The Voice, and you've got the makings for an entertaining evening.

I ask Jess, "How many do you want to sing tonight? I may be up for 4, possibly 5."

"I'm not sure. We may not get that many chances; this crowd is pretty thick. Oooh, look who just walked in. Remember the girl who sang all those Adele songs that first night?"

"Yes, I believe her name was Lizette. She was all over Sean, and I swear she was singing to him. Let's not forget that lovely warning I got from her." Rolling my eyes, I survey the crowd and smile when I see Ezra putting his name and some song slips in the jars. I'd love to sing with him even if he has a bad voice. He's just adorable and enjoys it as much as Jess, and I do. "So how many? I say we load up the song jar with our faves and then put in just the number we want to sing. This is a unique and fun way to mix up a regular karaoke night."

"Let's do it." Jess grabs the slips of paper, passes me half, and we get started. Occasionally consulting on the songs, we quickly make our selections as the rest of the crowd is doing. Jess takes our choices up to the correct jars and, with a wink and swish of her long skirt, heads back to the booth.

Without a word, we both pick up our drinks, clink the glasses, grin and take a drink. Sean finally breaks free and joins us as Charlie announces the first song, Miranda Lambert's Gunpowder and Lead and the first singer. He pulls out a name, laughs and says, "I'll pick a female, so we start out on a traditional note. Let's welcome a local, Eileen!"

Everyone claps as Eileen makes her way to the stage and tells us she's not sure she can sing Miranda Lambert but will give it a go. She does a remarkable job considering it's not her key, and she wasn't sure of the words. The next couple of songs end up being male country singers, Jason Aldean and Alan Jackson. Charlie then announces a group, Little Big Town's Day Drinking and calls up Ezra, Drew, Jess and me. We both love this song, so we jump up. Knowing Ezra is horrible, we tell him he gets to sing Phillip's part. Jess and I split the roles by hair color. I have a deeper voice, so I get Karen, and she gets Kimberly. That leaves Jimi for Drew. Ezra isn't familiar with the song, so he's happy to whistle and sing harmony. In the end, it sounded pretty decent for a first-time singing together.

"How about that match-up? Not bad, not bad at all." Charlie says as he comes back up on stage. "Let's see who gets to follow." Reaching in, he pulls out "Jolene by Dolly Parton. And to sing will be Lizette!"

Jess and I look at each other and quickly look away as we try to hold back our laughter. It may be petty and mean, but that song choice is perfect for her. She wants to keep women away from her man, Sean.

Lizette did her best, but you could tell she had never heard Dolly sing it. Charlie tried to get more applause for her, but it was lukewarm at best. Next up, he called Jess, me and a lady from the crew Tara that we had seen but never really talked to. We got to sing Dixie Chicks Cowboy Take Me Away. Tara likes Dixie Chicks, so we had fun with it and decided we wanted to add Goodbye Earl to the list. Laughing and hugging, we parted, and I barely returned to the booth when Charlie called my name.

"Andi, you'll need to come on back up. We've got another Little Big Town song, but it's really just one voice, so I'm not calling anyone else up. You get Girl Crush."

I'm smiling since I know Jess and I both can sing the heck out of this one. I use the tall bar table on the stage with the glass jars as a prop. The music starts, and I stand there singing and staring at the table as if I'm unsure of myself; I'm no professional, but I can sell this one for sure. I'm slowly moving my fingers around my bar napkin. During the entire song, I never lift my head until the very end of the song. For the last few chords, I raise my head and look straight out at the crowd, then put the mic down and walk off stage. Silence follows. I walk straight back to the booth, high-five Jessica and sit down next to her. All of this has taken about 3 seconds. Sean looks stunned. Sitting across from me, he has a look of pure shock on his face.

The bar suddenly erupts in applause and cheering. Charlie is standing there looking fairly shocked himself before he says, "I think we will take a break before we bring up the next singer. We all need to let that one sink in." He leaves the stage and heads toward us.

Sean finally manages to say something. "Christ, Andi. That was amazing. Truly amazing."

Charlie joins and agrees with Sean. "You really can sing, Andi. I mean, you've got talent."

"Not really. That's not the first time I've sung that song."

Sean says, "I'm not familiar with that song, but, damn, it was powerful. At first, I thought you were nervous since you didn't look at the audience like you had before, but in the end. When you lifted your head, it was piercing."

I feel myself blushing and turn away to look at Jess. She's giving me a look of such pride I get even more embarrassed. That is one of the songs we had in our hip pocket for the last country club event.

"Andi, you've never sounded that good before. These guys were right. You were absolutely amazing. I wonder who thinks that song is about lesbians?" Jess deadpans.

I choke on the remains of my drink which causes Sean to pat me on the back while looking quizzically at Jessica. No comments are made, which makes me laugh that much harder.

Charlie gets us all another round of drinks before he heads back to the stage and gets things started again. He spends a couple of minutes looking through the songs in the bowl before he selects one and says, "Let's see if we can bring some American bro-Country to the stage. Ezra, come on up and sing Luke Bryan's Shake It For Me."

Jess and I look at each other and snort with laughter. That song, sung by Ezra, who admits he cannot sing, is going to be hilarious. Sean even laughs, acknowledging he knows that song as well. The three of us settle in to enjoy the next three or four minutes. Ezra has fun with the song and even tries to mimic some of Luke Bryan's dance moves which throw us into fits of laughter again. He wraps up, and Charlie calls Jess up to sing Before He Cheats by Carrie Underwood. A couple of classics by George Strait and Johnny Cash let the locals have some fun. Charlie pulls out a song, grins really big and looks over at us. "Jess and Andi, you ladies get to come to sing Something Bad. Think you can do it justice?"

Jess immediately pops up, sashays to the stage and leans very close to Charlie's ear, saying, "Hide and watch." We take a minute to discuss who will sing Carrie and who will sing Miranda. We've switched back and forth a few times before when we've chosen this song. Sticking with our strengths, Jess takes Carrie's part, and I get Miranda's. We both reach up and take down our hair, shaking it out as Charlie starts the track. A little less than 3 minutes later, we're both twirling a strand of our hair around a finger singing the last line. Then we smiled hugely at each other and walked back to our table as the applause and cat calls commenced. We really love singing karaoke together, and it shows. Sean was laughing and saluted us with his drink.

"Well done, ladies. I think half the bar would give their eye teeth to be bad with you."

Someone yells, "I'd love to be bad with BOTH of them!"

Laughing at that, I sat down and grabbed a full, ice-cold hard cider. I know I haven't finished a whole one yet; this one is brand new. Charlie's work, no doubt which, makes me realize I need to be careful about how much I drink tonight. These automatic refills could sneak up on me.

Charlie called Lizette up to sing a Shania Twain classic, followed by two more male country songs. A local woman named Amelia sang a vintage song about cheating and had a fantastic voice. The crowd started to thin a bit around half past midnight when Charlie pulled a Lady Antebellum song out.

"We've got a trio for this one. Drew, Alec and Andi come on up for Just a Kiss."

Drew and Alec have good voices, and the song is one of my favorites. It's actually pretty interesting the lyrics of the song are about going slow at the beginning of a relationship and not jumping in. I've always been a Lady A fan, and the range is good for me, so I enjoy the company and the song.

When we finish, I decide I'm done for the night. Walking toward the table, I give a couple of high fives to some people and spend a couple of minutes chatting with a few I recognize from the production crew. I get to the table and turn to ask Jess if she's ready to leave. I'm willing to bet it's raining again, so that rules out walking.

Sean stands up as if to let me slide in the booth but then grabs my hand and pulls me down the hall to the back by Charlie's office. It's dark back in this area as it is off-limits to patrons. I turn to ask him what's wrong when I find myself propelled out the back door into the alley. Turning on him, I find myself backed up against the wall outside with Sean's hands buried in my hair and his mouth on mine. Holy Mary, Mother of God, the man can kiss. That's the only thought I managed to get through before my brain short-circuited. I stop thinking completely and just feel. I can attest to the fact the man is solid muscle, and there cannot be any fat on him.

Tearing his mouth from mine, he puts his cheek to the top of my head and holds me tightly. I can feel an energy around him that I'm unfamiliar with; he seems almost desperate but hasn't said a word.

We stay like this for several minutes before he loosens the pressure of the hug and pulls back to look at me, sliding his hands down my arms to my hands. "I know I seem mad, but I had to do that. I can't explain it."

"It's ok. It's not like it was a hardship on my part," I say with a small smile that shows my confusion, and I squeeze his hands. I'm still feeling that energy, and it's made me more than a little edgy. Add to it my own reactions and worries; I'm starting to feel the need to back away. "I'm actually ready to go, and I think Jess is too. Would you mind taking us home?"

He must have sensed my unease because he tugged me toward the back door and said, "Let's collect Jess and head out."

As the door closed behind us, we didn't notice the person in the shadows lowering the camera and slowly backing away.

Chapter 21

The next several weeks are consumed with the push to finish much of the outdoor production during a break in the seemingly endless rain. The schedule is packed tightly, and days often run into twelve to fourteen hours. I stay busy coordinating the rotation and transportation of the animals. I quickly realized I couldn't handle running all of this along with my business back home, so I've hired an extra two grooms to help coordinate the transportation as it is often the smaller animals are needed for only part of the day.

Sean and I text frequently and talk on the phone occasionally. We've spent a few evenings at Charlie's with Jess and several others. On one such evening, I got to meet Sean's co-stars, the two lead actors who have been filming on the location several hours south of here. Shannon Collins is a gorgeous female with flowing blonde hair and a figure that would make most women hate her. She is also one of the nicest women I have ever had the pleasure of meeting. Jasper Campbell is a flirt if I have ever laid eyes on one. He's about an inch taller than me, which makes him a relatively short man, but he makes up for it with a personality that is giant. His dark hair and equally dark eyes make him seem like a rogue, but he's a sweet man who has been married for almost five years and has two adorable children. The entire cast and crew get along very well despite being separated for more time than they are together filming.

The only dark spot in an otherwise idyllic period is the bad luck I seem to have come across. The first instance was finding something wedged into the lock of the barn office door. This required a locksmith to remove a shoeing nail. Several days later, the tack needed for the day's shoot was not in the trailer, and I personally loaded it the night before. We found it dumped in an empty stall, but the delay cost us an hour of daylight. Add to that string of mishaps the flat tires and blowouts that have plagued my team for the last ten days, and I am more than ready for a break.

After a particularly long day, I am helping Patrick, one of the new groom/stable hands, load up the horses to return to the barn when Sean stops and asks for a moment of my time. I step away to speak with him, leaving Patrick to finish. We haven't spent time alone together since the impromptu kiss in the back alley of Charlie's. I felt odd for a couple of days because I thought we were strictly friends. It seems to have faded, and we've been back to our usual banter for the last 24 hours.

"You look like you're ready to fall over. How much of that is makeup, and how much is exhaustion?"

He looks down at himself and gives me a tired smile, "It's probably equal."

"Are you finished for the day?"

"I am. I wanted to ask if you'd like to come over for a while tonight. I'll defrost something, and we can watch that African Cats documentary you mentioned."

"Are you sure? You probably need to be unconscious for about 10 hours."

"I'm sure I need to wind down and would appreciate the company. How long will you need at the farm? I need about an hour to get all this off and back to semi-normal."

"That works. Do I meet you at your house?" I ask with a tilt of my head.

"No, I'll have the driver stop by and pick you up."

"Ok. See you in an hour or so."

While I was talking to Sean, Patrick finished loading up the horses and gave them a bit of hay to munch on the way back to the barn. The trip is short, but we're all tired, so we take it slow. It's a good thing we did because less than a mile from the location, the back tire of the trailer blows. Normally, this isn't a huge hassle, but this makes the third one in less than 10 days. We have to unload the horses, tie them off away from the road for safety and then deal with changing the tire. From beginning to end, the process will take us about 45 minutes at least. There goes my night, I think, as I unload Zeus and Rock from the trailer.

Patrick looks at the tire and shakes his head. "I don't know what to make of this, Doc. I'm drivin' careful, and I've been checking the tires since that first blowout. Hell, I mean, heck, the trailer is barely a year old." Along with acquiring the animals from Lester, I had to outfit a truck and trailer to move them back and forth. I got a great deal on both, thanks to a friend of Charlie's, but I have had nothing but trouble with the tires on both truck and trailer. I'm beginning to think this entire country is full of nails and other debris that jumps out in front of my tires.

We're almost finished changing the tire when I see headlights on the road. I tell Patrick to move back to the horses to make sure they don't accidentally spook when the car passes, but it slows instead of passes. The back window rolls down, and Sean sticks his head out.

"Everything ok?" he asks.

"Another flat," I sigh with obvious frustration.

He reaches for the handle to start to get out of the car when I tell him, "No, don't get out. We're almost finished, and there is no point in you getting filthy again. But this does mean I can't hang out tonight. By the time we finish here, get them loaded back up, back to the farm and settled; I'll be ready to fall straight into bed."

Looking disappointed but resigned, he says, "Another time."

"Definitely." I like the man and have come to value my friendship with Sean. He's got a wicked sense of humor, eclectic tastes in music and can talk about pretty much any topic with an open mind. We've even discussed religion and politics without ruffling feathers. Two topics that I normally steer well clear of when in conversation outside Jess and the family. We've also become solid workout partners when time permits. I'm back on my regular routine of yoga and martial arts, with runs sprinkled in to give me a reason to explore the area. Jess joins us occasionally but usually bows out after a couple of miles.

***

"Goodnight, Doc," a tired Patrick says with a half-hearted wave of his hand.

"Goodnight, Patrick. Thanks for everything today." I wave him off as he climbs into his girlfriend's tiny car. It makes me laugh a bit to see him fold himself into that little car. He's tall and lanky and hasn't really finished filling out since he's only twenty. Watching him get in is funny, but watching him unfold himself to get out is downright comical.

As he and his girlfriend zoom down the drive, I walk back into the barn for one last check on everyone. They are all happily munching or snoozing in their stalls and pens. The sights and sounds soothe me and take away a lot of the stress that built up while we were on the side of the road changing the tire. Zeus sticks his head out and calls softly to me. I walk over and give him a hug and stroke his long neck. He's such a baby now that he leans on me when I pet him. I spend a few extra minutes giving him the attention he wants before a yawn makes me turn to leave.

I stretch my arms over my head as I walk toward the main door. Closing it and latching it, I turn toward the truck and promptly trip over a hay rake laid out. Falling, I reach out my hands to break my fall but end up face-planting in the gravel. Pain streaks up my cheek, and I roll over to catch my breath and take stock. I'd swear that rake wasn't there when Patrick left, but it must have been. It also felt like I was shoved because of the momentum when I fell. My face and palms sting like mad. I sit up and look at my palms. There are small pieces of gravel embedded deeply in a couple of spots and scrapes in a few others, but overall, I'm ok—no bone pain in my fingers or wrists. I reach my hand up to my cheek and come away with blood.

"Great, just great." I feel like an idiot, but I have to be happy no one saw my less-than-graceful face plant into the gravel. Picking myself up and dusting off, I continue to the truck after moving the rake to the side of the barn. I know I'll be sore tomorrow. A long soak sounds perfect, but I don't have that luxury in the tiny bathroom. I can soak my feet but not my body, so I'll make do with a long hot shower and some ibuprofen. The ride back is uneventful. I've been feeling more comfortable driving for a week now and enjoy the freedom that comes with having the truck at my disposal. Finding a parking spot is sometimes a challenge, but tonight I got lucky and got one in front of the building.

I'm relieved to see that Jess is out. I'm aching now and more tired with each step. I'm not in the mood for Doctor McSmarty to lecture me about clumsiness. I manage that hot shower and crawl into bed as my phone signals a text. I roll over and grab my phone. It's from Sean.

Too tired to sleep. Not watching the documentary until you can watch it with me. Save me from Social Media.

I laugh and text him back.

Try counting sheep.

Seeing the 3 dots, I can't help but smile and try to guess his comical reply.

They're too gassy. Stink up the whole place. Distract me, or I'm diving into Instagram.

I decided to admit my clumsiness to him, so I texted him about my fall and sent him a funny GIF.

Are you ok? Is Jess there to see to you? Do you need to go to the clinic?

Aww, he's so sweet. I start to text that but then change to

My phone rings in response. Rolling my eyes, I pick up and say, "No, Dad, I don't need to go to a clinic to have my boo boos looked at. I'm fine." I don't mention the nice scrape on my cheek or the small cut at my hairline.

"Boo boos? There are multiple? Anderson, are you really ok? Do I need to come by?" he truly sounds concerned, so I laugh under my breath.

"I'm fine. Really. I've had worse after vaccinating a cranky alpaca. Believe me; this is nothing compared to that."

"If you are sure. I can come to take you to the clinic."

"I'm in bed, and I live with a trauma doctor. I think I'll survive. I just want to go to sleep. It's been a long day."

"Ok, go count sheep." I hear the concern fade and humor come back into his voice. "Goodnight then."

"Goodnight."

That lecture I avoided last night came full force this morning when Jessica got a look at me. Apparently, my face was bad enough to jolt her awake without the benefit of caffeine. Standing in her pajamas with her hair going a thousand directions at once and standing on end, she promptly jumped all over me.

"Are you okay? Why am I seeing this now? And what in the fresh hell happened?"

I laugh and feel the skin pull at my cheek. Wincing, I say, "Calm down, Doctor. I fell. No big deal."

"No big deal? Let me be the judge of that." She takes my hands, notices the wince there and looks at them. They're scraped but nothing bad. I get a glare and a frown for that. She tugs me to the tiny table and sits me in the chair. Switching on the light, she grasps my chin and angles it to see my cheek better. "Did you clean it well and disinfect it?"

"Yes, ma. And I brushed my teeth and made my bed too."

With another glare, she smacks me on the leg. "Dork. Did you hit your head? What about your knees?"

"No, I didn't hit my head. I wasn't fast enough with my hands to break my fall, so I face-planted. Apparently, I fall faster than I used to. My knees are fine. I was in jeans, so not even a scratch."

"Humph." She looks annoyed, but it's obviously gone down a few notches. "Why didn't you call me?"

"Jess, it's a stupid accident that earned me some scratches. I'm fine. Relax, ok?"

"Ok. I guess I overreacted a bit. Your face looks like you got in a fight."

I open my mouth to respond when my phone rings. It's Knox, my other groom. "Good morning, Knox. What can I do for you?"

I listen as he asks me if I locked up last night, which I assure him I did. He then tells me when he got to the barn about 15 minutes ago, the door was open, and two of the horses' stalls were open. Barbie and Jessamine were missing. I grabbed my jacket and told him I'd be there in 20 minutes to get the feeding started and then set out a couple of buckets of feed to start the search.

Jess comes with me to help with the search, and while en route, she calls Rick to let him know there might be a problem and a delay in getting animal footage. Rick asks for us to let him know if we need help searching. When we arrive, Knox has Jessamine and is leading her by the halter back to the barn.

"She just came strolling up like she was out taking the morning air and decided she needed her tea."

"That's good. Does she have any scratches or wounds or anything of that sort?"

"No, but the funny thing is, she had a halter on. We take them off when we put them up, just like you told us to. Could it have been forgotten?"

"No. I hung up their tack myself. And I locked the door before I face-planted in the gravel."

Knox grinned and said, "I wasn't going to ask about your face. I was just gonna ask how the other guy looked."

"Ha ha, Mr. Funny Pants. Let's go find Barbie."

After a search of the nearby area, I decide to grab Zeus and take him around further out to see if we can find her. Barbie has a bit of a crush on Zeus, so I'm hoping she catches his scent and comes to find him. We have about an hour before we need to call Rick and delay the day's shooting if I can't find her. While I'm riding around the edges of the farm and looking for her, I'm replaying last night in my mind. I know I took off their halters and locked the door on my way out. I'm positive, so what is going on here at night, and why would someone let the horses out on purpose? Nearing a particularly dense copse of trees, I notice Zeus's ears flick forward and hold. He hears something, so I urge him forward and around the trees. Standing about 20 yards away with her head buried in the grass, munching away without a care in the world, is Barbie. She must have heard us because she raised her head, looked our way and then came trotting over to Zeus with a happy snort.

Dismounting, I hold on to Zeus's reins while I put a halter and lead rope on Barbie. She pays me no mind and is focused on tossing her head and giving Zeus flirty looks, in my opinion. He could care less if his bored expression is any indication. Mounting up, I turn the two animals toward the barn after calling Knox to let him know. Jess stayed at the barn to coordinate between myself, Knox, and Patrick. Arriving back with about 10 minutes to spare before we have to load up and leave for the location, I give both horses a quick look to make sure all is well after their little adventure. They are both fine, and we get everyone loaded up to transport.

Jess and I have to ride with the guys to the location in order to catch a ride back to town with the set drivers. It's a waste of time, but it gives me a chance to ask around about upgrading the security around the barn. I want to replace the locks again and see about getting some discreet cameras up. Jess and I split up and headed in different directions after we arrived on location.

This is a new location to film, and it's beautiful. I can't help but wander around a little bit before I force myself to get in gear and head into town to see about the locks and cameras. Within the hour, I'm settled in at my favorite coffee house with a tea latte and some amazing fresh scones.

By the time the crew calls it for the day, I've got the installation of locks and cameras set for the next day.

Back at the barn now, I am considering staying overnight to make sure there are no more incidents. It would be uncomfortable, but I've dealt with worse during college and my practicums. I know Jess will bring me some overnight things and even stay with me if I ask, but I won't. I bought myself into this situation, so it's for me to deal with alone.

Hearing a car pull up, I look out and see Sean getting out of the back with an excited Rab. I look at my watch and see it's later than I thought. I smile as he walks up. Zeus immediately recognizes him and wants his attention, so Sean walks over to give him a pat on the head. Rab takes off for parts unknown with a happy bark.

"Let's try our plans for last night tonight." He doesn't seem as tired tonight. I hate to say no, but I really should stay at the barn. Tomorrow is another long day, and I cannot have any more incidents like this morning. My face must telegraph what I'm going to say because he holds up a hand and says, "No excuses. We both need a night to relax. Patrick and Knox are going to camp out here tonight, so you have no reason to stay."

"I can't ask them to do that. It's my responsibility."

"You didn't ask; I did. Besides, I made it worth their time."

"Let me hear it from them and let them know I'll be paying them for it if they agree." I sigh and admit, "I wasn't really looking forward to an uncomfortable night out here without much sleep."

Raising his eyebrows at me in an astonished look, Sean queries, "Don't trust me, woman?"

"I just want to confirm with them for my own peace of mind. It has nothing to do with trusting you or not trusting you. But, truth be told, I haven't known you long enough to trust you."

"We will have to see to that, then, won't we?" Sean states quietly.

I feel a bit guilty like I hurt his feelings, but that can't be right. I'm frowning down at my feet when I hear Rab barking. Still concerned and thinking I need to apologize to Sean, I turn toward him only to find he's already walking in the direction of the dog.

I find the two grooms playing ball with a very happy Rab. I know they have already talked to Sean, but I'm not sure what he bribed them with or even if he bribed them. Knox and Patrick both look excited by the idea of camping out at the barn. They asked if I was okay with their girlfriends coming out but promised no shenanigans since they were working. I laughed at their excitement and earnest expressions. Agreeing with their request, I tell them to have their girlfriends bring plenty of provisions and pizza for the night and to give me the bill.

"No need, Mr. Miller has us taken care of for food and such."

"Ok then. Y'all promise to call me if there is any problem or anything out of the ordinary. 'Kay?"

"We promise. We will see you in the morning, Doc. There won't be any trouble tonight."

"Goodnight, then. I'll see you in the morning."

Knox has the optimism of a young man, and I could use that right now. I have not been able to puzzle out what happened all day. It's bothering me more than a little, and added on top of that is the nagging feeling I hurt Sean somehow when I said I didn't trust him.

A short while later, we are settled into the back seat of the car with Sean's driver headed away from the barn. Sean asks me if I'd rather get dropped off to get cleaned up, and he would come to get me in an hour, or if I would like to grab some things and take a soak in his tub. I don't even hesitate. I'm sore from my little trip and more than a little envious of that tub.

"I'm not sure you will get me out of it once I get in. I'm in love with your bathroom." Leaning my head to the side, I think and say, "And your closet. The gym isn't bad either, and your kitchen would make my heart beat faster if I cooked."

He laughs and gives my hand a squeeze. He has a habit of touching and holding my hand and does it without seeming to think about it. We ride in the back seat in companionable silence until we reach my building. I run up and grab a change of clothes, then head back to the car. Traffic is extremely light at this time of night, which allows us to be dropped off a short time later. Rab jumped out, stretched, and then took off for his usual tour of the property.

Sean walked me into the bathroom, showed me where to find everything then told me to take my time. I was suddenly very self-conscious about being naked in his bathroom. Glancing at the tub, I decided there was no need to feel awkward or embarrassed. That tub is calling to me, and Sean is a friend. Friends don't want to see each other naked, although I did have that image when I first saw his shower.

Sean told me his youngest sister Aileen left a variety of bath salts for sore and strained muscles. She is a physical therapist and understands how physically demanding his job can be at times. I take full advantage of those bath salts, and the scent of eucalyptus fills the air. The towel warmer may be another item I need to add to my bathroom back in Atlanta. I've never felt the need for one since it's rarely cold at home, but it would be nice to have one. I discovered his bathroom floor is heated, to my delight, and I can also appreciate that luxury in this climate.

Piling my hair on top of my head, I slide into the hot, fragrant water with a sigh. I may never get out. Closing my eyes, I lean my head back and hear…music. Michael Bublé starts crooning about wanting to be Home. I vaguely remember mentioning to Sean that he was one of my favorites in a conversation about music a couple of weeks ago. I smile and relax that much more. I spend more than a few minutes imagining the man in the house and creating some interesting scenarios involving the tub and shower. That shower already conjured up some wicked thoughts, and now the bathtub has me thinking sexy thoughts that make me blush even more. I need to stop this train of thought immediately before I embarrass myself.

My phone alerted me with a text from Sean, making me realize I'd spent more time in the tub than I probably should have, knowing he was likely waiting for me so we could eat.

Not rushing you, just want to make sure you've not drowned.

It's been more than an hour, and I haven't noticed the water has cooled, probably because of my wicked thoughts. I decide to text him back before I get out.

Still alive, just boneless. Have I told you how much I love your bathroom?

I unstop the tub and reach for a towel. It's toasty warm, and I sigh again at the luxury. I'm in danger of being spoiled, and I like it. I didn't bring my lotion with me, so I bypassed my usual routine and quickly pulled on my yoga pants and UGA t-shirt. I tidy up the bathroom and wipe down the tub with my towel, then look for the laundry bin. Not finding it immediately and not wanting to invade

Sean's privacy more than I already have, I carry the towel and washcloth with me down the hall to the kitchen. I can't find Sean at first and end up wandering around until I find him standing outside on his back patio.

"Where do I need to put these? I didn't see a laundry bin in your bathroom," I ask, gesturing with the towel.

Sean turns his head and smiles distractedly, "I'll show you the laundry room if you promise not to fall in love with that room too."

I stick my tongue out at him. I'm too relaxed to be prodded into a snarky remark. I follow him to a small room off the hall leading to the foyer. He has a state-of-the-art washer and dryer set along with a folding counter and an odd short bathtub/shower-looking tiled area. I raise an eyebrow in question, and he answers, "Dog bath."

"Fancy schmancy, Mr. Miller. Where you outside playing with Rab? I figured you would be hard at work in the kitchen."

He just shrugs and says, "I needed a bit of distance."

"Distance? From what? Is everything ok?"

"From a beautiful naked woman in my bathtub. I have a VERY vivid imagination, and it was getting out of control. Instead of making a fool of myself, I took myself outside for some air."

We stare at each other for a few moments before I walk forward and reach for his hand; without too much thought, I say, "Come on. I'm hungry."

"Hungry?" he says gruffly.

"Starving." I'm following my hormones here, and a part of my brain, or maybe my heart, that tells me this is right.

I pull him down the hall, but instead of turning toward the kitchen, I pull him toward his bedroom.

"I thought you were hungry?" Sean says in a quiet voice.

Chapter 22

When we reach his door, I turn and wrap my arms around his neck, raise up on my toes and whisper, "I am. For you" in his ear. His arms band around me with shocking speed, and once again, I find myself pressed against a wall with my mouth being plundered by a master. This time, I am more than ready for him and bury my hands in his hair, giving as good as I get.

Reaching back, he pushes open his bedroom door and backs me into the room, never lifting his mouth from mine. The intensity I've seen and felt in him has been released, and I feel both nervous and energized by it. This is what we both need. The last few weeks have been hectic and stressful; added to that, I haven't been able to get my mind off that kiss outside of Charlie's.

We both seem frantic, grabbing and gripping in a blind rush of need. Sean reaches behind his head with one hand, in that sexy way men have of taking off their t-shirts and rips it over his head, tossing it away. He returns to give me another sizzling kiss that makes my toes curl into the thick carpet. I drop my hands from his hair to his bare shoulders and slide them across and down his chest.

"Umm, I like this," I say as I lean forward and kiss his pectoral muscles. I've not been with many men, but I know I don't like a lot of chest hair; Sean has a sprinkling in the center of his chest, and that's pretty much it. I take my time running my hands across his chest and down to his waist. I can barely think, but I know the man does not carry any extra weight where I've inspected. Smooth, taut skin with the slightest bit of tan stretches across muscles that ripple and bulge as I run my hands across them. I'm not given a lot of time to explore before he kisses me again and reaches for my T-shirt.

Stepping back in an effort to slow us both down some, I raise my arms above my head and look him straight in the eyes as he pulls it up and off. It follows his t-shirt into a dark part of his room. He looks down and sees the demi bra I'm wearing, and his eyes dilate. I spend a half second thanking the lingerie ladies at home for ensuring my bras are pretty as well as functional for my job. Sean takes a finger and runs it along my collarbone toward my throat, where he lingers at the pulse, then slowly slides down to the cleft between my breasts. I can barely breathe as he continues to lightly trace that finger across the upper swells of my breasts, then back up across my other collarbone. My skin tingles everywhere he touches, and goosebumps cover almost my entire body now. He slides his fingers back into my hair, and we share another mind-blowing kiss.

There is a newness or novelty to kissing each other; we are tasting, shaping, exploring, and learning each other with a joint sense of discovery. We are both content to enjoy being skin-to-skin, sort of, while we kiss. After several minutes of drugging kisses, he slides his hands down my back and releases my bra. I feel no shyness with him as he tosses it behind him and looks at me.

"You have got to be the most exquisite woman I have ever seen." With gentle, calloused hands, he cups my breasts and leans in to kiss each one. What follows is enough to drive me over the edge, but before I leap over or fall at his feet, he leans down, picks me up and takes me the short distance to his massive bed. He sweeps back the thick comforter and then lays me down gently on the softest sheets which hold his smell. Inhaling deeply, I can't help but smile. Following me down, he carefully shifts to avoid crushing me. His strong chest touching mine is scorching hot and makes me intensify our kiss to an incendiary level. Clutching at his back, I can't help but try to move closer to him.

He slides slowly back and down my torso, kissing, nipping and licking as he goes, to slowly remove my yoga pants and panties. With a wicked smile, he states, "I know why women love yoga pants. They make your ass look spectacular." I don't get a chance to respond. He stands and removes the remaining clothes he has on without ever stopping his visual caress of my body. I'm usually very self-conscious, but the heat in his gaze has me mesmerized. I reach out my hands to bring him back as he slowly begins to work his way back up my body, murmuring, "You smell of a garden in summer with the heat of the sun warming the blooms."

He seems so in tune with my body and focused on me that every shudder, every sigh, and ripple that runs through me draws a murmur of encouragement from him. I'm getting frantic to have him inside me, and when I ask him to hurry, the response is a deep chuckle that I feel on my abdomen, "No."

Lifting my head to look down at him, I am incredulous when I breathlessly say, "No? You can't be serious."

He lifts his head, locks his smoldering blue eyes on me and kills me with his next gruff sentence. "You have no idea how long I've been dreaming of this, waiting for this. I refuse to rush myself or you. I'm savoring and drawing our first time out as long as I can, even if it kills us both."

Holy crap, I close my eyes and think I just had an orgasm from that alone. I reach down, grab a fist full of his hair and pull his mouth to mine. The kisses have turned greedy and deep again. We are both short of breath and panting when we part. I smile and then flip him to his back for a little retribution of my own. During my explorations, I discover a small scar just below his breastbone, a ticklish spot near his armpit and the most impressive set of abdominal muscles I've ever had the pleasure of feeling beneath my hands. Lightly tracing them, I say, "No wonder they have you shirtless so often. These are impressive." He catches my hand with a laugh and says, "A blessing and a curse." No more words are spoken for several minutes as my mouth, and free hand continue their exploration. Just when things are starting to get heated, Sean moves like lightning. I am on my back with him pressing me into the mattress with another hot, wet kiss before I can protest.

Without breaking the kiss, he reaches into his nightstand for a condom. My already racing heart speeds up a bit more, and I can't help but break the kiss and repeat my previous plea, "Hurry." A deep rumbling chuckle comes from his chest, and he gives me a soft kiss and then says, "Good things come to those who wait." I could growl with frustration at this point, but then he kissed me deeply and slowly pushed into me. It's been way too long for me, and he is bigger than I thought, so it's a bit uncomfortable. I let out a small gasp of discomfort, but my body quickly adjusts and eases.

Framing my head with his hands, he looks at me and asks, "Everything ok?" At my "oh yeah," we stop speaking entirely but continue looking at each other. Our bodies take over, and we just surrender to the sensations and emotions carrying us. It may have been a while since I was intimate with someone, but I don't remember the power of these sensations ever being this strong.

With a sharp cry, I dig my nails into his back as I fly over the edge into the best climax of my life. I honestly see stars as pleasure rolls through my body. Sean continues to hold me, drawing out the sensations until I loosen my grip. Then he kisses me fiercely, lets go of his control and surges forward. Our passion flares hotter than I can stand as I feel another orgasm beckoning. Sean's hand tightens around my hip as he growls his release, which brings on my own. How it could be better than the first, I don't know, but I think I blacked out for a bit.

Regaining my senses, I find I am pinned under the weight of Sean's body with his head pillowed on my breasts. I'm not being crushed by him; I can tell he's keeping the majority of his weight off me. Slowly, I raise my hand from his sweat-slicked shoulders to his hair and lightly run my fingers through it while my other hand slowly travels up and down his back.

"You can do that for as long as you'd like," he softly murmurs against my skin. I can't help myself; I give him a full-body hug and then continue. We lay like this for a long while before he shifts, kisses me softly and says, "I'm hungry."

Remembering I said that to him, and we ended up here, I laugh and raise an eyebrow. "Are you? Work up a bit of an appetite, huh?"

"That I did, my beauty, that I did." The man has no modesty as he moves away and out of bed to walk to his bathroom. I pull the corner of the sheet over my naked body and realize I don't feel terribly awkward myself. I stretch and feel the pull of muscles not used in a while. Smiling to myself, I think it's a good feeling.

"I like that smile."

Looking over, I see Sean has emerged from the bathroom and is headed, naked, to his closet. I can now swear on my life the man has a first-class ass as well as every other part of his body. He emerges in low-slung athletic pants and pulls on a t-shirt as he goes. He walks over, sits on the edge of the bed, places one hand on either side of me, leans in and kisses me stupidly again.

"That smile you're wearing lets me know I haven't scared you off."

"The smile I'm wearing ought to tell you you've more than taken care of things here," I say as I reach up and trace his mouth. He kisses my fingers, stands up and reminds me he's hungry. "I thought men went to sleep after they had sex?"

He pauses at the door and looks over his shoulder with an odd expression. Staring at me for a moment before he replies, "Not this one. Come on out when you're ready. If YOU fall asleep, I won't feed you." Smiling once again, he winks and walks out.

With a sigh, I slide over to get out of bed and find my clothes. I'm bending over to pick up my bra when Rab comes bounding in with a happy bark. It's strange to feel embarrassed because I'm half-naked in front of a dog, but I do. We end up playing a bit of tug of war with my shirt, but I prevail. I don't bother to put my hair up again, but I do take the band and smooth it back into a low tail.

We sit and eat some sort of breakfast casserole his mother made while we talk about my barn situation. I admit I'm stumped by what happened and fill him in on my plans to change the locks and get some hidden cameras up tomorrow.

"It could be some kids out for a lark."

"True, nothing was broken or taken. It doesn't seem like it was maliciously done, but something tells me it isn't right."

"Perhaps a discussion with the local constable might be in order. At least to alert them to the possibility of dubious behavior."

"Maybe. I'll see what the next few days bring. This may have been kids like you mentioned."

As we clean up the few dishes we have, Sean tells me about his day. I am happy things have not been awkward. We seem to have a rhythm when we spend time together that we slip naturally into. Before we leave the kitchen, he catches my hand and tugs me in for a kiss.

Holding me lightly, he asks, "Can I ask you some very personal questions?"

"We're friends who just spend the better part of an hour being as personal as two people can get, so I think you can ask me just about anything." I smile and lean back, waiting to see what his questions will be.

His expression froze for a split second, with an emotion I can't name flashing in his eyes before he continued, "I know that wasn't your first time, but I couldn't help but notice you stiffened for just a moment. Did I hurt you?"

"No, gosh, no. It's just been a while." Embarrassment has me ducking my head to his chest, "a very long while."

Tipping my chin up, he asks, "How long?"

"Five years." Watching his eyes widen, you'd think I said some astronomical number.

"Five. Years. Five years since you've had sex with a man? How can that be?" Sean is truly astonished and can't keep the shock out of his eyes or his tone.

"Um, well, yeah. Five years. I haven't really been looking for that in my life. I wasn't looking for you either, but here you are."

"Five years." Shaking his head in wonder. "That's 1825 days."

Pushing away because I feel like a specimen under a microscope, I raise my chin and reply in a haughty voice, "1826, you forgot leap day." I turn to walk away but find my hips grasped in two large hands. He leans down to my ear and nips the lobe before saying, "Don't get cheeky. I'm just surprised a woman as vibrant and gorgeous as you doesn't have men swarming around looking for the chance to get you into bed."

I lean my head back against his chest and reply in a cool tone, "Wasn't on my agenda, so I didn't pay any attention to it. Should I then assume because you are good-looking that, you have a pile of women in your bed when you get the urge? That they are lined up?"

"I'm not carving notches in my bedposts, but I can say I haven't gone five years. I'm sorry if I keep poking at it; it's just surprising in this day and age."

"I had other things to focus on. Things I don't want to discuss right now, ok?" I'm starting to feel uncomfortable and tense, like I'm some kind of freak because I haven't been having sex frequently.

He slides his arms around my waist to hug me close and puts his cheek on mine. "I'm sorry I made you uneasy. Truly. I didn't mean to. Forgive me?"

I nod and turn in his arms to wind mine around his waist and hug him back. We stand for several minutes, just holding each other in a newfound intimacy. He leans back and asks me if I want to watch that documentary I've been wanting to watch about African Lions.

We settle onto the big sectional in his living room, but I barely make it through the first twenty minutes before my head grows heavy, and I lean against Sean's shoulder. Another few minutes and my eyelids grow heavy. Sean shifts to put his arm around me, pulls me closer, and I drift off to sleep.

Several hours later, I slowly surface to hear a steady heartbeat, the feel of a solid body next to me, and ironically, a warm solid little body against my back. Realizing I fell asleep makes me stiffen slightly as I am embarrassed. I start to ease away, only to have the arms around me tighten and pull me back. The warm mass behind me shifts and lays his head on my butt. Rab. I reach a hand out to pet him and hear Sean's sleep-roughened voice say, "Did he wake you?"

"No. I'm sorry I fell asleep." I start to slide away again, and this time he lets me go. "I need to get home." I realize then that I have no car here.

Sean stretches and says, "No problem. I'll take you home."

"I can call an Uber; you need your rest. You said your call time is 5 am."

Sean gives me a hard look and repeats, "I'll take you home", in such an authoritative tone that I don't argue.

Giving up, I nod my head and reach for my shoes. Rab climbs down off the sofa, stretches, and lumbers off in the direction of the bedroom. I laugh and say, "He's not very energetic right now."

"That dog is worse than a teenager. Once he goes to bed, you can't budge him until he's ready to get up. I'm surprised he got off the couch. Usually, he won't move."

This embarrassment I felt when I woke a few minutes ago has disappeared. Sean has a way of putting me at ease. I grab my bag with my dirty clothes and head toward the garage. The ride back to my flat is quiet, with only the music on the radio between us. It's not an uneasy silence by any means. I think we are comfortable enough to understand there are times when a conversation is not needed. We arrive at my flat in short order, and Sean insists on walking me to my door. Once there, he asked me if I would consider going with him to a charity dinner the next weekend. He explains he and several others on the cast have donated different things for a silent auction benefiting a local domestic violence shelter. He tells me to think about it, and we will talk more in the next day or so. With that, he gives me a hot kiss and bids me sweet dreams. Guaranteed, I think.

I go to bed thinking it would be interesting to see what his public life is like. I feel like we have been somewhat isolated here. The people in the area treat the entire production crew as normal citizens of the area since they've been here for almost two years now. It will be insightful to see how things are when he has to be a public figure. As for my dreams, I doubt they will compare to reality, but it's worth checking into; they do not disappoint.

Chapter 23

" I'm out of my mind, aren't I?" I ask Jessica as we embark on a whirlwind shopping spree. "I must be crazy to leave myself one day to find something suitable to wear to a charity event that's black tie."

"Pshaw! Honey, you're with me. We only need a couple of hours." Jess smiles smugly and proceeds to direct the Uber driver to drop us off on the corner of a boutique shopping district. As we step out of the car, my phone pings with an incoming text. I glance down and see it's from Sean.

Good luck with your mad dash shopping trip!

He's got a full day of shooting today, but it's on set and not on location. That translated into a day off for me, which worked out well, except it was the day before the event. If I were in Georgia, it would be as simple as grabbing one of my go-to dresses. I didn't pack any formal or semi-formal clothing, so I've got to buy something quickly and hope it doesn't need alterations. I smile as I remember my mother and I shopping for a dress for a country club dance when I was 11 or 12. She always said buying off the rack is fine if you have a tailor touch it up to make it look perfect on you. She always looked like her clothes were made for her. Shaking off the touch of melancholy, I text Sean back.

Thanks. I've unleashed Jessica – there could be chaos and havoc in our wake.

Five hours later, I'm in possession of not one but two gorgeous dresses. Two, because I couldn't decide between floor length or knee length and midnight blue or black. Jessica was no help because she encouraged me to buy both since she bought two of her own. I also ended up with a new pair of shoes which I know I won't be wearing tomorrow night. Another rule my mother taught me, and Jess's mom reinforced, under no circumstances do you wear a new pair of shoes to an event. That guarantees sore feet and a short evening. Right before we decided to call it quits, we hit the lingerie store and both spent way too much money on pretty, lacy things. Jess and I both agree when you spend your day wearing scrubs and comfortable shoes, you tend to want to look pretty and sexy underneath, even if no one sees it. Having recent first-hand knowledge of how my underwear affected Sean, the devil in me decided to up my game a bit.

We had a great time, as always, but now I want a drink and to put my feet up. We decide to order pizza and spend the night at our flat. Arriving at home, I hang each dress up in the living room so we can make a joint decision on which one I wear tomorrow night. Jess calls in our pizza order, and we both change into lounge pants and t-shirts. Shoes and bras are banished for the remainder of the evening. Sitting side by side on the tiny loveseat with our feet propped up on the coffee table, we discuss the merits of both dresses.

"The midnight blue has the shimmer and sparkle that really catches the eye, plus the back is the bomb," Jess states as she raises a diet soda to her lips.

"They both look fantastic from the back. Good call on going with a low cutback." I say, toasting her with my own soda. I can't stand diet drinks and refuse to drink them on the rare occasion I indulge in a carbonated drink.

"You are right. The bow and ruffle on the back of the short one draws attention to the low cut back, and sis, you've got a spectacular back and shoulder look goin' on."

Sitting my bottle down, I gesture toward the dress on the left and say, "I'm leaning toward the short black one. It's classy without being too showy, and since it's a fundraiser for a domestic violence center, I think the more conservative, the better. Plus, I haven't been to this type of event here, so I have no clue what is acceptable."

"The midnight is conservative enough, even with the shimmer and sparkle. But if you wear my strappy Louboutin's, your legs will look amazing in the black. The shoes will be lost in the long dress." Jess tips her head to the side, considering, then says, "Go with the black. Save the midnight for New Year's Eve."

There was a knock at the door just as she said that. I got up and checked, then opened the door to pay for our pizza. Thanking the teen who delivered it, I took it to the coffee table where we had already set out napkins. This fancy dinner did not lend itself to plates.

"Ok. Black dress, your strappy black Louboutin's, and next up will be hair and earrings. I'm thinking of either sleek tail or up do to show off the back of the dress. I don't want long earrings; I think the simple diamond studs would be best."

"Let's play with your hair after we eat. What are we watching on Hulu while we decimate this pizza?"

"Documentary?"

"Boring. Let's have some laughs. Sitcom."

"Well, let's see what's available. I Love Lucy is always good. Cheers. Scrubs. Difficult People. Wait, this is it. Designing Women."

"Oh yeah. I love that show."

We sit back and enjoy our pizza while binge-watching the first few episodes of a show set in our hometown. After we finish and clean up the remains, Jess grabs a brush and makes me sit on a cushion on the floor. We used to do this same thing many nights when we were teenagers. Jess loved playing with my hair. She was the one who did my hair for prom, graduations – all of them – and several weddings I've been in.

"Go try the dress on with your hair up like this. I like it from behind but need to see it with the dress."

Groaning, I get to my feet. I'm almost too tired to bother, but I don't want to have to deal with it tomorrow. I want to pamper myself with a mani/pedi and relax until I need to get ready. I skip the shapewear and slip into the dress. Glancing at the back, I think she's right about the updo. It looks sharp. Stepping out of the bathroom, I strike a pose against the door jam and almost die. Charlie's got Jess in an embrace so hot I start to blush.

"Oops, don't mind me. I'm not even here." Whipping around, I duck into our bedroom and start to laugh. Imagining how ridiculous I looked but feeling pretty confident neither of them noticed me. I change back into my comfy clothes and decide to get ready for bed to leave them some time alone. This is one of the times it stinks not to have two bedrooms—or separate flats. Oh well, it worked before, and it will work now. I quietly slip out into the hallway and hit the bathroom. My nightly ritual is short, and I'm ready to hit the sack in under 15 minutes, then I remember. My phone is sitting on the table by the sofa. I look out and notice the living room is empty. Hmm, ok. I grab my phone and head to my bed.

I noticed a couple of missed calls from Sean and a few more texts. Reading the texts, I call him back. "Hey, what's up?" I ask as he answers almost immediately.

"I need to speak with you. Can I come over? I want to speak face to face." He sounds anxious about something.

"Sure. Jess left with Charlie, so we could speak privately. Come on over. Is everything alright?"

"I hope so. I'll be there in two minutes." He disconnects. Knowing how far it is from his house to my flat, I realize he was driving here already. I wonder what has him worked up? The knock on my door tells me I don't have to wait long.

I open it and admit a frazzled Sean. He sweeps past me into the room, runs his hands through his hair in obvious frustration, and sits down. He immediately pops back up, crosses to me, pulls me into his arms and kisses me. Holding on to me, he says, "I am going to jump right in." Pulling away, he takes my hand and leads me to the loveseat.

I have no idea what's going on, but his demeanor is starting to unsettle me. "What is going on? You're starting to scare me."

"There is a picture that someone released to POPSTOP of us in the alley at Charlie's." He looks like he's waiting for me to react, but I just raise an eyebrow and say, "Okay."

He pulls out his phone and pulls up the photo on POPSTOP. He hands it to me and waits. I read the article, which is really just a couple of sentences saying Sean's been spotted hot and heavy with an unknown female. Another couple sentences about how he's obsessive about keeping his relationships quiet and no one has seen him out in public with a woman since Gabriella, his last girlfriend, two years back. I look at the picture and see the two of us, but it's hard to really tell who we are. If I weren't there, I wouldn't know who I was looking at.

I hand his phone back and give him a cheeky smile, "Pretty hot pic."

The look he gives me is a surprised shock. I laugh and ask, "What's the problem with this? They don't know who I am and aren't likely to find out from that photo. Hell, it is difficult to recognize you in that image."

"Are you really this laid back about this? I thought you might get upset. We haven't really discussed any of this since the other night when we made love."

That sentence gave me pause. I was trying to put us back in the friends, maybe friends with benefits, category by thinking of it as sex only. His calling it making love puts it in another category completely, and I'm not sure I'm ready for that.

"Let's just wait and see what happens. You've been at work for almost 14 hours and likely aren't thinking straight. Sleep on it, and you'll see it's not a huge deal."

Still looking frazzled, he says, "If you're sure. I don't want you pulled into anything you aren't prepared for, and this can get out of control fast."

"Go home, sleep, and we will see what POPSTOP says tomorrow. Okay? If you are still this uncomfortable tomorrow, I'll skip the gala."

"What? No. I want you to go with me. If you are okay with the possibility of more photos of us."

"Tomorrow. Let's discuss it then." I know he thinks I'm pushing him out the door, and in part, I am, but I need to process this alone. I give him a sweet, quick kiss on his cheek, then shove him out the door. "Go to bed. We'll talk tomorrow."

Putting myself to bed, I lay there and think about Sean's concerns. Do we have a relationship, or are we just friends who happen to have slept together? Do I want whatever it is to be splashed out across the tabloids? That seems strange to think about, but it's a reality in his life, so I have to consider it. How will it impact both of us? My brain is spinning and spinning until I decide enough is enough. I push it out of my mind and go to sleep.

I vaguely remember hearing Jess crawl into bed a couple of hours later, and it makes me smile. I feel like we are back in college again, but we're a bit wiser than we were then.

Chapter 24

Sean calls me a bit after 8 the next morning. "There's been another photo posted. This one was on set when you confronted Lester. I'm standing in front of you, about to knock his teeth down his throat. They clearly identify you, Andi."

"Ok. Ok. Let me pull it up." I grab my iPad and pull up POPSTOP. The photo clearly shows how infuriated Sean is, and I'm equally pissed looking, but you can't see what we're looking at. It does say plain as day who I am and what my profession is. "I didn't realize at the time how fierce you look when you're pissed off. Then again, I'm not looking very calm myself, am I?"

"Andi…"

"I know. Relax Sean. We just need to talk and decide how we want to address it, if we even want to address it. Honestly, is there anything to address? We're friends. They can't say for sure I was the girl in the first picture."

"This is just the beginning. Other photographers will start now that there has been something to sell to POPSTOP. Are you okay with that?"

"With being someone's gossip site photo? No, but neither can I control it. Are you okay with being romantically linked up with me even though we're just friends?"

"What? Yes. No. Yes. Damn it. I don't like my personal life out there for all to see."

I'm not really sure how to take his vacillating answers. I decide to take a stand that will keep us both out of the limelight, so to speak. "How about we have your publicist deny the first photo by saying it's impossible to identify either party? Then say I am, indeed, working on the production, and we are becoming friends. That's innocuous enough to appease the media. Plus, it's accurate."

"Is that all we are, friends?" he asks in a voice that almost sounds hurt to me.

"Aren't we friends?" I ask. Feeling the nerves blossom in my stomach, I realize this topic is starting to scare me. If he admits we are more than friends, I'll have to admit it to myself. I am not sure I'm ready to unpack my feelings.

"I thought the other night proved we are far more than that, Andi. Or was I wrong?"

"I enjoyed myself immensely, but we need to be realistic here. We've been hanging out and getting to know each other as friends. Things happen sometimes that are one and done. This doesn't mean what we have as friends must change. Neither one of us has time for anything but friendship, right?"

My statement is met by silence for long enough to make me check my phone to see if we were disconnected. "Sean, are you still there?"

"I am. You're exactly right, Andi. We're friends, and this is a non-issue. I'll have my publicist treat it as such. I'll pick you up tonight at six. Enjoy your day." He disconnects, and again, I feel like I've hurt him somehow. Confused and feeling bad because I may have hurt him, I almost called him back.

Jessica comes out and asks me what's going on. I dump the whole mess on her and ask for her advice. She spends a few minutes looking over the two images and articles on POPSTOP, then asks me a few questions about Sean's tone and his exact words.

After a couple of minutes of quiet contemplation, she stands up, stretches and tells me, "You're afraid and being an idiot."

"What are you talking about? How am I being an idiot?" I realize I'm afraid already, but it's not because of Sean. Or rather, not what he's doing or how he's feeling. It's totally because of how I'm feeling.

"You are pushing that man into the friend zone and basically nailing him to the wall there even though he wants to be in the boyfriend zone."

"Whoa. No one said that."

Exasperated, Jess reaches out and smacks me lightly upside the back of the head and says, "Andi, you had sex with the man. Great sex that he's more than happy to repeat, I'm sure. He's basically spelt it out to you numerous times that he is interested in more, but you keep flinging friend back in his face."

"I don't know that we are more than that or that I'm ready to let anyone be more than that. I can't do that again, Jess."

"Honey, you are going to sabotage this before it ever has a chance to bloom. Stop doing it; let yourself live again and love again. See where this thing with Sean goes, and if it doesn't go anywhere, you'll know that you finally took a step forward."

Through a sheen of tears, I say, "I don't know if I can."

Jess walks over and hugs me tight; she says, "I know you can. I'd bet money on you every time."

I made it a point to be ready well before Sean was due to arrive. Knowing he worked so long the day before, plus had the added stress of the POPSTOP thing, I don't want to poke the bear. I'd be a raging lunatic if I had worked crazy hours like that. I need my sleep. He says he's conditioned to it and gets bursts of energy when he needs it, but I can't imagine it. Add the POPSTOP photos and our discussions to it; I imagine he may not be in the best of moods.

I am more certain of the dress choice than I was last night. The clean lines highlight the fact I don't skip the gym. It's simple but elegant, with a neckline adorned with diamantes around the shoulder straps and along the edge of the low back. The back takes the dress from simple LBD to simply elegant. The low-scooped back will show off my shoulders and back, but the best part is the ruffle detail. A small, tasteful bow that sits low on my spine starts a waterfall of fabric to the hem. Nothing that calls undue attention to my backside but neither does it hide it. I am feeling pretty good about the choice.

Jess did my hair, and it looks better than it did last night when she was playing around. She's got a talent for it; I told her she was a cosmetologist in a past life. She laughed and said it was her fallback plan if the whole trauma doctor thing didn't pan out. The entire outfit has come together and looks great. I feel confident enough to go out in public with a famous actor and not embarrass either of us. Jess also had a dab hand at the make-up tonight. She does great smokey eye makeup. If I try that, I look like a raccoon or junkie. It's a toss-up. Normal make-up, I can handle it, but dramatic looks are beyond my ability.

The knock at the door that signals Sean's arrival is just a few minutes early, but I'm ready. I open the door with a smile, then lean over to grab my clutch from the table by the door. Vanity prevents me from bringing a jacket tonight. Looking back at Sean, I stop short. Sean is in a tux. Wow. My brain stutters as my eyes enjoy the sight in front of me. Wow. What is it about a tux that makes a man look like James Bond? Realizing I haven't said anything, I smile again and say, "Hey."

Noticing he hasn't said anything either, I focus on his eyes. He has a very intense look in them that quite literally raises the hairs on the back of my neck and brings goosebumps to my arms. "Uh, um. Is everything ok? Am I dressed wrong?"

The intensity remains, but he smiles and says, "You are exquisite. Stunning. I couldn't speak for a minute there." His voice is deep and rough, but his eyes have changed to the smiling eyes I'm used to, so I smile back.

"Thanks. You clean up pretty well yourself." I say with a wink.

He leads me out to his car and opens the door for me. When I turn to slide into the front seat, I hear a sharp intake of breath from Sean. I turn my head and say, "What's wrong?"

"I just saw the back of the dress, that's all. I think it stopped my heart."

I laugh lightly, "You are such a charmer and full of all the right words tonight. Just like always. Thanks for making me feel pretty." He closes the door but stands there a few seconds before moving around to slide in behind the wheel.

"Anderson," he begins slowly, "you are a beautiful woman. You don't need me to make you feel pretty."

"No, I don't, but you're my friend. Friends always build each other up. Jess helped me tonight with the hair and makeup, and now you are helping me with the charming words and compliments. See? Friends helping friends." I smile at him until I see the muscle in his jaw twitch and his hands tighten on the steering wheel. I realize I've said friend too many times and begin to see what Jessica mentioned earlier. Am I sabotaging something that could be wonderful because I'm afraid of what happened before?

He opens his mouth to say something, then shakes his head and reaches for the console to turn on the music. He gives me a look that I don't understand but says nothing. For several miles, we sit in relative silence with only the music on the radio as background. I am nervous that Jess is right, and he wants more from me than just being friends. Or maybe he regrets bringing me. Surely, he would have found a way to bow out if he had changed his mind. Just as I turn to ask him, he exhales a deep breath and says, "I know we talked about how tonight would likely go, but I want to make sure you are okay with me leaving you alone here and there. There will be a lot of people who will ask for a chat or a photo. Don't feel like you have to stay with me."

"Are you sure you want me to come at all? You seem tense since you arrived, and now," I trail off and turn to look out the window. He reaches for my hand and holds it tightly.

"I want you to come with me, but I don't want to ruin your night by making you stand there while other people monopolize my time."

Looking over at him to gauge the truth in what he is saying, something occurs to me. He's a successful actor; how will I know if he's being genuine or acting? I've never watched him at work. All I know is the Sean I have been around all these weeks. His face looks earnest, and the grip on my hand tells me he's serious. I shake off the doubts that have suddenly taken hold of me and squeeze his hand back.

"I'm a big girl; I can entertain myself. Plus, you said there is a silent auction. I'll make sure and spend some time checking that out before you get to announce the winners of the big items. What did you say those were again?"

"There is a boating adventure with a footballer and his wife, a VIP race experience with an open wheel driver, some kind of music package that I can't remember and mine. Plus a lot of other great items to bid on. Whisky, wine, technology, holidays, and more. I should have given you the book they sent me."

"No worries, I'll get ready to do some shopping."

"Anderson, I didn't bring you so you could spend money. As a matter of fact, let me buy anything you want to bid on tonight."

"That is a firm negative, sugar," I say with a deepened Southern drawl. "It's for charity, plus, it's one specializing in helping women out of horrible situations. I'm all in. Keep your money or spend it on what you want. Besides, I might outbid you."

Squeezing the hand he never released, he says, "Bid on my adventure; save me from the middle-aged women who have more money than the treasury and only want my body."

I'm stunned for a brief second, then burst out in laughter. "I can't believe you just said that. More money than the treasury. I need to remember that one."

"Wait and see." He pulls up outside a posh hotel. The bellman opens my door while the valet walks around to give Sean a claim ticket for his car. There are a couple of flashes as people take pictures of us, but I don't pay any mind to it. It's odd, but this has happened at a couple of fundraisers I've attended, where celebrities are on the guest list. Realizing I'm with one tonight, not just a random attendee, I almost stop walking.

Sean is walking next to me but not touching me, which, for him, is odd. He is a toucher and always finds a way to touch me. Having already discussed how private he is, I assume it is because he doesn't want to add any more fuel to the fire that we are a couple because we are attending together. I'm his friend, his plus one; he has no reason to touch me. We walk through a gorgeous lobby that I'd love to stay and look at. It's got to be historic. I paid no attention to the name of the place and was distracted when we arrived.

Sean has barely left the lobby, walking down a long corridor, when he is noticed by several women in evening gowns. They waste no time in calling his name and walking over. He smiles, but it seems different from the smile I usually see from him. We slow as they reach us. One woman already has her phone out and is snapping pictures.

"Ladies, lovely to see you again. The Rise Up Women's Gala is such a wonderful event, is it not?"

"Absolutely. We wouldn't miss it. Who's this with you? We don't recognize her."

The events of last night and this morning have me a bit on edge, so the last statement catches me off guard. They've seen me for all of twenty seconds at most. How could they have even seen me well enough to recognize me or not? Slapping my country club smile on my face, I reach out a hand to the lead woman in fire engine red sequins, "Hello. I'm Dr. Sullivan. Pleasure to meet you," I pause and wait for her to give me her name.

She takes my hand in a brief handshake and replies, "Lydia Presley."

The woman to her left in white and silver is next to shake my hand, "Melody Cartwright."

And the last woman on the right, in a black gown with a slit almost to her navel, says, "Margo Westinghouse."

"Ladies, if you'll excuse us, I'd like to introduce Dr. Sullivan to our hostess for the evening. Enjoy the event." He smoothly moves away from the women, and we continue down the corridor, where a larger open area opens up to the left. It is obviously a cocktail hour as there are several bars set up and high-top tables scattered around the area.

"You were very smooth in extracting us without telling them any more detail than necessary."

"I've had a lot of coaching and practice."

Before we enter, Sean leans closer to me and says, "You just met exhibits A, B and C that I mentioned before."

I choke on a laugh as he walks into the room smiling and is immediately greeted by a lovely lady who looks to be about fifty years old. Unlike the other women, she does not come to Sean. He walks over to her, gives her a hug, and kiss on the cheek, then turns to introduce me.

"Eliza, meet my friend Dr. Anderson Sullivan from the US. Andi, meet a true icon among women, Eliza McIndree. She leads the Rise Up organization and is responsible for tonight's event."

I reach out to shake hands and say, "Ms. McIndree, it is a pleasure to meet you. I look forward to the evening."

"Please call me Eliza. Any friend of Sean's is a friend of mine. Doctor, you say? What kind of physician are you?"

"I'm a veterinarian. I think Sean wants to make me feel important by introducing me using a doctor. I'm just Andi, who works with animals."

"You are lovely, and I want to talk to you more as soon as the crowd thins. Please do get a drink and mingle around. There are a lot of youngsters like you here tonight, so the conversation will be lively." Turning to Sean, she says, "Did you already get greeted by your trio of admirers?"

"Yes, I did. Andi got the pleasure of meeting them as well."

Eliza turns to me and says, "If they didn't spend a mint or bucket of money each time they attended, I'd not allow them to be here. They chase after him all night; it's embarrassing to watch. See that you keep him safe tonight." Turning back to Sean, she says, "It's about time you brought someone to keep those women at bay."

I barely contain the laughter that threatens to erupt. Sean takes one step toward the bar and is greeted by a man who obviously knows him. He's built like Thor but looks more like the guy next door. They exchange man hugs and slaps on the back so hard I feel the wind getting knocked out of my own lungs.

"Phillip, good to see you, man. How've you been? Is Tess here?" Sean is smiling now with more enthusiasm than before, and I start to notice the difference. He turns to me, reaches out to take my hand and draws me in. "Andi, meet a right good chap and one of my brother's oldest friends, Phillip Larson. Phillip, meet Dr. Anderson Sullivan."

My hand is quickly swallowed up by Phillip's much larger one and shaken vigorously. "Pleased to meet you, Anderson."

"Andi, please," I say with a smile. This man gives off the most pleasant, jovial vibes that I feel like I've known him for decades without ever speaking to him. We move toward the bar to get a drink while the two men are talking. Phillip turns to me and says, "You'll have to meet my wife, Tess, of course. She sent me over to get her a drink. She's found a comfortable spot and refuses to budge until it's time to go in for dinner."

Sean claps Phillip on the back again and says, "When is the baby due? I remember she got a bit cranky toward the end with Liam."

Phillip grimaces and says, "We've got another four or five weeks. I may not survive. She's more tired now since she's got Liam to chase around. Won't let me get her any help either."

"I look forward to meeting her."

Another group of people intercept Sean as we leave the bar with our drinks, so I ask Phillip if he will introduce me to Tess now. He obliges and takes me to a small seating area close by where a heavily pregnant woman is sitting. "Tess, I've brought someone for you to meet. She's a friend of Sean's."

"Hi, I'm Andi," I say and extend my hand. "I'm pleased to meet you. I hear you have a son named Liam?"

She shakes my hand, smiles warmly and says, "Yes, he's two and a half. I'm pleased to meet you too. I'd get up, but that would take an hour."

I smile and sit down next to her. "How's this? I'm always good to sit down and chat at events like these. Too often, you're standing in one spot, and your feet end up hurting."

"Exactly. Add to that being 1,000 weeks pregnant, and you are straight-up miserable. You're from the States, aren't you? I can tell by your accent."

"Me? I don't have an accent. You do." I say with a laugh. She's another one I can tell I will like. "Seriously, yes, I'm from Georgia. I'm here working with the production company for a while."

We spend about ten minutes talking about being in Scotland, their one trip to the US for their honeymoon, and their soon-to-be addition. Sometimes when you meet someone, there is an initial click of like meeting like. That is exactly what has happened here. Phillip and Tess are great people, the kind of people you will know for a lifetime, no matter where you live.

"We really need to go have a look at the auction items and see if there is anything we want to bid on. Remember that chalet in France we got for a bargain last year?" Phillip turns to me and says, "Two weeks in a chalet in the wine country of France. It was amazing."

Tess adds, "It was lovely, but it was far more entertaining for you than me. Andi, my husband, runs a group of restaurants around the country that specialize in fine wines. While I was chasing an 18-month-old, he was off tasting wines and comparing grapes." Phillip helps her up with a bit of effort, and she hugs him. Seeing the two of them make me smile, and I've just met them. They're such a cute couple.

I tag along with them to the row of linen-covered tables that house the silent auction. There are no items displayed, as with some auctions I've attended at home. This one has an image in a crystal frame with a description at the base along with an iPad to enter a bid. I'm surprised to see a wide variety of items ranging from ski weekends to Disney tickets, cruises to wine tastings, hot air balloon rides and spa days, a nanny for a week, training by a local, well-known dog trainer, and even a safari in Africa. At the end of the row of tables in large crystal frames are the special celebrity items. I don't know sports celebrities outside of the US, but I see a VIP package to an upcoming Michael Bublé concert that I am excited to bid on as well as Sean's Highland Camping Adventure Weekend.

I make another pass around the auction items and bid on several things. I notice the three women are dividing their time between following him and hovering near Sean's adventure weekend to immediately top a bid once someone enters one. I see exactly what he means now, and the little devil in me decides if they want it that bad, they might as well help the charity out and push up the price. I stroll over and glance at the current bid, then top it by a thousand pounds. I glance at the Buble package and smile when I see I'm still ahead on that one. I also bid on the week of nanny services, which I will gift to my new friends, The Larson's, as a baby gift. I know Jess will love the hot air balloon ride, so I bid on that one too.

I have that tingling sensation at the back of my neck seconds before a warm hand lands on my back at my waist. Sean leans over and says, "Hot air balloon ride? Looking for an adventure, are you?"

"Jess will love it." I turn to smile at him and see that strange smile firmly in place. I'm going to call this his working smile. It doesn't make his eyes sparkle the way some of his smiles do. "Did you finally break free, or is this a temporary lull?"

"It's a lull. Eliza asked me to speak to a few reporters who are here. Have you had a chance to meet the footballers and their wives? Great lads, even if they don't play for my team."

"Point them out, and I'll go meet them when you get pulled away next time." He gestures over to the opposite side of the room, where a group of about a dozen are standing. They are very boisterous, and their wives are all wearing sequins with sky-high heels. "I got to spend some time with Tess and Phillip. They are amazing people and so adorable together. I like them."

"I forgot they were coming, but I'm glad you got to meet Tess. She changed a lot of things for Phillip. He was in a bad place after his first wife died from cancer." He lifted his head in acknowledgement of someone's greeting and then continued, "There is something about Tess that makes you smile. Plus, she has a wicked sense of humor and a razor-sharp wit."

I chuckled as I recalled her saying she was 1,000 weeks pregnant. Telling Sean this, he laughed and said, "That sounds like Tess." Out of the corner of my eye, I see the Trio approaching and nudging Sean. "I'm being a bit mean to your Trio."

He raises one eyebrow in the inquiry but says nothing.

"Forgive my crudeness here, but they are eye fucking you and basically hovering over your adventure weekend to ensure they win it. I've decided to make it worthwhile for Eliza, and I keep raising their bids."

His eyebrows flew up at my crude description, and then he let out a bark of laughter that had more than a few heads turning our way. Just as he starts to respond, the Trio arrive and insist on knowing what is so funny. Lydia, the front runner, has managed to wedge herself next to Sean and press her more than ample cleavage against his arm.

"I was telling Sean about the lack of morality in certain bovines I've run across during my practice."

Sean chokes and quickly excuses himself. I turn to face the ladies and smile. "I don't normally get into detail about my animal practices, but tonight it just seemed to come up naturally."

All three women gave me somewhat shocked looks and sputtered responses. I realize that I never stated that I am a Doctor of Veterinary Medicine. I took pity on them and clarified, "I'm a vet, ladies. I work with animals for a living."

The ladies made the appropriate responses and then trailed off after Sean. I took the opportunity to go raise the bid on his adventure weekend by another thousand pounds and also bumped up my Bublé bid before heading toward the soccer players. I can't call them footballers; they play soccer, and to me, that will never be football. I'm an American Football fan who will not be calling soccer football anytime in the next hundred or so years.

I walk straight up to a lovely blond woman wearing amazing shoes and compliment her on them. She introduces herself as Priscilla, the wife of James. I introduce myself, and we have a nice chat about fashion. I admit to her that I'm not a big fashion follower since I usually wear scrubs for work. That segues our conversation into the kind of dog that would be best for their family. They have three children under the age of 5 and feel it is a good time to add a family pet to the mix. Our conversation draws several other wives over, and I end up meeting the entire group by the time Sean comes to tell me it's time to sit down for dinner and the program. I ask him if he has been introduced and end up introducing him to several of the players and their wives.

On the way to our table, we detoured ourselves by the silent auction one more time to up the bid on Sean's adventure. This time I made it a really obnoxious increase and up it by ten thousand pounds. As we walk away, I hear a screech and know the Trio has discovered my trick. Sean seems to be oblivious to it, but I know he isn't. The hand at the base of my spine slides up until his thumb is on my bare skin. He rubs it slowly as he leans in and says, "You have a wicked sense of humor, and I like it." He doesn't move his hand but keeps that slow slide of his thumb across my skin, and I shiver a bit. Hoping he didn't notice, I quickened my pace a bit and tossed a sassy grin behind me at him as we arrived at our table.

The next hour is spent in companionable conversation with our table mates as we enjoy a meal and some exceptional wine. Eliza excuses herself to start the program. She is a gifted speaker who has the ability to grab your heart as well as your attention. When she queued up a video about some of the women they have helped over the last several years, I was truly touched and on the brink of tears. Looking up at the screen and hearing the stories of what these women have endured at the hands of men who should be protecting them makes me want to weep. I feel a hand on my thigh and reach down to grasp Sean's hand in a tight grip. He looks at me, and then away as if he senses he will unravel my grip on my emotions if he says anything. We continue to hold on to each other tightly as one of the survivors gets up to speak.

She doesn't tell us her name but starts out with a powerful story of the first time she was ever abused by her father. She tells us another story of being virtually neglected as a teen with the exception of beatings delivered for various innocuous reasons. Moving forward into young adulthood, when girls should be shopping and dancing in clubs with friends, she tells us of living with a boyfriend who beat her so badly she was unable to move for two days. He didn't like the way she looked at a friend of his on the previous day. The examples continued until she ended with the day she excitedly told her then-husband they were pregnant for the first time. She went on to tell us of the rage that comment sparked and the beating that ended the life of their unborn child almost as soon as it began. She looked up then, scanned the room and said, "This is not just my story. This is the story of so many of my sisters here tonight and many, many more who are still on their journey to freedom and healing. My story changed when the doctor slid me a small business card that had contact information for a place called Rise Up. I had no idea what it was, but she explained it was a place where hope was born, freedom was gained, and the cycle could be broken. I sat at the bus stop, my husband said I didn't deserve a car, and decided it was time to do something for me. I called the next day after my husband left for work and took the first step to regain my dignity, my life, and my freedom. Every person here has the opportunity tonight to help someone like me take that step. Donations for Rise Up help women like me believe again; in ourselves, in society, in each other, and most importantly, in being free. Before I reached out to Rise Up, I was like so many of my sisters - a no-one, a face in the crowd that did her best to stay hidden. Now, my name is Marla, and I will Rise Up for women like me. Thank you for helping us.

At that, every member of the audience stood and clapped for so long that our hands were red. I managed to barely keep the tears in check, but it was a struggle. I had let go of Sean's hand when we stood up to applaud Marla, and I would have liked to hold it again for some of his strength, but he needed to go on stage for the next portion of the program. He walked up there, clapping until he reached Marla. He extended his hand to her, shook her hand, spoke to her for a brief moment, and then hugged her tightly. When he backed up, both of them were smiling and looking a bit misty-eyed.

Walking to the podium, he took a moment to compose himself before looking up and saying, "That's the hardest thing I'll have to follow; I guarantee that. Marla, you are an amazing woman, as are all the women given the chance to start a new life through Rise Up. I had planned to inject a lot of levity into my portion of the program, but I'm scrapping that now, and I'm going to say one thing and one thing only before we announce the auction winners. Get out your donation slips now and double what you planned to donate tonight. Triple it if you can. Take a moment now to fill them out, and a volunteer will be around shortly to collect them. Think of your daughters, sisters, cousins, nieces, and those friends you had at university. This could be one of them. Help them now."

There was a murmur of voices as those around the room reached for pens, glasses, checkbooks and the donation envelopes at each table. Sean stood quietly for a solid five minutes before he said another word. He beckoned the volunteers to come forward to collect the slips then began to highlight some of the items the silent auction boasted.

"I hope everyone had ample time and opportunity to bid high and often. I saw several hovering near their favored offering in hopes of keeping the high bid. Let's see how you faired."

He announced high-bid winners on all the silent auction items before building up excitement and hype around the celebrity items. The happy winners were all given the crystal frame that held the picture and description of the offer and instructions on how to make payment. The murmur of happy voices was interrupted occasionally by good-natured bantering with those who lost the bidding war. I can't help but smile at Phillip and Tess. Phillip outbid me to win the nanny services for Tess, who appeared relieved to know she would have a week of help at any rate.

"Now, ladies and gentlemen, Eliza has given me the envelope containing the winning bidders for the celebrity adventures. She has also advised that for those who did not win but want the opportunity to match the winner's bid and receive the identical adventure, all you need to do is visit the close-out table outside the ballroom. A rare treat for the second-place bidder! Shall we see who won?"

The applause and cheers around the room were boisterous and loud. Sean had to reach his hands out and motion for everyone to calm down and bring the noise down. He announced the winners of the four footballer adventures, and everyone who was runner-up immediately stood to take advantage of the matching offer. The Michael Bublé concert VIP package was announced, and I was not a winner or a runner-up, which disappointed me a bit. I have seen him in concert several times and really enjoyed it.

Sean's Highland Camping Adventure Weekend was the last to be announced, and Lydia Presley was the winner with the highest bid of the night at twenty-five thousand pounds. I was the runner-up and debated about whether or not I was going to take the matching offer or just donate and be done. Sean decided that for me when he looked right at me and said both the winner and runner-up for his adventure would be going the same weekend. To me, that said he wanted me there as a backup to help him deal with the trio. The adventure was for the winner plus three, and I feel confident it will be the Trio plus one other lady. I tilt my head to the side, raise an eyebrow and appear to contemplate the offer. I know it will be fun to bring Jess and maybe Charlie along, plus it will prove to be an entertaining weekend watching Sean dodge the women. I finally smile up at him a bit mischievously and nod.

With the last adventure-winning bids announced, Sean steps away to allow Eliza to close out the event. She announced tonight is the largest fundraiser they have ever had, and the final tally will be announced on the website on Monday. Everyone appears to be extremely happy and pleased with the outcome of the evening as they stand to depart. The Trio don't look very happy, but they also do not look angry. The line to make payments for all of the auction items has grown, so I sit back down and decide to finish the glass of cabernet sauvignon I have been sipping during dinner. Phillip and Tess stop by to say goodnight, and Tess and I exchange phone numbers.

Priscilla, James and several of the other soccer players and their wives come by to say goodnight as well. Priscilla asked if we could continue our conversation about the family pet over lunch one day, so I exchanged numbers with her as well. There are several other wives who appear to want to be included, so Priscilla decides to coordinate a group lunch. It should be fun, and I'd love to introduce Jessica to all of them. I am happy to have made new friends this evening.

The payment line has dwindled down enough that I decide it's time to pay the piper, so to speak. I stand and walk in the direction of the table when Eliza interrupts.

"Andi, I'm so glad you came tonight, and I was able to meet you. I hope you will keep in touch?"

"Of course, Eliza. I enjoyed myself immensely and have to give you kudos for your program. I was almost in tears several times and will be showing my support for your work. I've got to go pay for the Highland Camping Adventure; I was the runner-up, you know."

Eliza looks a bit confused and says, "But Sean already took care of that; he said he owed it to you. I'm not sure what he meant by that, but he's paid for it already."

I look around and don't see him. "Hmm, I'll have to ask him about that. Either way, I am still donating, so I'll be taking care of that right now. If you see Sean, please tell him I'd like a word."

Eliza beams and tells me she will and to give her a call at Rise Up so we can get together for lunch. Another friend has been made, and I smile at her, give her a hug and walk over to the table. I'm a bit irked that Sean paid for the trip even after I told him I would pay for my own items. I'm mulling over whether or not I'll give him a bit of my sharp tongue when I feel the tingle at the back of my neck. I glance over and give him a bit of a pissed-off look, then turn back to the volunteer who is handling my credit card transaction. I've given a small deposit and advised my accountant will be wiring the balance in the next few days.

Sean walks up as I finish. I turn to face him and give him a bit of the stink eye. "Why?"

I don't say anything else but that. The Trio is closing in on us from the opposite direction, which causes Sean to take me by the elbow and propel me down the hallway toward the foyer and exit of the hotel. His car is already pulled up, which tells me he has an escape plan in mind. I slide smoothly into the passenger seat as he rounds the car and gets in. As we pull away, he says, "I know you wanted to pay for your own auction items, but I feel like I begged you to take that match offer. I didn't think about who may buy it when my assistant and I put it together for the auction. I am not spending two days and nights in the wild with those three women, to be honest, any three women whom I don't know. The Trio, as I am now calling them, will be sure to make it a bit of a difficult weekend. Having you and three others around can help keep the balance right, and I won't feel so…" He trails off.

"Hunted?" I supply with a small grin.

He snorts and says, "Aye. That's a good word."

"Well, I'll let it slide, but I donated more than that amount anyway. It is a worthy cause, and, goodness, Marla just about ripped my heart out and threw it on the stage—her story. I can't imagine. How did you get involved with Rise Up?"

"Eliza is my father's sister, my aunt. She's a favorite one too."

"Why didn't you tell me that? Neither of you mentioned it."

"I try my best to keep my family separate from my work to keep their lives private. As evidenced by the recent POPSTOP debacle, my life is often more public than I am comfortable with, but it's part of the job, so I deal with it. They didn't ask for it, so I do my best to keep it away from them."

"That's commendable. It has also got to be hard at times."

"It is. Now, tell me how you liked the evening. You seemed to enjoy it with the exception of Marla's story."

"I had a wonderful time. Phillip and Tess are lovely, and I plan to catch up with Tess soon. Priscilla and several of the soccer, um, football wives also want to get together to talk about family pets and such. They seem like a fun crowd, and it's nice to have more new friends."

"Several of your new friends' husbands had a difficult time keeping their eyes on their wives and off of your legs."

"That's funny; I didn't notice." We slowed to a stop and were lucky enough to find a parking space in front of my building. Sean parked and came around to help me out.

"I overheard one of them say you had a world-class arse, too." He said this in a tight, almost angry voice.

Laughing lightly, I pat his chest as I pass him and through the door to my building. "You almost sound jealous. Better watch out, or someone might think you see me as more than a friend."

He doesn't say a thing as we ride the elevator in silence. I can feel the tension around him go up a few dozen notches and wonder what's bothering him. As the elevator door slides open, I walk out and say, "Don't worry, Sean. I know you don't think of me that way. We're friends, good ones, I'd like to think."

As I reach my door, I find myself spun around, backed up against the door, and my mouth covered by a hard, hot male one. Sean shoves one hand in my hair as the other wraps around my back tightly. His hand is hot against the bare skin of my back as he presses my body into him.

Just as abruptly, he breaks the kiss, and I hear him say harshly, "Yeah, I only think of you as a friend. I never think of doing this." He kisses me again, just as fiercely. "Not since I first met you." Another slightly softer kiss follows. "And not every day since then. I don't think about making love to you like I did the other night or how I want to do it again, and again, and again. How's that for not thinking of you that way?" He then melts the last of my brain cells with another scorching kiss.

I am leaning up and into him by now and start to reach my arms up and encircle his neck when he steps back from me, shoves his hands into his hair, and gruffly says, "I'm sorry. I shouldn't have done that."

My brain hasn't reengaged yet, so I'm slow to catch up. Dazed, I look up at him in the dimness of the hallway light and say, "Wait…what? What?"

He then grabs me again in a bear hug, kisses the top of my head and says an abrupt goodnight before turning and leaving, leaving me weaving in the hallway outside my flat with no real clue what just happened and why. I know the man kissed the daylights out of me, but then he apologized and left. After he hugged me? More confused than anything, I lean heavily against the door, only to squeak and almost fall in when it opens behind me.

"What happened? I thought I heard Sean out here?"

"I'm not really sure." Walking past Jess, I head to the sofa. Sitting down with a plop, I lean my head back and replay the events of the last two minutes. There is a serious possibility my brain is somewhere melted in the hallway. I can't wrap my mind around what just happened.

"Andi, you're freaking me out. What happened? Did the two of you have a disagreement?"

"What?" I shake my head to try to clear it. "No, he kissed the living shit out of me, told me he thought of me as a friend, or maybe that was sarcasm, I don't really know. I think he said he wants to have more sex. Anyway, then he hugs me and leaves. I can't figure it out. Probably because my brain imploded after the first kiss."

Jess does a little jig and then plops down next to me and says, "Here is where I say I told you so. Now tell me every tiny little detail."

An hour later, I'm no closer to sorting it all out than I was when it first happened. Jess was no help. She kept smiling like the Cheshire Cat and telling me she'd been waiting for this since we first arrived. I keep turning the whole scene around and around in my head, and nothing gets clearer. I have decided the man is a shockingly good kisser who may be insane. Telling Jess this, I get up, grab my shoes and announce I'm going to bed.

I catch sight of myself in the mirror above the dresser and realize my hair has fallen, and I look like I rode back with my head out the window. The realization that it was Sean's hand in my hair that caused the disarray gave me a shiver and brought that first kiss back into sharp focus. My brain stutters every time I recall those kisses, which then brings up our night together and those hot memories. Shaking my head, I push it away and jump into my nighttime skincare routine.

Chapter 25

My dreams are as confusing and tumultuous as my reality. I wake up shortly before sunrise, cranky and tired, with a heaviness in my chest that is all too familiar to me. Rolling over, I reach for my phone to check and almost drop it when I realize the date. My eyes fill with tears as my mind fills with guilt. This is the first year I won't be there, and I basically forgot about it because of everything going on with Sean.

Deciding not to expose Jess to my mess, I dress quickly and quietly then head out to my favorite coffee house. The second level is a series of nooks designed to allow a modicum of privacy to enjoy conversations, read, work, or just gaze out the window. I find an isolated spot in a window seat to sip my tea and stare out at the weather. My mood is as dreary as the rainy, cloudy sky.

I am confused. About my feelings. About Sean's actions. About how much he excites me and makes me feel. I haven't reacted like that to a man since I lost Justin five years ago. That realization leaves me melancholy and lost in a sea of memories. Those memories get jumbled up with more recent memories of my time with Sean, which causes even more confusion. The guilt is overwhelming me, and I almost give in to tears.

Not caring about my surroundings, I draw my knees up in the window seat and rest my chin on them. My heart aches. My head is beginning to follow. I truly don't know what to do. Does Sean have feelings for me? Did he get caught up and kiss me in the moment? Can I risk finding out? Can I risk not finding out? The timing of all of this really sucks. Am I ready to finally let Justin go? If I admit my feelings for Sean, I have to finally say goodbye to Justin.

My phone buzzes, drawing me out of my dark thoughts. I pick it up absently and glance at it. Noticing it's after 9 a.m., I check my messages and see that Jess has texted me several times. The last text said to order her a very large latte because she was on her way. I'll bet the Find My Friends app has given her my location. A small smile breaks through my gloom as I unfold myself, rise and order both of us beverages and pastries.

Jess comes in wearing an ancient hoodie that belonged to her brother, yoga pants and a raincoat dripping with water. She sheds the raincoat and looks around to find me. Starting toward me, she barely notices the heads turning her way. Several men eye her with approval, but she's focused on me and breezes past without acknowledging them.

"Where are we sitting?"

"Upstairs. It's quiet and somewhat private."

"Window seat? Looks like a good brooding place for you." Jess tries to make a joke but stops when I smile wanly. We settle in without talking for several minutes. Jess reaches over and taps me with her spoon. "How long have you been up?"

"Just before sunrise. I didn't want to bother you."

She brushes that away with a wave of her hand and settles back in the overstuffed chair. "Let's unpack all this, shall we?"

"I really don't want to unpack it until I have it sorted out in my own mind."

"And heart," Jess says.

Shaking my head, "No, that's not involved yet. I just don't know what to make of Sean's actions and his words."

"Have you heard from him?" she asks.

"Not since he said goodnight last night," I say with a shake of my head.

Jess takes a sip of her latte and stares down at it for a minute. Lifting her gaze, she says, "He woke me up this morning. Knocked on the door around 7:15, looking for you. He didn't seem happy when I told him you weren't home, and I had no idea where you were. I think he thought I was lying about you not being there."

I look out the window, "Hmm, should I reach out to him?"

Jess takes another sip of her latte, sets it down and says with conviction, "No. He needs to reach out to you and clear up some of the confusion he's caused. In the meantime, we need to cheer you up. You don't need a mani/pedi, and we just went shopping. What about renting a car and taking a drive through the countryside? Or find a yoga class?"

"Jess. Stop. I am fine. I know you've seen the date. I don't need you to distract me or cheer me up. It's a bit ironic that I am so emotional and worked up about Sean on this date. It's not ever easy, but I knew I would be here and not able to visit Justin's grave this year. I'm okay, really."

"I really don't know what to say." Jess looks sad and worried about me, so I force a smile I don't feel and reach for her hand.

"I'll be fine. I am going for a run when the rain stops. That will help me work a lot of this out, I'm sure. For now, let's just sit here and enjoy the coffee house vibe, good lattes, sweet pastries and great friends. Okay?"

"Okay. I'm here if you change your mind and want to go on a spur-of-the-moment adventure."

///

The clouds clear out around midday, and the sun attempts to shine down, albeit weakly. I've eaten enough sugary pastries to make me groan and drank enough tea lattes to float a boat. I'm still no closer to understanding things than I was last night. My somber mood is compounded by the knowledge that this is the first year I won't be visiting Justin's grave. The first year after he was killed, I spent the whole day there. I missed him so badly; I still do. It's gotten easier each year, but I still have a solid ache in my chest when I think of him.

Jess offered to run with me, but I need to be alone, and I know I'll go further than she likes to run. It's best for me to go solo. Jess knows I'll keep my phone but won't answer any calls or texts. Lacing up my runners, I check the arm strap that holds my phone and grab the lightweight tech hoodie. Ready to meet the Uber driver who will take me to a park outside of town that has a wonderful old ruin. I want fewer people and more moody landscapes for my run; this place suits me perfectly.

I know the Uber driver probably thinks I'm a nutty American because I took a car to go run but I don't bother explaining myself. He drops me off, and I start walking around the trail that leads towards the ruins. I warm up my muscles, stretch and start a slow run as the wind picks up. There is an eerie howl to the wind that suits my mood as I set a slow pace. I don't bother to use my earbuds; music isn't what I want. I need to work through the tumultuous emotions rolling through me like spring storms.

After an hour, I feel no closer to resolving my feelings than when I started. Reaching a secluded area that overlooks the ruins, I sit and take stock. I need to talk to Sean and get him to lay it all out for me. Once we clear things up, I think I'll be able to resolve my own conflicting emotions. As for Justin, my heart still hurts from the loss, but it's time I move on. I know he would have wanted me to already have moved on, but I couldn't do it. I'll always miss him, but I can't live my life avoiding serious relationships.

A hawk cries above me, and I jerk out of my deep thoughts. I watch the hunter land on a tree close to me and stare at me with those sharp eyes. I don't know why, but the bird's eyes remind me of Justin. Highly intelligent and piercing, they seem to see straight to my soul.

"You are beautifully scary; you know that?" I say softly. "Why are you so close to me?"

The bird gently flies down to stand just out of reach at my feet, startling me. "Ok, this is strange. You need to go on. Shew. I'm not in the mood to find out how sharp those claws are, and I am way too big to be considered a snack for you."

He stares right back at me without moving so much as a feather. Again, I'm struck by how much this bird reminds me of Justin. I look up to the sky and say, "I've finally lost my mind. The next thing you know, bird, I'll get in my head that you are Justin; come to tell me it's okay to let go. Then you'll fly away as Sean comes up to take me to the sanitarium." I am speaking to an avian; I have decided an obviously domesticated one, who responds by cocking his head and giving me that intense stare. I'm really losing my mind. Sighing, I decide it's time to go explore the ruins. Standing up, I assume the hawk will startle and fly away, but he doesn't.

Walking away and heading toward the ruins, I look back to see the hawk take flight and follow. It takes several minutes to reach the ruins which are almost completely deserted at this time of day. I'm fascinated to think about the people who built this structure and lived here. It's a nice break from the deep thoughts I've been mired in all day. Hearing the sharp cry of the hawk, I look up and watch as he flies toward the entrance of the ruin. I nearly trip and fall on my face as I see Sean standing there. I have to have imagined him, so I close my eyes tightly and then reopen them. He is still standing there, somberly looking at me but not coming any closer. I look up to see where the hawk is and see that he is gone. Could this get any stranger? Maybe I'm still asleep.

Sean walks over and stops a short distance away. "Are you alright? You look like you've seen a ghost."

Shaking my head, I look at him with a furrowed brow. "How did you know I was here?"

"Jessica finally told me. I needed to talk to you and didn't want to wait until you came back. I've been looking for you for most of the day since you won't return my texts or calls."

"I," sighing, I try again, "I needed some space to sort things out in my mind."

"I owe you an explanation and an apology for my behavior last night. I was a fool." Sean shakes his head and runs his hand through his hair in a gesture that I now know means he is either very uncomfortable or very frustrated. "Can we walk and talk? Will you let me explain myself?"

"Yes, I'd like that. I need to understand." We turn and start a ramble around the ruins that eventually lead us out the back to an area that must have once been a garden of sorts. It has crumbling walls around most of it and wildflowers blooming everywhere.

"Anderson, I want to apologize for being an utter ass at the end of the evening last night. I was so frustrated and uncertain that I lashed out at you. I'm sorry. My behavior was unforgivable, and I should never have manhandled you as I did. Will you accept my apology?"

"Apology accepted, but Sean, tell me why you were frustrated. I feel like it was because of me, but I'm not sure why." I turn beseeching eyes on him and reach out my hands as if to ask why.

"I don't know what to say, really. I like being around you, talking to you, laughing with you, sparing with you. You're an incredibly intelligent woman, not to mention unbelievably sexy. I want to touch you, hold you and kiss you, but not as your friend. Can't you see that? Can't you see I want more than to be your friend?"

"But what changed? You never gave any indication of that when we first met. I know when I'm being pursued, and you didn't act that way. Why?"

"I've always felt this way. I could see you were skittish and backed away from me whenever I got too close, so I decided to work slowly until you relaxed around me. There are times when I see your hesitation as clearly as crossing arms at a railroad. What makes you step back from me? Is it my profession?"

"No, it's not that." Looking away, I close my eyes briefly and then reply, "It's a long story. One I'd like to share with you if you want to hear it."

"I do."

I walk several steps away before I begin. "I got engaged when I was just out of undergraduate school to a wonderful man named Justin, who was a soldier, a Marine. We knew each other a bit from high school and connected again the summer before Jess and I went to college. Justin was two years ahead of us in school, and when he graduated, he planned on enlisting. We dated for several years before he proposed after I graduated from UGA. He knew I was going to graduate school and then vet school, so we had a plan to be engaged until I finished. We had so many plans, but all of them came to an end five years ago today. Justin had been deployed in Afghanistan and constantly on missions I couldn't know about. He contacted me as often as he could, but sometimes, it would be weeks between calls or emails. I didn't worry much and was blindsided when the officer and chaplain showed up at my door."

Sean didn't touch me, but I could feel him close to me. I turned and looked up at him. His blue eyes were alive with sorrow for me. I turned away quickly before I broke down. I took several deep cleansing breaths before I went on, "I don't think I really knew what was going on around me for almost a week. Jess stepped in and took care of everything; Justin had been raised in foster care, so he had no family to speak of but me. My entire world just….stopped."

"It was different than the accident that took my parents. I'm not really sure how, but it was different. I was so angry when my parents died, but with Justin, I was just numb. I didn't feel anything for a long time, and then, when I finally surfaced, I embraced the numbness. I decided I was never going to feel again. If I didn't feel, I didn't love. If I didn't love, I didn't lose." Sean settled his hands on my shoulders now and drew me back just a bit until there was barely a breath between our bodies. He still didn't speak.

"I'll always have Jessica and her family, but I've avoided any and all emotional entanglements since the day I lost Justin. You know what's funny? About three years ago, at a bachelorette party, we all went to have psychic readings. My friend Nancy is an Earth Mother who is into crystals, tarot, psychics, etc. The psychic, Mahala, told me I was stronger than most because I endured so much sorrow and heartbreak, but I was destined to have a full heart and happy life. I laughed at her. Outright laughed at her and said that was never going to happen because I would never give my heart away again; there was nothing left."

Looking out over the rolling landscape, I catch sight of the hawk again. He is gliding so elegantly as he flies away. I hear one last piercing cry, and he's gone. My eyes sting with unshed tears, and I realize I am finally letting go. "I've kept that vow without a thought and assumed it would always be that way. Until…" My voice fades, and I feel Sean's hands tighten slightly on my shoulders.

"Until now," he says, "Until me." Nodding, I take a shuddering breath but still can't look at him.

"Jessica was right when she said I was sabotaging whatever we have and forcing you into the friend zone because I was scared. Hell, I'm terrified. I'm moving into uncharted territory; I'm saying goodbye to Justin and stepping forward without knowing where my feet will fall."

Sean steps fully into me then and wraps his arms around my waist, brushing his lips against my head and says, "Step to me; I'll keep you steady."

Turning in his arms, I finally gain the courage to look up, "I'm afraid," I admit in a choked voice. He leans his forehead against mine and says, "I am too."

Closing my eyes, I nestle into his chest and let the feeling of safety wash over me. The strength of his arms and the steady beat of his heart smooth out the ragged emotions I've been fighting all day. I feel him let out a long breath and hold me a bit tighter. We stay this way for several moments before I ease back and smile at him.

"So, you like me?"

With a hearty laugh, he picks me up, swings me around several times and then says, "A little bit."

"I like you too. A little bit." I say, with a lightness of heart, I have not felt in a long time.

"No more friend talk?" He says with a bit of a frown.

"Well, I feel like we are friends, right? That we started as friends, and now we are moving toward being more than that."

"Darling, we moved past that a while ago; you just haven't caught up yet." With a wink, he reaches for my hand, catches it and raises it to kiss the back. "Let's talk this through a bit more, shall we?"

We begin to slowly walk along the paths that wind in and around the ruins with our hands linked. He breaks the comfortable silence, "You fascinate me. The more I learn about you, the more enthralled I am. That psychic was right, you know. You are stronger than most, certainly stronger than anyone I know." Another squeeze of our joined hands followed by another kiss on the back of mine. He is most definitely demonstrative of his affections.

"I admit to initially being fascinated by the outside, which is gorgeous, but there is so much more to you. I'm comfortable around you and let my guard down, which I rarely have the luxury of doing these days. You don't treat me differently or look at me like I'm some kind of prize."

I can't help but choke back a laugh at that. "You are a prize. If what we dealt with last night is any indication, women look at you like a prime piece of meat. I'm ashamed of my own gender but will give other women a bit of credit because you are extremely attractive."

"Thank you. It's things like that, being real with me, that adds to why you fascinate me. You have no hidden agenda or ulterior motive for spending time with me."

"That's not completely true," I say, deciding we need to lighten things up a bit. He stops abruptly and looks at me in question.

"I love your dog and want to see him too."

Shaking his head, he reels me in for another hug, followed by a sweet kiss that slides right on into heavy. Both of us are breathing heavier as we part and continue walking. Neither of us sees the person inside the ruins with the camera aimed at us.

He continues as we walk, "I'd like to continue exploring what is growing between us but also keep it quiet so it's just ours. If the media gets wind of it, it will become a headache neither of us wants. What do you think?"

"I doubt the media will have much interest in me, but I do like the idea of keeping things between us. I will let Jessica know; she and I don't keep secrets, plus she knows me too well not to guess."

"Need I remind you of the two images already on the POPSTOP page?"

I wave my hand and say, "Speculation. Nothing solid." Stopping, I turn to him; in a serious voice, I say, "Thank you for being upfront with me and listening. I don't tell many people about Justin; I haven't had a reason to before now."

"I'm glad we spoke and cleared things up. I'll always listen. I'd actually like to hear more about the man who stole your heart so young. When you're ready, I'll be there."

I smile now with more feeling than I have all day. My heart is no longer heavy, and there seems to be a weight I wasn't aware I was carrying gone from my shoulders. Looking at Sean, I feel a sense of excitement as well as peace. It sounds contradictory, but I'm excited to explore what we may have but also feel a sense of peace and contentment that has been missing since I lost Justin. For the first time, I feel confident enough to walk over to him in the wide open space of the park, pull his head down to me and kiss him soundly. "Can we go to your place for a while?" Eyes sparkling, I give him a saucy smile accompanied by a wink. Being bold like this is new for me, so I'm jittery and nervous.

"I'm already halfway home." Tugging on my hand, we trot off toward the car like a pair of teens.

On the way to Sean's, I make a call to Patrick to check on the animals. I've been really impressed with his leadership since I hired him weeks ago. He assures me all was well when he went by to feed this morning, and he has Knox on tap to handle the evening chores. A quick check of my email lets me know there are no issues with Doc on a Walk. I check in with Jessica and let her know not to worry when I don't come home. All is right in my world.

Chapter 26

I had no idea what I was getting myself and Jessica involved in with this Highland Camping Weekend with Sean. The shooting schedule allowed for a variety of weekends, but Sean wanted to get this completed before the coming two-week break. His assistant had everything organized prior to the auction, then had to double it. I included Jess and Charlie in my group, and the Trio brought in another female to round out their foursome.

We met up in Glencoe at the famous Kings House Hotel, where introductions were made. I held back with Jess as Sean introduced everyone. I got the sense the ladies were not happy to have both groups going together, but they made all the appropriate comments and smiles. The new addition to the foursome, Pamela Evans, took an immediate shine to Charlie, which amused Jessica. After all the necessary paperwork was signed and given back to Sean's assistant, we headed to our starting point of Glen Etive, which led to the trail going to Glen Ceitlein.

Jess and I had camped and hiked before, but not on this scale. Our guide, Gareth, asked us if we wanted to carry our own backpacks or send them up in advance by quad to make the hike easier. Not one to back down from a challenge, Jess and I quickly said we would carry our own. The ladies opted to have their gear taken up to our campsite. Sean and Charlie had packs that made them look like professional guides like Gareth. Obviously, they have done this a time or two.

"So, how many times have y'all done this kind of hiking camping adventure?" Jess asks as she shoulders her pack and starts buckling the straps.

Charlie shrugs and declares he goes at least four or five times a year with friends and has been twice with Sean. Sean nods and adds he tries to go several times a year, but lately, it's been difficult.

"Jess and I haven't been on any treks like this, but we went a few times in college with a group. Of course, we had cabins and a lot of adult beverages, so it wasn't really roughing it." I say that as I strap on a pack weighing about twenty-five pounds. "I'm actually looking forward to this. We haven't been out in the country to explore too much."

I quickly realize that the ladies were going to monopolize Sean and Gareth's time as well as attempt to draw Charlie in as well. Sean shot me a wink and a smile before being the dutiful host. Walking with the ladies and entertaining them with additions to the rhetoric Gareth provided, Sean seemed to walk with little to no effort despite carrying the pack that had to be close to 40 pounds. Jess and I shared a look, an eye roll and a soft laugh as we continued trekking through the somewhat muddy path.

We stopped several times at lovely vistas that had all of us taking out our phones to take photos. There was no cell service, so taking pictures was all we were going to do. Gareth advised us to put our phones in Airplane Mode to conserve the battery as we would not be able to charge them until we descended. The break from technology was welcomed. However, I was glad to be able to take photos. I took several of Charlie and Jess, and he returned the favor so Jess and I could memorialize the moment. I didn't bother asking for any pictures with Sean. The ladies were wearing him out with individual and group photos at just about every possible photo spot on the trail. I cannot imagine how he does this type of thing without losing his mind. I am obviously not designed for public life; my mouth tends to overload my good sense from time to time. That thought makes me ponder how I could negatively impact things for Sean if our relationship goes on and becomes public.

Our trek for the first day was short as it was Friday, and we got a late start due to filming. We made camp on a flat, dry area where we found the quad had delivered the ladies' packs. Gareth helped get us all started setting up our tents, which seemed to shock Lydia. She thought it would already be set up, and a fire started.

With a smile, Gareth patiently disabused her of that notion. "No fires in advance, ladies; we must find our own wood and create our own fire circle. As for your tents being set up, that's part of the adventure. Learning to set up your own campsite. Let me help you get started."

There was some quiet discussion among the ladies, which I can imagine centered around where Sean's tent would be located. Gareth put all the ladies' tents on one side and the men's facing on the opposite side of the clearing. Jess and I helped each other get the tents up and then went inside to set up the thin inflatable mat and sleeping bag. My tent was on the end with Jess next to me, then the other four ladies. I took several minutes to relax and think about the short hike, as well as speculate about what the ladies would entertain us with over the next several hours.

We spent about a half hour finding materials for a fire, and Charlie showed off by using flint and steel to light it. Dinner was entertaining as well as delicious. Gareth shared some history of the area, folklore, legends and such while we ate a wonderful stew. Charlie brought out a bottle of whisky, telling everyone you couldn't camp in the Highlands without a dram of good Scottish whisky.

I decided I was ready to call it a night before any of the others. I bid everyone a good night, then left to take care of my personal needs before crawling into my tent. I wasn't tired so much as ready to decompress and have some solitary time. My internal batteries needed a recharge, so to speak. Jess poked her head in and said good night, then whispered, "Don't check on me overnight...I may not be in my own tent." With that statement and a wink, she was gone.

Camp got quiet about an hour later, and I switched off my flashlight. Rolling to my side, I was getting situated when I heard the zipper on my tent flap. Looking up, I saw Sean poke his head in.

"I didn't get to say good night properly." In the darkness, I couldn't see his face, but based on his tone, he was smiling. Reaching out my hand, I sat up as he grabbed it. "I'm sorry it's been a tedious evening for you."

"It hasn't. It's been very entertaining and educational. I enjoyed all of Gareth's information as well as watching the ladies give the come-on to you, Gareth and even Charlie. It was amusing."

"You didn't get upset? I wondered why you left early." He moved over to sit next to me now and continued to hold my hand while speaking in low, soft tones.

I let out a snort and said, "Not likely. I would like to ask who gave you the biggest push to stay with her. Jess and I have a bet."

"I am not dignifying that with a response, you minx. Now kiss me like you mean it, and then I must leave."

I give him a kiss that is guaranteed to keep us both up for a while, then push him toward the tent flap with "Go lock your tent flap."

Several hours later, I was awakened by the screeching of Lydia Presley. I quickly stuffed my feet into my boots and went out into the rain. Lydia was standing next to what used to be her tent; a large limb had fallen onto it and crushed it. Everyone was starting to exit their own tents with Gareth in the lead.

I reached Lydia first and grabbed her shoulders, "Mrs. Presley, Mrs. Presley, stop. LYDIA! STOP!"

She finally quit screeching and looked at me with wild eyes. "Calm down, tell us what happened."

Lydia took a deep breath and stammered, "The wind was howling, and then the limb suddenly crashed down on my tent. I was almost crushed."

Gareth and Sean lifted the limb off the tent and tried to resurrect it, but the tent poles were broken in too many places to hold the fabric up. Lydia looked miserable, so I went to her and offered to let her sleep in my tent.

"I am happy to squeeze in with Jess in her tent. We can get your things out of your tent and put them in mine. I just need a couple of minutes to make the swap, and you can be inside and dry in no time."

Lydia looked at me with rain dripping off her face, "Why would you do that for me?"

"Why wouldn't I? We women have to stick together, right?" I say with a smile. The poor woman looks like she is one swift wind away from a complete meltdown. Her friends seem almost equally shocked, and no one is stepping forward, offering her a dry place to stay for the remainder of the night.

Sean walks over to us and speaks quietly, "Lydia, I'm so sorry this happened. We can shift some things around and get you another tent."

"Miss, I mean, Dr. Sullivan offered me hers already. She is going to get my things and put them in her tent and sleep with her friend." She says with a sniff and a smile at me. I excuse myself and head to my tent to clear out my things. Jess follows, and under her breath, "Good thing my tent is empty."

"You'll need to bunk with me since she is likely not to sleep the rest of the night or at least for a couple of hours. She's wound up tighter than an eight-day clock right now. She'll be listening for the slightest things. If you aren't in here with me, she'll know. Do you want questions tomorrow?"

"You are right, darn it. Charlie and I aren't really broadcasting our relationship, but then again, we aren't really hiding it either—no big deal. I do need to let him know I won't be back. Want me to help move her things?"

"No, I've got it. You give Charlie the heads up. I'm not sure how the two sleep mats are going to fit in the tent, but we'll make it work."

It took about fifteen minutes to get things transferred and get Lydia dry and in my former tent. Charlie brought her over a flask of whisky to take to bed with her, and she immediately drank a couple of swallows. She needed something to calm her nerves, and he had the best medicine. The other women retired back to their tents, leaving the rest of us in the drizzle. Sean came over to me, said thank you and kissed me softly before everyone. I was a bit shocked that he was so open in front of our audience. It must have shown on my face because he chuckled, kissed me again and said, "The wind is picking up and promising a downpour. Best get tucked in for the rest of the night."

We all agreed, bid each other a second goodnight and returned to our tents. Jess and I wedged into the little tent and spent several minutes trying to dry off and get situated. There was some giggling and several elbows and knees colliding. We were both in a sweat by the time we got organized and on our sleeping mats, which went about four inches up each side when placed side by side. I was wise enough to pack extra clothes, so I had a set in the bottom of my sleeping bag to be warm in the morning and laid out the clothes I got wet on top of the bag so they may dry if possible. We both fell asleep quickly despite the recent events and slept undisturbed for the remainder of the night.

Gareth, Sean and Charlie were the first to wake up, and the ladies slept another hour. Jess and I rose before the other four and were given coffee and advised to let them sleep. Today's hike would be a bit strenuous, so the added sleep would help. Plus, Lydia deserved to sleep in after her ordeal.

Taking my coffee mug, I wandered down a barely worn path and discovered a lovely overlook where I could watch the morning mists and fog roll over the glen below. Standing there, I was mesmerized by the power and mystery of nature. The countryside was vastly different from Georgia, even the mountainous parts in the northwest part of the state. The Smokies are majestic and can take your breath away, but seeing this vista gripped my soul somehow. I decided I was going to stay until I was forced to go back to camp to begin the first full day of our adventure.

"I've been looking for you. Most tourists don't wander too far off the marked paths, but somehow, I knew you'd find a beautiful spot regardless of there being no path."

I turned to find Sean smiling at me, leaning against a tree with his arms crossed. I waved my hand to encompass the view and said, "This is simply amazing."

His smile softens as he pushes off from the tree to come toward me. He wraps his arms around me from behind, takes my coffee and takes a drink before lowering it and leaning his jaw against my head. We stood there for several minutes, just watching the sun burn the mist away and reveal a beautiful day. We were so wrapped up in each other and the view we didn't notice Lydia on the path. Her eyes widened, but she didn't say anything, just backed silently away.

"We need to get back," Sean says in a voice tinged with regret. "We've got a solid six, maybe seven hours of hiking today."

I turn in his arms, wrap mine around his waist and smile up at him. "Let's do this!" Giving him a smacking kiss, I pick up my coffee mug and slip past him down the path. I hear him laugh and follow.

When we get back to camp, Gareth has everyone eating a breakfast of dried fruit, protein bars and hot coffee. Sean changed direction and came in from a different path completely, so it did not look like we were together. We said good morning to each other, and the others then joined the group for breakfast. Several minutes later, we were organized into teams to get our campsite packed up and packs ready for the journey. Gareth let us know a member of his team would be up shortly to get the ladies' packs and take them to our next campsite. He let Lydia know she would have a new tent for tonight.

The hike was strenuous, but we didn't try to break any records, stopped when we needed to, whether for photo ops or for short periods of rest and made it to the campsite on time. As promised, Lydia had a new tent when we met the quad with their packs. Gareth walked us through the set-up again, and we all agreed Lydia could be in the middle. She deserved a good night's sleep after last night. Despite the long day and physical exhaustion, everyone was in a fine mood, and dinner was a light-hearted affair with a lot of jokes and laughter. Lydia, Melody, Margo and Pamela seemed to really relax and, strangely enough, become less haughty and more likeable. They teased Sean about gag reels of the first season of the show and some of his early work. He took it all good-naturedly and laughed a lot of it off. Some of the gag reel scenes got even funnier to the ladies once he told some of the backstory. I know I'm definitely going to search for that one when I get the chance.

All of us opt to turn in early. I walked off to take care of my personal needs, then took a few moments to listen to the sounds. Jess showed up and asked me if everything was ok. I'm tired, but nothing is wrong. I just wanted a few minutes alone. She told me she thought Sean was looking for me and hoping for a few minutes alone with me. I headed back, leaving her to her privacy.

Right before I got to the clearing, I heard a sound to my right and saw Sean walk out. He put his finger to his mouth in the universal sign for be quiet and motioned me to follow him. I turned and followed him as he led me to another small clearing that could overlook a nice view, but in the dark, it was impossible to see anything. He must have read my mind because he grabbed my hand and pointed it up.

I looked up and gasped. The sky was clear, and the stars were so bright it was almost as if we could touch them. "Wow, how beautiful."

He sat down and tugged me down, so I sat with my back against his chest. He was literally surrounding me. I leaned back with a sigh and relaxed against him. We sat quietly for quite a while without speaking. It was a comfortable silence where neither of us felt the need to fill the quiet. I already knew Sean was a toucher, but if I didn't, sitting here with him would have proven it. He rubbed my arm lightly, traced my fingers or played with my hair absently. It's been so long since I let myself enjoy this kind of intimacy; it felt like a balm to my soul.

Leaning back a bit, I look up at him and say, "Glad you intercepted me. This is nice."

He leaned down and rubbed his nose against mine, then kissed me softly. "I was hoping to spend time with you this weekend; I didn't realize how busy the ladies would keep me."

"Have you noticed they seemed to have chilled out today? I mean, Lydia had reason to be wound up tight today, but she wasn't."

"They do seem a bit less hyper-focused on me. And dinner was pretty funny."

"More than pretty funny, I'm going to look up that gag reel."

He laughed and hugged me tight. "Have you ever watched the show?

"Jess has, but I haven't. I'm not a huge tv person. I think I'll watch this one, though. I can't just watch the gag reel. I assume you've seen all of your episodes, right?"

"I usually see them once edits are finished; we all sometimes watch together. I don't usually sit down on the sofa with popcorn and binge-watch the season if that's what you're asking. If I watch something I'm involved in more than once, I start to get overly critical, which messes with my head when I go back on set. Once is enough."

"That makes sense. I don't have a way to see what I do in front of me on a screen, so I just get to second guess myself in my own head."

"Do you do that? Second guess yourself?" he asked, leaning me to the right so he could look at me. Darkness made it hard to see each other clearly, but we were close enough to make do.

"All the time. Especially when I lose an animal, I get mired down in the details and try to figure out what I should have or could have done differently. Jessica calls it brooding, but I think it's just overanalyzing. I think it's human nature, really. We all do it, just in different ways."

"True. You're a wise woman for such a young one."

I laugh at that, "I'll be thirty next month, so not very young, I'm afraid."

"You're younger than me." He says with another wink and a quick kiss. "We need to head back before someone comes looking for us."

He helps me stand and pulls me close again for a longer kiss. This man makes me breathless with these long, drugging kisses. "Come home with me tomorrow night. I'll let you take a swim in my tub again."

"On one condition," I say, leaning up to his ear, "This time, you join me instead of leaving me in there to think about it." I take a small nip of his ear before easing back down. I'm immediately preoccupied by more of those delicious kisses, which makes me forget my lascivious suggestion.

"You've got a deal, darling," Sean states gruffly before tugging me along toward camp.

"What's a deal?" I ask, dazed. He chuckles but doesn't say anything else.

It only took us a few minutes to get back to camp and discover everyone, but Gareth was tucked away in their tents with their LED lanterns off. Gareth acknowledged us with a nod before he headed into his own tent. Sean stopped in front of mine and gave me another long, deep kiss before he peeled my arms from around his neck and said good night. Whew, the man really gets my blood pumping. It's not the best way to be sent to bed when you're alone.

Chapter 27

Sunday morning dawned clear and crisp, with winds blowing to make things interesting for our trek down the mountain. Taking the most direct route down versus the winding trails that allowed for many stops and detours made the trip down a short five hours. The wind stayed at our back most of the time, which made the pace seem faster. By the time we reached Kings House Hotel again, we were all laughing and teasing each other about windblown hair, mud-covered boots and general silliness. I will admit I honestly thought the weekend would be tedious with few moments of pure enjoyment, but I enjoyed myself immensely and didn't have a problem with The Trio Plus One (Jess and I coined that name on Friday's trek), especially after things seemed to thaw considerably on Saturday. Before we all split up to return home, Sean invited everyone into the bar for a farewell drink. Lydia pulled me aside as we were heading into the bar.

"Anderson, can I have a moment?" she says with a happy smile.

"Sure. What can I do for you?"

"I'm going to sound ridiculous, but I'm saying this anyway. I like you for Sean." I try to keep my shock from showing, but I am no poker face. She continues, "I noticed the two of you on Saturday morning, and it struck me how right you look together. I've been a huge fan of his since he first started doing television, and I know I come off a bit stalkerish from time to time."

"My children are grown, with my middle son only a few months older than Sean. I think that's part of what makes me feel so protective. Anyway, my husband has never really had time for me, and with the children gone, I seemed to be lost until I watched Sean in a play in London. He's got such talent and is such a genuinely nice man. I want him to be happy, and I think you will do that for him."

After dropping those bombs, she pats my arm and walks into the bar, leaving me stunned and gaping at her near the entrance. What. The. F---. I must have been standing there with every thought crossing my face when Jessica and Charlie walked over to me.

"What happened to you?"

"Lass, you look a bit shell-shocked. What's the matter?" Charlie asks, reaching out to touch my shoulder.

Shaking it off, I laugh and say, "It's too bizarre to get into now. It's nothing bad, not bad at all. We'll talk later." I walk off toward the others and can't help but laugh and shake my head. Wow. We thought we were so discrete.

As we approach the group at the bar, Sean catches my eye and raises a brow in question. I shake my head, smile and turn to Charlie. We all enjoy a couple of rounds before going our separate ways. For Jess, Charlie and I, that means we head out with Sean. He offered to drive all of us, saying he wanted to test the car out on a bit of a drive. We had barely made it out of the parking lot and onto the road when Charlie asked what happened with Lydia.

Sean glanced over at me and said, "I was wondering the same thing myself. You had the strangest look on your face when you walked in from speaking with her."

Laughing, I turned slightly to face Sean and to be able to see Jess and Charlie in the back seat. "Y'all will not believe this. The woman, who we deemed a cougar by previous actions, told me she – and I quote here – liked me for you, Sean. She had apparently come up on us Saturday morning when we were sharing coffee, decided she liked how we looked together and started paying closer attention."

Sean's eyebrows went up like I'm sure mine did when Lydia spoke to me. Barely taking his eyes off the road, he glanced over and said, "You've got to be kidding me."

"I promise, I'm not. She went on to tell me she's a bored housewife whose kids are grown, and her husband doesn't pay her any mind. She saw you in a play in London, and you became her hobby."

Jessica and Charlie tried not to laugh, their shoulders hunched forward and their heads bowed together until they saw Sean's expression. It was a mixture of incredulity and disbelief with a dash of something undefined mixed in. I glanced back at Jess, and we burst out laughing. Charlie joined in, and the three of us laughed until we noticed Sean was not laughing along.

"Sean," I say, reaching out my hand to lay it on his arm briefly, "I'm sorry we laughed."

"It's not that, Anderson. I don't want to be anyone's hobby." He reaches over with his right hand to take mine. "It sounds so…odd. Like I'm an inanimate object or a collectable to be put on a bloody shelf in the library." He seemed to mull it over for a few more moments while idly running his fingers over my hand. The burst of laughter from him was so sudden Jess and I jumped, and naturally, that started the three of us laughing again.

"I suppose it could be worse," I say, biting my lip to hold back the laughter and the grin. "She could have seriously been a cougar who was after your rather fine self, Mr. Miller."

"What's everyone feel like for dinner?" Sean said in an obvious attempt to change the subject. "I've a mind to cook. Let's stop at the market and pick up something good."

"Is cooking a bit of a...." Jess begins and pauses dramatically, "Hobby of yours, then?"

Charlie had been taking a drink of water when Jess asked her question; he promptly choked and sprayed water all over the back of the Audi. Jess was laughing so hard she could barely pat him on the back to help with his choking. I was trying desperately not to laugh but lost the fight and dissolved into giggles. Sean chuckled once but did no more than shake his head at the hilarity running amok in his car.

"Sean, haven't you had enough of us this weekend?" Jess asks after she catches her breath.

"Maybe one of you," he deadpans, looking as serious as I've ever seen him. Until I looked into his eyes, which were sparkling with humor, Jess couldn't see since he ducked his head below the rearview mirror. I started to giggle when I glanced back at her, and she was struck silent.

"He's kidding, Jess." I reached over and swatted his leg, only to have my hand captured and held there.

"Am I kidding?" he queries as he squeezes my hand against his thigh. "Maybe I've had enough of Charlie and want the beautiful American women all to myself."

"Dream on, mate." Charlie chimes in. "I'm inclined to stick around and keep you away from this one. Plus, you're not a half-bad hand in the kitchen."

"Sounds like you're all in for dinner. Let's hit the market. You three choose the menu, and I'll handle the prep and cooking."

"That, my friend, is a deal," Charlie answers for all of us. "Ladies, I'm claiming meat. You two can handle sides and dessert."

Jess immediately claims dessert, which leaves me sides. "How do I choose sides when I have no idea what the entrée will be?" I ask.

"That's half the fun of this little game," Charlie answers. "He's got to make something delicious out of it. We're off the hook until clean-up time."

Twenty minutes later, Sean pulled into a local organic market that he favored. He parked and got out with us before Charlie told him he wasn't allowed to walk with any of us but could choose a wine. Good-natured and relaxed, Sean saluted and gestured the rest of us to precede him. Once we entered the market, each of us grabbed a basket, and we parted ways. Charlie seemed to have a familiarity with this market, but Jess and I spent a lot of time wandering up and down aisles. I ended up in the best produce section I've seen since we arrived. I swear, everything seemed to be fresh from the farm. I may have gone a bit overboard; I bought fingerling potatoes, several different colors of carrots, two kinds of lettuce, tomatoes, cucumbers, and several other colorful vegetables.

Jess and I almost collide at check out, and I notice she's had a bit of fun shopping also. Both our baskets have way more food than we need for one meal. We start laughing and poking through each other's baskets when I catch a glimpse of Sean and none other than Lizette. She seems to have him backed into a corner in the wine section. He's got several bottles of wine in his basket and keeps nodding and trying to move, but she shifts and blocks. I can't see her face, but he has a polite smile. Nudging Jess, I gesture my chin toward the pair.

"Should we rescue him," I ask.

"Looks like Charlie's coming in hot. He'll handle it."

"Mate, we need to get going. Hey, Lizette. Gotta steal the man. He's got cooking to do." Charlie says with a smile and a wink.

"Sean is cooking?" Lizette asked with shock. "Why don't you have someone do that for you or order takeout? Cooking is for normal people, not celebrities."

"I enjoy cooking, Lizette. It relaxes me."

"I'd love to try your cooking. I'm free tonight to join you and Charlie if you'd like." Lizette says hopefully with a flirty smile.

"Sorry, doll," Charlie responds. "This is man time. Take care!"

The pair moved away from Lizette without Sean saying another word. Her face had flamed in anger, and she turned as if to follow but didn't. Jess and I checked out a few cashiers down from where the group were chatting, so Lizette didn't seem to notice us. I don't know why, but I'm actually happy she didn't see us or notice that we all came in together. Jess and I walk out and head to Sean's car without a backward glance.

"Is she always that intense with him?" Jess asks with a raised brow.

"She definitely has a thing for him, but that seemed a bit much, even for her. Then again, I am not normally around either of them, so it could be new or her normal behavior. Charlie seemed to know how to handle it."

Jess glanced at me and said, "From what Charlie's told me, he and Sean are close enough friends that Charlie steps in and rescues him from time to time when a fan or a female gets too persistent. I think it's an unspoken agreement, or maybe they have talked about it, but either way, Charlie knows Sean well enough to know when he needs an assist."

"I'm still struggling to wrap my mind around what he has to deal with," I say, "The long ass days alone are not something I would have thought an actor put in frequently."

Jess laughs and says, "Did you think they worked banker's hours? 9 – 5?"

Rolling my eyes, I glanced back to see the guys exiting before responding, "I never thought about it either way. I rarely think about the amount of time any profession truly works. I know your schedule, but that is because we live together, and we're framily."

"You haven't said framily in a while. I missed it, tear."

"Don't be snide; it makes your nose scrunch up and look piggish."

We both look at each other and burst out laughing again. Then, she hip-checks me and calls me a very unsavory slur under her breath as Sean pops the trunk, and we put more than enough food for one meal into his trunk. Both men are giving us quizzical looks, but we just brush them off and keep laughing. Sean starts the car, and we are once again on the road. It takes less than 10 minutes to reach Sean's house, where we grab all the bags and food, heading into the kitchen while Sean takes care of Rab. Rab runs happy circles around all of us as he barks his welcome. Then, Sean and Rab exit to the backyard, where they play his favorite game of fetch. That dog could fetch a ball for hours and hours with little to no rest.

A short time later, Sean returns to the kitchen, where he washes up. We've made ourselves at home and opened the wine, sliced a block of cheese and settled at the bar side of the massive kitchen island. Three expectant faces look at Sean as he dries his hands.

"What do I have for my ingredients?" he asks as he looks at the clear counters. "Have you so little faith in my abilities that you've already ordered takeout?"

Charlie speaks up first and says, "I've got a couple lovely tenderloins of beef as well as a filet of salmon for you. I'm hoping you can handle both surf and turf sounds spot on after our meager meals."

Glancing at me as if to say, your turn, Charlie lifts his wine glass in a toast. I take the queue and launch into the list of veggies I bought. Sean looks a bit shocked at all of it, which makes me blush a bit and stammer, "I know you won't use them all. I'm going to eat well this week on the rest."

"I'm the easy one; I bought a bunch of things as well but only bought Brookies for dessert. You don't have to do a thing but open the package!" Jess says with a wink and a toast of her own.

He leans forward with his palms braced on the granite, head bowed as if in defeat. Then, he straightens, smiles brightly and says, "Get ready for a feast, my friends. We're eating well tonight."

The next half hour is spent with Sean leading the charge and the three of us acting in various roles as sous chefs and wait staff. The outside dining table is cleaned and set; Jess went and cut some of his flowers and made a lovely centerpiece, I chopped vegetables while Charlie was responsible for scrubbing pots and pans as Sean discarded them. In between our assignments, we enjoyed a relaxed conversation that flowed from sports to music, back to sports and then to theater. It came as a surprise that both Charlie and Sean had seen Hamilton, the latest Broadway craze, but Jess and I had not. Both had attended when the tour was in London a few years back. Jess and I shared a look and admitted we were bad Americans for not seeing the musical.

Sean laughed and said, "With your schedules, it's a wonder you see each other, much less a musical."

"We find time to do a lot of things, but I'll admit, seeing a popular musical dropped out of my top ten things to do on my days off," I say with a bit of sass. "We went zip lining last year in Costa Rica. We did a snorkeling adventure in … St. Lucia?" I continue, looking at Jessica.

"St. Bartt's. Don't forget our ski trip to Banff." She laughs. We both share a long laugh about that one. Our shared looks and laughter piqued the interest of both men.

"Tell the story," ordered Sean with a severe look and stern tone.

"There really isn't much to tell. We had a long weekend trip planned to ski in Banff, and we both ended up getting food poisoning and never seeing anything outside our room for four days. The closest we came to skiing that weekend was when we both slipped on ice and landed on our asses in front of the van that brought us to the resort." Jess shares the memory with a careless wave of her hand, but we both remember how sick we were that weekend. Sharing a bathroom when you have food poisoning is not pleasant; we never had a problem when we were roommates before because we always had two bathrooms and were never sick at the same time.

"So that trip was a complete disaster," Charlie concludes as he dries the last pot. "When was that?"

"Last year," I say. "This year's adventure was a few days in London before we came here. We haven't gotten over the memory enough to try skiing again, and I think I'll pass on Banff for another few years."

"Surely it wasn't the food in the city that made you ill?" Sean said.

"No, we grabbed something at the airport before catching the shuttle to the resort. The ride was about an hour, and we were starving. Lesson learned."

"No worries that you'll be off color after this meal, and I guarantee you won't be speaking Welsh!" Sean advises as we carry platters to the outside table.

"Speaking Welsh?" Jess asks.

"Sometimes the sounds you make during those, um, moments, sound like the Welsh dialect," Charlie answers.

That makes everyone chuckle as we sit. The table looks amazing and the food even more so. I hope it tastes as good as it looks and smells. My stomach has been quietly rumbling for several minutes, and I know a loud growl is coming if I don't eat soon. Sean stands back up with his wine glass and proposes a toast to open the meal.

"I'd like to thank you for sharing this weekend with me."

"Saving you is more like," Charlie interrupts.

"Too right. I cannot imagine what the weekend would have been like if it were just Gareth, me and the ladies. In addition, I want to thank you for agreeing to have dinner with me. I don't get to entertain like this very often, and I enjoy it. I hope you enjoy it as well."

Sitting down, he passes the salad dressing to me. He plated up the salads and made a homemade vinaigrette dressing that tastes so light and tangy. Sometimes, salad dressing is heavy and completely overpowers the vegetables, but this is perfect. Charlie made no comment, but Jess and I both asked for the recipe. The rest of the meal is just as delicious as the dressing—braised beef tenderloins in a burgundy reduction, lemon garlic salmon, roasted fingerling potatoes and pan-roasted carrots.

"I think you may have missed your calling," I say after slowly leaning back in my chair. "That was freaking amazing."

"You don't think I can be amazing at more than one thing at a time?" he says with a wink. Immediately, I'm overcome by a blush because I remember some other activities he excels at. Looking away, I reach for my glass of wine with a hand that trembles slightly and almost drops it as I feel his warm hand on my thigh. He gives me a gentle squeeze and then retreats; the only indication he did anything was the slight wink he gave me before he, too, reached for his wine.

Dinner was a relaxed event full of laughter, camaraderie and plenty of wine. The four of us were as comfortable together as if we were all old friends instead of relatively new ones. The ease with which we shared stories of our awkward teen years, first loves, and most embarrassing moments was that those who like and respect each other.

Under the cover of darkness, the figure watched the couples through binocular lenses and seethed with anger. This is not how it is supposed to be. This is not how it will be. This American woman needs to leave and never come back. She's caused nothing but trouble since she came, and it is high time she went back to where she came from before she ruined everything.

Lowering the lenses, the figure slowly climbs down from the wall and moves steadily back to the car. Sitting behind the wheel, idly tapping gloved fingers on the dash while making plans to drive the American away for good. With a smile, those same fingers started the car and drove toward the next move in this game.

Chapter 28

Monday mornings are often difficult when you are out late the night before and indulged in a bit too much wine. This Monday was even more difficult because the sun was bright and showed no signs of dimming for the next several days. The perpetual rain and overcast sky were gone, at least for the foreseeable future. The production team was scrambling to get as much accomplished during the meteorological reprieve as possible, which meant everyone was on high alert.

I headed into the barn at my usual early hour of seven am, armed with a very tall Earl Grey and a Clif bar to fuel me for the next several hours. Liam had been scheduled to handle the morning feeding and preparing for the afternoon and evening shooting schedule. That left me the time to organize the remainder of the week and put in some time with my email inbox. I rarely unplug for a full weekend, so I imagine the fallout will be felt in the vast number of emails I have to read and respond to this morning. After a few minutes spent greeting each of the horses, checking out the goat pen and letting the chickens out of the coop, I headed to my small office.

Noticing the door handle looked odd, I reached out and opened it while making a mental note to get the tools to tighten the lock. Turning to flip the switch for the overhead light, I stopped short and couldn't help but gasp. My office looked like a very bloody battle had been waged. The lone file cabinet had been emptied, and the drawers pulled out and bent badly. The small sofa and chair that sat opposite my desk had been shredded, and what remained of the cushions were scattered everywhere. My desk, where my laptop sat, was covered in red paint. It looked as though the laptop had been opened and paint poured on it as well as on top of it. I carefully walked around to my desk chair only to find it had been smashed to kindling. I turned to continue my survey of the damage when I saw the solid wall opposite me had a message.

The red paint had obviously been left over after the message had been scrawled on the wall. My eyes kept circling the room as my brain refused to process any of it. I was standing there several minutes later when Liam came to the door.

"Holy God, Doc! What happened here?" he asked in a shocked voice.

His exclamation snapped me out of my fog, and I strode to the door, nudging him out as I passed through. I closed the door with a snap and whirled to face him.

"I need you to handle the horses and the production schedule today. I imagine this is going to take some time. I'm going to call the police then the insurance company, but I know they will need a police report. Do not, I repeat, do not say anything about this to anyone. I'll handle it. If anyone asks where I am, I've got some other business to deal with this morning."

With wide eyes, Liam nodded and slowly backed away. I reached a shaking hand into my back pocket for my phone and dialed the local authorities, who quickly advised they would send someone straight away. I put in a call to the local insurance company I had engaged when I purchased the animals from Lester, as well as the owner of the farm the production company leased from, to advise them of the damage. My next call was to Rick to advise him of what was going on and let him know Liam would be on time for the day's shooting, but I would likely be absent. Within a half hour, there were several police officers, a crime scene investigator and a detective on site, as well as my insurance agent, Rick and one of the senior producers. Knowing the barn would be buzzing with activity; I sent the horses to the filming location several hours early to ensure they remained calm.

"Doctor Sullivan, have you had any other incidents of this nature?" the detective, who introduced himself as McMillen, asked in his heavy brogue. "Even things you may not think are related but stick out in your mind?"

I knew this question would be asked sooner or later. I spent the time before they arrived thinking of all the odd little things that had happened over the last few months. Some things had to be coincidences, but maybe they were all connected, and I was too oblivious to notice. Trying to put some of this into perspective and some kind of order helped calm me down a bit, but I was still very shaky.

"I've had numerous flat tires on the truck and horse trailer. I don't know if they are related, but there seemed to be several weeks where there were more incidents like this than I would consider normal," I mentioned as I continued thinking about the last few months. "A few weeks back, I tripped over a rake that was left in the wrong place but initially thought I had been pushed. And Jess and I found a note on our door that told us to go home recently. We didn't think anything about it at the time. Figured a couple of the local ladies took a dislike to us being here and garnering more than they deemed our fair share of male attention."

"Do you have the note?" the Crime Scene tech asked.

"No, we threw it away. We didn't think it was anything other than a bad prank."

The detective dismissed the tech and returned his attention to me. He was writing in a notebook and surreptitiously looking around. "Have you seen anyone around lately who was out of place? Or new?"

Looking around, I think before I reply, "I don't have any new help. I haven't seen anyone, but I'm not here as much as some of my employees. I'm only here a couple hours a day and not every day. I haven't been here since Friday mid-day. I also run a business back in the US, so I often work in town in a coffee shop or my flat there. I suggest asking my grooms, but please be discreet. I don't want word of this spreading around the production or, worse, the town."

"Dr. Sullivan, I'm afraid something like this will get out likely before lunch today. I suggest you come to terms with it. As for your employees, I'll need a list of them as well as anyone else you have had around here. I know you recently purchased the business from Mr. Lester," he paused and looked at his notes before replying, "Reid, Lester Reid. Can you run through that transaction for me? Did you come here looking to buy into the production?"

Detective McMillan and I spent the next ninety minutes going through the story of how Jess and I came to be affiliated with the production, how I rubbed Lester wrong and how I lost my temper and ended up with a bunch of animals. I told him there was more to Lester's story, but it was not my place to share as I was not involved, and it would be hearsay coming from me. I gave him Rick's name and number since he has a professional history with Lester. While we were talking, my phone kept alerting me to incoming text messages. I ignored them until the detective told me he wanted to check with his crime scene tech and the others who were cataloging the scene.

I stepped away and checked my text messages. Jessica texted several times, and by the last, she told me if I didn't answer, she was sending a search party for me. I sighed and hit call to connect to her. She needed to hear this sooner than later, and I wanted her thoughts. My mind was still racing around in circles, and talking to her would surely help me calm it.

"It's about time, Andi. I started to wonder if you'd lost your phone again."

"No, I didn't lose it. I've had my hands full this morning. Have you got some time? I need to talk." I must have sounded shakier than I thought because I could almost hear her stop what she was doing and focus completely on me.

"What's wrong? Are you ok? Is it Sean?" she asked rapidly. "I know you're at the barn. Is it one of the horses?"

"I'm ok; I just had a bit of a shock when I got here this morning. I went into my office, and it was trashed." I went through what I saw, the subsequent calls to police and insurance, the realization some of the things that had happened recently may not have been accidents or coincidences, and the frightening thought that someone was truly upset with me. The more I articulated my thoughts and feelings to Jess, the more frightening the entire situation became to me.

"I'm not easily upset or scared, but Jess, this is some strange shit. If it's all tied together, I've been oblivious to it for weeks, almost two months. How can I be that blind to someone being so close to me and doing these things?"

"Criminals don't usually announce their presence and intent, Andi," Jess says with a sigh. "I'm coming out there."

"No, don't bother. They're almost finished here, and the detective wants me to come down to the station to sign a formal statement. I'll be there for who knows how long. I'll grab a bite and head back here to start cleaning up after that. I want this mess gone as soon as possible."

"Will the police let you clean it all up today? Don't they need to leave it tapped off or whatever as a crime scene?"

"It's not something major like a murder scene or anything. Detective McMillan told me once their techs are finished, I can let the insurance adjuster walk through and take photos. After that, it's okay if I clean it all up."

Jess didn't hesitate; she immediately said, "I'm coming to help. I'll meet you at the police station."

"Ok. I don't really want to be out here alone anyway. Not yet, anyway." Looking around, I shudder and think that someone could have been watching me, and I never knew it. I've been here alone late at night on several occasions and never thought a thing about it. Now, I wonder if I'll be comfortable here in broad daylight.

"What did Sean say about all this?"

"I didn't tell him yet, and I don't want you to say anything to Charlie until I can. He's got a packed schedule today and likely won't be finished until late. I don't want to distract him."

"Won't he notice when you aren't there with the horses like you normally are?"

"I sent Liam and told him if anyone asked, I had some other business to attend to this morning, and I'd be around as soon as I wrapped it up. I doubt anyone will question him; they know I often deal with Doc on a Walk emails and such. It'll be fine." Noticing the detective heading my way, I end the call by promising to text when I head to the police station.

Several hours later, Jessica and I return to the barn, and she gets her first look at the mess that is in my office. Knowing how upset this has all made me, she turned her own concern into righteous anger on my behalf. We dove into the clean-up and had most of it done by the time Liam got back in the early evening with the horses. Jess kept up a steady stream of chatter designed to keep my mind off the puzzle of who trashed my office and possibly caused the other mishaps. Liam's arrival and the routine of settling the horses for the night helped calm me and clear my head. The grooming and quick physical exam of each of the horses acted as a balm to my battered heart and mind.

"Jess, we can't do any more tonight. It's as clean as we can make it without ripping out drywall and replacing it. Let's call it a night." I stretch my tired back and neck as I reach out to give Zeus one more pat on the neck. "I could really go for some comfort food and a stiff drink."

"I'm all in on that suggestion. Pizza and beer?" Jess says as she tosses the tied-up trash bag into the bin. "I'll buy since you've had a rough day." She adds with a wink.

"You've got a deal."

Closing the door to the office, I turn and jump as a figure rounds the corner.

"Roxy, what are you doing here?" I ask the woman who is slowly approaching us. She's a few years older than I am but has some developmental delays that have left her younger in her mental and emotional years. She has a fascination with horses and comes by frequently after her shifts with the catering for the production company.

"I wanted to see the horses," she says without looking at me. "You said I could come see them."

"I did say that, but today isn't a very good day. We are getting ready to go home. Why don't you come back tomorrow or Wednesday? I don't think they are needed for shooting on Wednesday, so you can help me take them out to the paddock for some exercise."

"But I am here now. Why can't I see them now?" she asks with a pout.

"We're leaving for the day. Who is giving you a ride home?" I ask, looking around.

Roxy shrugs and starts walking away. Darting sullen looks back at me, she continues down the path leading to the road. Seeing a sedan near the road, I figure she has a ride, so I dismiss her from my mind.

"Who was that?" Jess asks, watching Roxy walk away.

"She works with craft services and comes by to see the horses. She loves them and is always so excited to see them and help feed them. She's a sweet girl, and I don't think many take the time to talk to her. I just don't have it in me today, and I know it hurt her feelings."

Jessica always thinks first with her doctor's brain and looks at me in question, "Autism spectrum? She seems much younger than she looks."

"That's my guess. She speaks like she is in her teens, and her behavior matches. But she has a job she loves with the catering company that runs craft services and talks about it a lot when she visits. I think she has a good life, which is a blessing."

"How long has she been visiting you?"

"She started coming shortly after I took over from Lester. I don't think he let her around the animals. She catches a ride with various crew members, so I never know when she will show up. All the grooms know her and treat her like a kid sister, answering her questions, letting her help carry feed buckets and all."

"I meet someone new every day."

"I should have introduced you, sorry."

We walk to the truck and watch as Liam gets into his little car and leaves. Turning back to the barn, I double-check the new locks on the office door and then make sure the barn is closed up. I always leave the security lights and turn the radio off, but tonight, that seems almost eerie, so I leave the radio on.

Jess opens the passenger door, then stops and asks, "What about the security upgrades you made? Did the cameras catch anything?"

"Nope. They weren't even on. Apparently, that storm we had on Friday night tripped the breaker, and they never reset. Ironic, but the crime scene tech didn't see any evidence of tampering. They're back on now, and you'll bet your Great Aunt Fanny's prize silver; I'll be checking them daily."

"Maybe you need to upgrade again and get the ones you can get alerts on your phone and see that way. Like those Ring doorbells. Those have caught a lot of people stealing packages off of porches, you know."

"I'll think about that tomorrow."

"Ok, Scarlett O'Hara, let's get cleaned up and order that pizza."

The ride back to town and our flat took less time than usual, given the hour. Most of the light traffic from commuters had died down, and folks were tending to their dinner and families. We kept the conversation light during the drive, pizza toppings, beer preferences and what we wanted to watch while we gorged ourselves on carbohydrates.

Jessica volunteered to let me shower first while she called in our order for pizza and grabbed some beer from the Quick Mart on the corner. I was more than happy to take her up on it. The day wasn't overly long, but I was tired and weary to the bone. The shower may be compact, but at that moment, it was better than any spa Vichy shower I had ever experienced. I stood in there until I felt guilty taking the hot water from Jess's shower.

Within an hour, we were both refreshed and enjoying a beer and the beginning of a rom-com on Netflix. My phone pinged an incoming text just as the doorbell announced the arrival of our pizza. We both got up and went in opposite directions. Jess answered the door and grabbed the pizza while I went into the bedroom to grab my phone.

R U OK? Just heard about what happened. Finishing up soon, will call. Plz txt me back so I know all is ok.

I sighed and showed the text to Jess. She laughed and shook her head.

"I guess the cat's outta the bag now, huh?"

"How much do you want to bet I don't get a call, I get a knock on the door?" I ask with the beginning of my first smile of the day.

"No bet, that man is one smitten kitten."

"Not the phrase I would use to describe a man over six feet tall, but ok." I text back, telling him I'm ok and didn't want to interrupt his day. I know I'll be telling him about it soon enough, so I send the text and reach for the pizza. "Gimme those luscious carbs!"

I collapse on the couch next to Jess, who has already consumed most of her first piece. We always end up eating way too much when we split a pizza. Both of us sit back, content to watch a romantic comedy, eat pizza and do nothing for a while. In short order, the pizza is history; we've downed three beers each, and neither one of us wants to do more than fall into bed.

Rolling my head to look at Jess, I mumble, "I wonder what's in store for tomorrow? I doubt anything could top today."

"Don't tempt fate, sis."

"True, very true." I sit up and stretch just as someone knocks on the door quietly. I look at Jess, who shrugs and points at me. My turn to get up, I guess.

I walk over to the door and hesitate, not something I've done before and evidence of how much the events of the day have shaken me. I look through the peephole and see Sean. I open the door, and before I can get a word out, he's pulling me into a bear hug. I've said it before, but it bears repeating: the man gives a good hug. It was exactly what I didn't know I needed. Closing my eyes, I sink into the hug and into the comfort Sean is giving me. We stay like that for several moments before I realize we are standing in the hallway of my flat where anyone could come upon us. I step back and tug him in, closing the door softly.

"Good to see you," I say with a small smile. "I really needed that hug, thanks."

"I think I needed it as much as you did. I wish you'd have called me. I wouldn't've minded."

"I knew how busy today was, well, this whole week. I didn't want to interrupt, and besides, there was nothing you or anyone else could have done."

"She didn't even let me come and help until this afternoon," stated Jess as she waved and headed to our bedroom. "Good to see you, Sean and goodnight. I'm toast."

"Good to see you too, Jessica." Turning to me, Sean says, "She's drunk?"

"What? No." I say in confusion. "Why would you say that?"

"She said she's toast."

"Oh, no, that means she's tired, done for the day. She's toast."

"Ahh, got it. Now, sit and tell me everything."

We sit down on the couch, and he wraps his arm around me, pulling me into his shoulder so I can rest my head on his shoulder while I tell him the details. We spent several minutes trying to figure out who might be the cause of the vandalism, and both came up with Lester as the only possible suspect. I told him Detective McMillan planned to speak to Lester this afternoon. Sean insists on upgrading the cameras and adding more, but I tell him I've already thought about it but put any decision off until tomorrow.

"Tell me about your day," I say to change the subject. I'm not going to argue with him about the security system when I feel so relaxed and finally calm.

As he tells me about his day, we sort of slide down the small couch and end up snuggled together with my legs pulled onto the side, and his long legs stretched out on the coffee table. I didn't notice when I closed my eyes and ended up drifting off.

It seemed like minutes later, I was pulled into a dream with red paint dripping off every surface I touched and a voice repeating the words go home over and over again. I tried to turn and find the voice but kept slipping on the red paint. Each door led to another corridor dripping in red until I got to the last door that had whore written on it. I opened the door and, stepped into nothing and began to fall. Jerking awake, I almost fell off the tiny couch. Sean jerked awake as soon as I did.

"What is it? Are you alright?" he asked in an alert voice as if he had not just been rudely awakened.

Closing my eyes to try and calm my breathing, I jerked them back open as the image of the red paint came back vividly. "Bad dream. What time is it?"

Sean looked at his phone and grimaced. "Three-thirty. I've got to be on set at 5 for make-up."

"Ick. You're going to be exhausted."

"Come and let me hold you while you tell me about your nightmare."

"I'd rather not. I prefer to forget it. But I'm all for some more time in your arms." Knowing I won't sleep again but hoping he dozes back off, I snuggle back into his arms as he shifted to cover the majority of the couch and prop his feet on the table again.

Outside in the shadows of the night, a shadowed figure cloaked in dark clothes from head to toe opened the door to the truck. Taking out the red paint and pouring it all over the interior of the truck, then pulled out the paring knife and carved "whore" into the dash of the truck. Slowly opening the door and exiting the truck, the figure walked away without a glance.

Chapter 29

"Jessica Jane, you could try the patience of a saint. Hurry up, or I'm leaving you here. I've got both coffees, get your ass moving." I said in a very testy voice as I grabbed the coffee mugs and my backpack. I had planned to drive by the police station to ask how the conversation with Lester went, but I woke up late.

Heading for the door, I grabbed the keys and juggled the two mugs. It was definitely a coffee morning. Tossing and turning after Sean left, I didn't really get much more sleep. What little I had was plagued with strange dreams of red paint and shadowy figures. Waking up late was the icing on the crappy cake of my Tuesday. Coffee was my first step in restoring order to my universe.

"I'm right behind you," Jess calls as she leaves the bathroom. "I'll lock up."

We trotted down the stairs, coffee in hand and bemoaning the lack of a decent elevator. The entry door was propped open as it was on most mornings. The truck was parked a half block away, and the sidewalk was still damp from the rains the previous night. People were bustling by on their way to work or school with their heads down, and most were looking at cell phones. There was a crispness to the air that made even the heartiest duck their head and shiver just a bit; autumn was around the corner.

My Georgia blood was not thick enough for this climate, so I wear a hoodie more days than not; today is no exception, and I send a silent thank you for having it. Unlocking the truck, I watch Jessica toss a smile at a young man as she pulls her hair out of the collar of her jacket. Jess feels the cold more deeply than I do. Turning toward the truck, as I open the door, I stop, not believing what I see.

"Well, shit," I say when I find my voice. "We're going to be later."

"I don't think so," Jess says as she reaches the passenger side. "Why would we be later...oh shit. What the hell?"

I sigh, put my insulated cup on the roof and reach for my phone. "Will you call Rick for me? Let him know I'll call him later. You may want to get an Uber so you aren't derailed by this mess."

Jess just stares blankly inside the truck at the destruction and puddles of red paint. Her eyes shift around the cab of the truck at the puddles and smears of dried or drying paint. She doesn't seem to hear me call her name until I sharpen my tone.

"Jessica! I need you to look at me."

"What the hell happened here, Andi? I mean, who the hell would do this?"

"I need you to focus for me, Jess. Call Rick and let him know what I've got to deal with."

Jessica seems to shake off the shock and reaches for her phone. I didn't think I would need the detective's phone number, but I saved it in my phone yesterday. I press call and raise the phone to my ear. Despite the hour, the detective answers on the second ring.

"Detective McMillan, this is Anderson Sullivan. I've got a bit of a mess again and will need your help."

"Dr. Sullivan, are you alright? Are you safe?" he replies in a serious tone that tells me I have his full attention.

"Yes, I'm fine. My truck isn't."

"Where are you? I will get our dispatcher to send someone and be heading that way directly."

"My apartment, I mean, flat. About a half block down the street."

"Can you secure your truck and go back to your flat? I'd feel better with you there instead of standing on the street."

"Yes, but don't you want to know what happened to my truck?" I ask.

"I'd rather see it first hand and make my judgement from there. If I hear about it now, it may not strike me as strongly," he says. "Go back to your flat, and I'll call you before I come to your door. I'll have the uniform park and wait for me. Sound good? You're sure you are all right?"

"I'm fine. Getting pissed and maybe a bit scared, but I'm ok. Is it too early to drink?" I say, trying to inject a little levity into the situation and in an effort to calm myself.

"Are you Irish, Dr. Sullivan? I'd guess you are based on your last name."

"My family has roots in Ireland, yes," I say, wondering.

"Then you have the ancestry that will allow you a shot of whisky in your tea. No one will think less of you, I promise. I'm going to ring off now and call dispatch. Go back to your flat, lass. I'll be there soon."

Ending the call, I sigh heavily. "What a shit show."

I look over at Jessica, who has ended her call with Rick and looks at me with concerned eyes. This is not what either of us was looking for when we set out on this adventure. I cannot wrap my mind around yesterday's and today's destruction. Obviously, someone thinks I need to leave or, at the very least, that I'm stealing someone's man. I mentally shrug it off, grab my coffee from the roof and shut the truck door, depressing the lock on the key fob as I walk to Jess.

"I've been advised to go back to the flat and wait for Detective McMillan. Did you call for an Uber?" I ask Jess as I get closer to her.

"You are out of your mind if you think I'm leaving you right now," Jess says sternly. "Uncle Rick is on his way over as well. He said to tell you not to argue. Did you call Sean?"

"Not yet. I'll do that when we get back upstairs. Jess, he left at 4:30 am. Did this happen before then? After then? Does it have something to do with him? I mean, with our, whatever we have going on?" My voice is starting to shake as much as my hands are; I'm sloshing coffee all over the sidewalk.

"I don't know, And, but I can tell you this, someone's pissed."

"Ya think?" I look at her incredulously, only to realize she's trying to distract me so I'll stop my mini-freak out. We side-hug and walk, arms joined, back to our flat building. I can't help but glance back at the truck several times. Pausing on the steps of our building, I look around and wonder if the person who did this is watching me. I don't feel like it but these days, I don't trust my senses much.

Waiting anxiously in our flat, I text Sean about the latest vandalism. He's already in make-up for the day's shooting, so he's got time to text me for a while. I assure him several times that I'm fine, more pissed off than unnerved. He wants to get involved, but I tell him it's not necessary; after all, what can he do? He also texted that he wanted to cancel the trip he has to take at the end of the week. There are promotional stops the cast makes throughout filming to keep the interest and buzz about the show high. I text again that there is no reason for him to alter any plans and remind him the police have this under control.

Noticing the three dots that indicate he is typing back, I remained focused on our text thread so intently that the buzzing of an incoming call startled me.

"Sean, I thought you were texting me back," I say.

"I thought I'd better call you and talk some sense into you," he says curtly.

"I beg your pardon? Talk sense into me?" I'm not sure what he means, but his tone gets my back up.

"Yes, you are not taking this seriously enough."

Now that gets me started, I tartly inform him, "I hate to sound like a broken record here, but I beg your pardon. I am definitely taking this seriously."

"Are you pushing the police to resolve this and find the perpetrator immediately?"

"Sean, this started yesterday. Not months ago or even weeks ago, barely even days ago. Why are you so pissy about it?" My tone is sharp, and my Southern accent has thickened as it always does when I get annoyed.

"Because it's my fault," he says with a sigh, the energy draining out of his voice.

"What? How is this your fault unless you trashed my office and my truck? I'm feeling pretty confident here when I say you didn't do this." My voice softens as I picture his expression. "This is not your fault."

"I feel that it is because people know we are," he pauses for a brief moment, then continues, "close to each other and that brings you under the scrutiny that is my life. If it weren't for that, you'd not have these problems."

"Sean, I don't want to seem harsh, but you're really taking too much on yourself here and being a tiny bit egotistical as well. This could be nothing more than petty vandalism or a local being upset by me being here, or it could even be Lester, for all we know."

He chuckles slightly, and the sound makes me shiver slightly, "Egotistical, huh? Well, you've put me in my place again, haven't you?"

"If you need to be, yes. And you definitely needed to be after that."

"You're amazing, do you know that?" he says with another sigh, but this time I can tell he's smiling.

"Of course I am. I'm the most amazing woman you've ever met, and I have to go because I think the Detective has arrived."

"Text me updates, no matter what. Ok?"

"You're shooting today; I'll catch you up when you've wrapped for the day."

"No, I'm keeping my phone on me, text me, or I'll leave here and come find you."

"Egotistical again, but fine, I'll text you."

"Thank you," he says in a formal tone, which makes me think he's no longer alone.

"Go do great things, and we will talk later."

Detective McMillan sent over two officers and arrived only a few minutes later. The ensuing hours were filled with my truck being towed to the police compound for a crime scene review, questioning for both Jess and myself, and the arrival of Rick and the production company's local attorney. I sigh, thinking of my conversation with Sean and his assumption that this is related to him. Apparently, the production company seems to think this is related to them and the hiring of Jess and myself versus locals. This time, I keep my mouth shut and let them work out their multiple theories. I stand in the kitchen and wonder if maybe I'm wrong and it isn't just kids being vandals or a random local female who doesn't like outside competition.

Jess comes into the kitchen and hugs me. She seems as stressed out as I am, so we both stand there hugging for a few minutes until I hug her tight and step back. Looking at her, I see how pale she is and can't help but think this has really scared her.

"You ok? You look pale."

"I'm ok. This has freaked me out more than the office did yesterday. Plus, I'm not feeling 100% already. Maybe this weekend wore me out. I'm not as fit as you are, so all that hiking did me in." she says with a small, tired smile.

"That's a load of crap, and you know it. You may not run as far as I do, but you run daily, and I don't. You are in every bit as good shape as I am, maybe better."

"Yada, yada, yada," she says, smiling a bit brighter. "I heard you call Sean egotistical in a very snippy voice. What happened?"

"He thinks this mess is his fault. As if he had the red paint in his own hands." Shaking my head, I glance out at the detective talking to Rick and the lawyer, whom I've never met. "Everyone assumes it's something huge when it could just be something simple like teenagers with too much time and not enough discipline."

"Andi, this isn't that simple. This is targeted toward you, not the production, not the random populous you. And I think there may be a thread of truth to what Sean said. It's not directly his fault, but what if the person or persons responsible for this are doing it because you and he are dating?"

"We aren't dating, Jess." I feel a jump in my belly at that label. I'm not ready for anything like that.

Scowling at me, she sneered, "Ok, you're just screwing and spending a lot of time together."

I raise my eyebrow at her and quietly advise, "Keep your voice down, damn it. I don't want my private life tossed around in front of everyone here. That's not like you to be so crass. And we are not screwing; you make us sound like horny teenagers or rabbits. I'd say that description best fits what you and Charlie are doing."

Instead of the angry retort I expect, Jess responds with a cheeky grin and "True, very true." She weaves a bit as if unsteady on her feet. "I'm going to the bathroom for a minute."

Detective McMillan looks up and beckons me over to stand with them. The trio look like they have come to some sort of détente. I walk the few steps from the kitchen to the living room and send a silent prayer that he and the others didn't hear our conversation.

"Doctor Sullivan, we have had the vehicle taken to our holding lot to continue dusting for prints, etc. You can have your insurance adjuster stop by to start processing the claim at any time. We will be able to release the vehicle in 48 hours. With that said, there really isn't anything else we can do until the initial investigation is complete. Obviously, call us if you have any other incidents."

"Thank you, Detective. I'll call the insurance company shortly.

Chapter 30

The remainder of the day is quiet, as are the next few days. The insurance company authorized a rental for me, and life seemed to get back to what could be called normal. Even the weather cooperated by not raining until late on Thursday. I've got the little office at the barn cleaned up and painted. Liam offered to paint it for me, but I refused; I needed to take care of that chore personally. My new laptop came in Thursday; downloading everything took several hours, but my personal and professional life is now digitally restored. I'm still a bit edgy, but I stay busy to keep my mind off it. I've taken to having one of the barn staff or grooms with me whenever I'm at the farm. I haven't heard anything from Detective McMillan, but that does not worry me. I know these things take time. My two incidents won't be resolved in 40 minutes as they do on a television show.

Jess is still fighting some kind of virus that has her feeling rundown and upset at her stomach. I've tried to steer clear of her to avoid catching it or, worse, give it to Sean when he has to travel this weekend. His shooting schedule has been intense this week to finish the block they are filming before many of them head out for the promotional appearance. They've finished early today, if you can call 8 pm early. Sean invited me to come hang out with him for a while. I know he is exhausted, but I agree to drive out. I won't see him for four days and haven't really seen him much more than in passing the last few days. I try not to think about how important he has become to me in such a short period of time; when I do, I get a panicky feeling in my stomach. I don't think I'm ready for this…whatever this is, but I can't seem to stop myself.

Rab is barking happily at me as I park and get out of my rented truck. He darts around my legs with his wagging tail and bright eyes. I can't help but laugh and spend a few minutes roughhousing with him and giving him the vigorous side, and belly rubs that he enjoys. When he's had enough for now, he jumps back up and bounds off toward the back garden area. Dogs are such a joy to have, and one as intelligent as Rab makes it all the better.

I straighten and turn to the front door, smiling as I see Sean propped against the balustrade, arms crossed over his chest, feet crossed at the ankle with a soft smile on his face.

"Hi," I say as I approach. "Rab's a bit frisky today."

Pushing off, he straightens and reaches for my hands. He kisses my cheeks and then lightly touches my mouth before responding, "he knows a pushover when he sees one."

I laugh and lightly shove him with my shoulder. He doesn't move an inch, which is typical given his size and build. I'm no dainty waif, but then again, I'm no husky girl either. He's just that solid. "I'm a vet; I'm supposed to love animals."

"There's loving animals, and there is being a pushover. So far, with Rab, you're a pushover."

I put my hands on my hips, rounding on him as he closed the door. "I beg your pardon; I'm no pushover."

Rab barks at the front door, and I walk back to open it while waiting for Sean to respond. He just looks at the door, at Rab and back at me, raising an eyebrow. "Really?"

I realize I've just been treated like a doorman by the dog and laugh. "Ok, I admit it. He's so cute and too smart for his own good. I think he's smarter than some people I know."

Rab makes a sound of agreement before walking ahead and into the kitchen, where we hear him loudly drinking water. Sean rolls his eyes and follows. I'm not the only one Rab has trained. Sean follows behind the dog with a towel to clean up from his messy trip to the water bowl.

"How did it go today?" I ask, trailing behind master and pet.

"Great. The weather helped us a lot this week, and Ciaran wasn't as much of a tyrant as he normally is. I think it was the prospect of going to New York for a few days. He says he's never been."

"I'm not sure New York is ready for him. Or will survive if he gets crazy." Ciaran is very intense and a perfectionist when it comes to his work, but when he relaxes and lets loose, he is a maniac—more than one evening out had ended at dawn when he was involved. I made it through one night but passed on all the others. I'm definitely out of shape for those types of all-nighters.

Sean grins and looks at me with laughing eyes, "Several of us are pooling bail money in case we need to rescue him. Wine?"

"No thanks, I've got to drive back later, and it will make me sleepy. I'd ask for a glass of tea, but I know you don't have it. Lord, do I ever miss iced tea."

Sean wrinkles his nose and shakes his head, "I will never understand you Americans and your affinity for cold tea. It's disgusting."

"It's the house wine of the South but must be perfectly sweetened," I state in a superior tone. "I believe we will never agree on this point. For now, I will be happy with a Coke."

He gets our drinks while I head to the sofa and slip off my shoes. I really love his living room. The sofa is plush and seems to wrap around me, making me feel like I'm being hugged. Sean hands me the cold can and sits next to me. He picks up the remote to the huge television and starts surfing through the guide to determine something to watch. Neither of us cares much about what we watch, mostly landing on documentaries or travel shows. Tonight, he stops on a popular show about ghost hunting. I glance at him, wondering if this is really what we will watch, but decide to go with it.

He settles back against the sofa and leans slightly toward me so our shoulders and arms touch. "Do you watch this show?"

"No, I've never seen it. Do they really think there are ghosts?" I ask doubtfully.

"There most definitely are, especially around here and most of Europe. You can't live in a country as old as this one and not feel those spirits. Do you not believe spirits can linger in a place?"

"No, I don't believe that," I say in a flat voice, taking a drink of my Coke to cover my reaction somewhat. I have had friends before who went on ghost-hunting adventures, mostly during the fall and before Halloween, but I am not a believer. It makes me think of my parents and their death or Justin and his death. If spirits can linger, why didn't my parents or Justin stay with me or come back to see me or whatever?

Sean senses my discomfort and quickly wraps his arm around me, "Andi, I'm sorry. I didn't think of your past. I hope I haven't upset you." He makes a move to pick up the remote again, but I stay his hand.

"No, it's fine. It's just a TV show, after all." I lean into him, and we shift until we click together almost like puzzle pieces. The television investigator tells us the history of the castle ruins they will be visiting, and I have to admit, I am intrigued by the story and the castle itself. I can't help but think about the people who built it and lived there. Did they know that what they built would last hundreds of years? Did they think of those who would come after them and how the story of their existence would be told and retold? Or did they just live their lives from one day to the next?

"My mother's family have been known to have the sight," Sean says when the investigators bring in a local parapsychologist. "For more generations than I can remember, her family has these dreams that are sometimes fantastic and at other times so mundane, but they are always filled with some kind of truth about the present or future that is unknown at that moment."

He spoke so quietly that I almost didn't catch it all. Underlying his words is a vulnerability I have not heard before. He is still looking at the television, but his hand on my thigh has tensed. This topic is important to him, and my reaction is important to him.

"Your family can foresee the future in dreams?" I ask just as quietly.

"Somewhat, but it isn't as straightforward as that. There is a female or two in each generation that has the gift. I know it sounds absurd, but I've been around it my entire life and can assure you it is as real as you and I are."

"Ok," I say, not really knowing what else to say. His face is still blank, but his eyes seem to be asking me to understand and not laugh or scoff at this information. "I'd like to hear more about it sometime. It must make for some great stories during family dinners." Deciding we need to lighten our mood, I continue, "Do you see dead people?" I try to ask with a monotone and no hint of a smile and think I succeed.

Sean slowly takes my Coke and places it beside his lowball glass on the coffee table, his expression showing nothing. I start to think I've gone too far and should apologize when he flips me onto my back and says, "No, Bruce Willis, we don't see dead people." Then he laughs and tries to tickle me.

The wrestling match that ensues is intense and lasts for several minutes. I'm pretty good at defending myself, but it ends with my hands pinned above my head and him grinning down at me triumphantly. I watch as his expression changes and his eyes darken with desire. Slowly, he leans in to kiss me, which makes me forget about ghost hunting, his interesting family legacy and every other thought in my head. The man is truly like a drug to me. His lips are firm and strong against mine, moving expertly and coaxing me to open to him, which I do without hesitation. There is no rush in his kiss, no fervor or overwhelming passion; he's taking his time and, I think, savoring our kiss.

I'm hyper-aware of the vulnerability of my hands held above my head and the feel of his body pushing mine into the soft confines of the sofa. We are touching from torso to knee, but somehow, I don't feel crushed. I tug at my hands, and Sean releases them to slide into my hair and angle my head to allow deeper access to my mouth. The kiss turns hotter, no longer languid, but fanned into flames that threaten to take us both under. I grasp his biceps and feel the strength and heat of his muscles. I slide my hands to his back and feel the muscles corded along his spine before I slide up to his shoulders and slowly rake my nails down his back.

The shirt he's wearing is the softest cotton and completely in my way. I start to tug it up and succeed in getting it about halfway when he abruptly ends our kiss, straightens and reaches up. He does that guy thing that is so sexy, where he reaches behind his head with one hand and pulls the shirt off in one effortless motion. I bite my lip to keep from moaning because, damn, he looks hot. Before I can finish the thought, the shirt is tossed aside, and he's kissing me again. Now, I am treated to warm, firm skin and those mouthwatering muscles flexing as I run my hands and nails along his sides and back up along his spine.

He breaks our kiss again, and I smile as I feel a shiver run through him, "Again," he says gruffly and arches his back just a bit. My smile turns sultry as I oblige and watch his eyes go almost black. "I love your hands on me."

"I happen to enjoy the experience myself," I say as I lean up and softly bite his bottom lip, pulling it before releasing it and sweeping my tongue over the spot to soothe. That's the last thing I remember for several minutes as things heat up to incendiary levels.

My next conscious thought surfaces when I feel my bra release. Momentarily confused, I realized I never noticed my shirt disappearing, and now I'm bared to the waist. Then all thought slides away again, and I'm gripping Sean's head as he lavishes attention on my breasts, neck and shoulders. My legs wrap around his thighs, and

I push my pelvis into him, desperate for some kind of release. Sean seems to understand my body without my words and kisses his way slowly down to my jeans. He takes little nips at my stomach as he slowly unbuttons and unzips them, tugs slowly, slowly down just a bit, until the edge of my bikini panties shows. My mind races to remember what panties I'm wearing, but then I feel his tongue in my belly button and tracing a moist line down to the elastic. Another little nip, and I cry out, clutching at his arms. I'm so hot and so close to the edge that I know I'll climax the moment he touches me. He leans over and gives my lower belly a hot open, mouth kiss and growls as he tugs my jeans down and off my legs with an agonizing slowness that almost makes me scream with impatience.

Instead of coming right back where he left off, Sean lightly runs his fingers from my ankles to my knees as he settles back between them. He slowly slides his fingers under my knees and draws them apart. In no hurry, Sean stares intently at the most private part of me, which makes me blush and move my knees back together. He stops the movement, moves between my knees and leans in to kiss my cheek lightly, softly saying "Beautiful" before he kisses my other cheek and repeats the word. Each kiss on my lips, my collarbones, the pulse at the base of my neck, the valley between each of my breasts and each of my scars was punctuated with "beautiful" in a deep, barely discernable voice before he settled to kiss me in my most intimate place. I inhale sharply and stiffen slightly, which brings another soft "beautiful" before he proceeds to get me the most intense orgasm I have ever experienced. I cry out, clutching at his head and the edge of the couch as wave after wave of pleasure ripples through me. When the last wave fades, I release my grip and let my hands slide uselessly to my sides.

Sean proceeds to return to the same path, repeating, "beautiful" after each soft kiss. He reaches my lips, but I can't seem to open my eyes as he breathes, "Absolutely fucking gorgeous" and kisses me deeply. I just experienced the most fantastic of orgasms, but this kiss, this man, flames those flames back into life with ease.

I reach down to his waist and realize he is still wearing pants, "One of us is overdressed," I remark. I feel his smile as he kisses me softly and moves away. "Wait, what?"

He says nothing but scoops me up as if I'm a child and carries me, stark naked, through his house to his bedroom. Let me tell you, any man that can carry a woman like this will get just about anything he wants when he gets you to the bedroom. I'm no tiny little waif, so it's impressive to be picked up like that. I sigh at the romance in the gesture and spend the short trip nipping at his earlobe and neck.

The romance faded as I felt myself flying through the air to land on his king-size bed. With a startled laugh, I start to push up but see the look on his face. Gone is that tender, romantic lover and in his place is a man with rapidly unraveling control and a face full of raw passion. I'm frozen as I watch him push off his jeans and boxer briefs, then reach into the bedside table for a condom. As he crawls toward me, I feel a sense of pride that I've driven him to this point. The kisses that ensued showed me just how close to the edge he was, which ramped my own arousal back up. We both became frantic, and with one powerful thrust, Sean was fully seated inside me. We both seemed to pause for just a fraction of a second before the passion once again roared through us. Hands gripping, bodies straining to be closer, we climbed that summit together before we reached the peak with one more powerful thrust. I cried out again. I may have screamed, and Sean let out a long, guttural groan before collapsing on me.

Long minutes were spent getting our breath back and heart rate to a more normal rhythm. I think I came back to my senses first and started idly running the fingers of my right hand along his back and shoulders while my left hand remained in his hair. I feel a moment of panic because of how strong my feelings are at this moment. Am I really ready for this? Do I really want to risk losing someone else?

I must have stiffened because Sean lifted his head and pushed up to his elbows.

"You okay?" he asked. "Not having second thoughts, are you?"

Pushing away my thoughts, I smile and pull him down for a soft kiss. "Not even a little."

I'm rewarded with another hard kiss and him saying, "Excellent, because it's time to shower."

///

The promotional tour lasts four days and is chaotic from the outline Sean gave me before he left. I figure I won't hear from him often between the packed schedule and the time difference, so I spend most of the day on Friday dealing with insurance and checking in with Detective McMillan. It's still too early for the crime lab to have anything, but he hopes to have their report by Monday.

Jess and I made plans to try a new restaurant Friday night, but that was put on hold when that virus reared up again and kept her tied to the toilet, vomiting off and on. By Saturday afternoon, she swore she was fine, so we hit our favorite shopping district and did some exploring. I couldn't help but tease her a bit while we were out.

"It's a good thing you're on the pill, sister. Otherwise, I might think you were pregnant." I quip as I reach for a cute blouse in the boutique we just found.

"Bite your tongue, Andi," she tosses back and shakes her head at the blouse. "Too yellow. Try the one behind you."

I turn around but catch sight of her puzzled expression in the mirror. I turn back around and whisper, "Jessica Jane, could you be pregnant?"

"No, of course not. I just can't remember where I am in my cycle. It's such a routine action that I don't pay attention anymore. It's not that at all," she assures me with a smile that doesn't quite hit the mark.

A couple hours later, we run into Roxy at the pizza place closest to the apartment, where we stop because I am starving. Roxy usually speaks to me every time I see her, but today, she gives me the oddest look and quickly turns away to leave. Two minutes after she leaves, the teenage boy at the counter calls her name, announcing her order is ready. We offered to deliver it to her since she's in our building. When our pizza is ready, along with the order of garlic knots, Jessica swears she wants, we head back to the apartment.

"Do you know which apartment is hers?" Jess asks as we open the entry door.

I stop abruptly, realizing I don't. "Maybe it's in the mailbox?"

We walk over and scan the mailboxes but don't see her first name listed, and I have no idea what her last name is. The only conversations we've had are about the horses. I try to think of where I've seen her here in the building but can't remember.

"Wait!" Jess says and snaps her fingers. "I saw her going into an apartment on 2 when I was rounding the corner in the stairwell. Grabbing the door, she gestures me through it. When we reach the second-floor landing, she opens the door again and then pauses, closing her eyes in memory. She spins, points to the second door on the right and says, "That one!"

Jess knocks since my hands are full of pizza, and we wait patiently. The smell of gooey cheese and spicy marinara sauce, as well as those garlic knots, has my stomach rumbling in protest. The door was opened by Lizette, and I couldn't tell you who was more surprised. I almost dropped the pizzas, and she looked like she stepped in something unpleasant.

"Lizette, hi! Um, we thought a young lady named Roxy lived here. Sorry." I said and started to turn away.

"What do you want with Roxy?" she asks tartly.

Wrinkling my forehead in confusion, I hold up the pizza and inform her, "We have a pizza for her. She left Dominic's before her pizza was ready, so we thought we would bring it to her. We weren't sure what apartment she had. Jess thought it was this one."

Lizette impatiently gestures with her hands, "Give it to me."

I didn't say a word, only raised an eyebrow at her.

"She's here, in the other room," she rushes in a clipped voice. "Now let me have it and go away."

I give up and hand her the cardboard box, happy to end this encounter and get on with dinner. Jess looks back as the door slams with a quizzical expression, as if she isn't sure of what she just heard.

"What the heck just happened back there?" she asks with a thumb gesture over her shoulder. "I know you said she's snippy, but that went beyond that and straight into bitchy."

"Who knows? Maybe she is off gluten and dairy and wants pizza more than her lover. Maybe she thought we were a super hot guy coming to whisk her away from it all. Maybe we hit her on the first day of her period. I don't care; I just want to eat. I'm starving."

We get to our apartment, and my cell rings. I don't even bother to reach for it. Jess opens the door, and I immediately head to the couch, putting the pizza on the coffee table. I don't even wait for plates or napkins; I grab a slice and bite into it. Moaning in culinary pleasure, I sit on the floor with my back to the loveseat. Pizza when you are starving is the absolute best. Noticing Jess doesn't dive in, I take another bite and look at her.

"What's up? I thought you were dying for those garlic knots?"

"Yeah, I'm not really feeling it right now," she says quietly. "I'm going to take a shower. I'll eat when I get out if there is anything left."

I continue chewing while I watch her go into the bathroom. I'm starting to get concerned that this bug she has may be something more than a short-term virus. I resolved to get the doctor to see a doctor or, at the least, to talk to the doctor about seeing one. I remember my phone rang in my hunger-induced pizza frenzy, so I wiped my fingers off and dug into my purse. I see a missed call and text, both from Sean. Trying to calculate the time difference just to know what it is, I read his text. Short and to the point. He's got a half-hour free and hopes I am able to call back. I'm smiling as I'm dialing, I really like this guy.

"Hey," I announce when he picks up.

"Hello, gorgeous. Glad you could call me back. I won't have another break for about four hours." I hear sounds in the background that make me think he's on the move, perhaps to get some privacy. "That's better. I've put some space between me and the others."

"How has your trip been so far?" I ask. "Your texts make it seem like you're in a whirlwind."

"It's busy, but I'm finally getting used to it. It also helps to have people who are here just to keep us all organized and on time. Now, I want to hear about your day."

"I had the most exciting day imaginable. I cleaned, did laundry and then went shopping with Jess. Now I'm inhaling a pizza. Sounds positively thrilling, doesn't it?"

"It sounds normal. I could do with some normal right about now. Are you and Jess going down to Charlie's tonight? He mentioned he had a new band coming up from London. Should be good music; he's got a good ear for it."

"No, Jess doesn't feel well, and I just feel like comfy pjs, a blanket and a good book."

"Jess still sick? My sister was ill last month for the better part of a month off and on. Oh! Speaking of my sister, Frances Catherine and her partner, Simon, are going to be in town for a few days and staying with me. I want you to meet them. Can you come to dinner on Tuesday? That will likely be my only half-decent day."

I pause in the act of drinking from my soda. "You want me to meet your sister?" I ask with just the slightest tinge of panic in my voice.

Hearing that panic, Sean gives a small laugh and retorts, "I'm not asking you to run a 5k naked. I just want you to meet one of my annoying sisters while she is in town. Ok? Nothing more than that."

I'm quiet for a minute before I say, somewhat shyly, "I've never met a man's family before. I don't know what to think."

There was a brief pause, and then, "You've never met a boyfriend's family? You were engaged; surely you met Justin's family?"

"Justin didn't have any family. He grew up in foster care."

A pause, and I can practically see Sean run his hand along the back of his neck and look up. "What about boys in secondary school, uh, American high school? Surely a dance or something had you meeting up and taking pictures of corsages and such?"

I laugh and say, "I didn't date for a few years because of my accident and then I dated Justin. Sorry, I'm out of my element here."

"So, will you, then? Have dinner with me, my know-it-all-all sister and Simon? He's a good bloke. You'll like him. You'll like Frances Catherine too, I'm sure."

"Why not? I've had a lot of firsts on this adventure; why not add meeting the family."

"Excellent. They're flagging me down. I've got to run. Talk soon. Be careful!"

"You too. Don't work too hard."

I hear him laugh and say, "Not a chance," before he disconnects.

I'm meeting his sister. I'm meeting. His. Sister. The butterflies have escaped and taken residence in my stomach. I'm finished with pizza and start to pack it up when I notice Jess come out of the bathroom and retreat to our room. I really want to talk to her about this, but I don't want to be inconsiderate if she's feeling awful. I'll think about it, ha. Who am I kidding? I'll obsess about it tonight and talk to her about it tomorrow.

///

I spent a restless night thinking about meeting Sean's sister. I would drift off and dream of being under a bright light, interrogation style. I woke up several times, sweaty and uncertain, before giving up around 7:30 a.m. I grab my book from the shared bedside table between our beds and head to the living room. A cup of coffee sounds decent and can help clear out the cobwebs.

An hour later, Jessica comes out of the bedroom, yawning and looking pale. She promptly collapses on the tiny couch, grabbing the throw on the back. Snuggled in, she glances my way with bleary eyes and a small smile. "Up early on a Sunday, aren't you?"

"Rough night. From the looks of you, we both had a rough night. Stomach still giving you fits?"

"A bit, yes. I'm just so damn tired. I swear I slept like the dead last night, but right now? I think I could sleep 12 more hours."

"I'm going to make you a cup of tea. Mom always says that helps an upset stomach." In the kitchen, I rummage around the find two kinds of tea bags: a detox tea and a lemon green tea. Deciding she's had enough detoxing lately, I heat up the water and bring her the steaming mug.

"I know why I look bad; what's your excuse?" she asks, holding the mug in two hands.

"I don't want to unload this on you if you aren't feeling well." I start, pausing long enough for her to gesture 'go on' with her hand, then continue in a rush, "Sean wants me to meet his sister and her partner."

"Partner? Is she gay?"

247

"Jess, focus. HIS SISTER. He wants me to meet his sister. I've never met the family member of a guy I'm," I pause and try to decide on a word.

"Dating, the word you are looking for is dating," she drawls as she takes a sip of the tea. "Yuck! This tastes like dish soap. What did you give me, Lemon Fresh Dawn?"

"It's Lemon Green Tea. Just drink it. And I guess dating is a good word to use. I've never done this. Isn't it serious when you do this, aren't you? And partner here is the same as a husband, but it could be same sex. In this case, his name is Simon, so I'm going with not gay."

A weak but sincere smile splits Jessica's face, but it is quickly replaced by a grimace when she takes another drink of tea. "You're really frazzled. I'm going to enjoy this."

"Errrrr. Could you be serious for one minute? I've stressed about this."

"All night," she interrupts. "Andi, honey, we may be pushing on thirty, but in a lot of ways, you are still so green. Tell me this: Did he invite his sister here, or did he ask you to go with him to his sister's?"

"No, he said she and Simon are in town for a few days and staying with him." Not sure what her point is, I sit back down in the chair and pull my feet up.

Ok, so he's asked a woman he is seeing, as well as sleeping with, to his home where his sister is visiting and staying. It's simple— nothing to read into it. You spent the night there Thursday night. Wouldn't you think it was odd if he came back from being gone and didn't want you to spend the night? Heck, he may anyway, but at least this way, you know who is there. He wants you to meet his sister, plain and simple."

I muddle over that for a few minutes before she breaks in, "Did you ever think maybe he's nervous about his sister meeting you?"

"Why would he be nervous?" I dismiss with a wave of my hand.

Jessica repeats the gesture, "Why would you?"

Chapter 32

I'm just finishing up with the boys at the barn when Jess calls me. Instead of answering, I ignore it and opt to finish feeding and locking up before I call her. Two more calls from her and I give up. It's obviously important if she's called me three times. Tapping her name her name in my Favorites list, I wait for it to connect.

"FINALLY!" Jess exclaims in obvious frustration.

"What is wrong? Are you hurt? Is someone hurt?" I ask, feeling a little guilty for not answering.

No, no. I'm sorry. I'm just in the midst of my own personal freak out."

"Slow down and talk to me."

"I'm late," she says quickly.

"Late for what? Do you need a ride?" I ask, the confusion obvious in my voice. I am twenty minutes or more away from our place. She can get an Uber there faster.

With a strangled sound of annoyance, "Not THAT kind of late. Late, late."

I pull my phone away and stare blankly at the screen as if it will give me a sign then it hits me. "OH! You mean, you're LATE."

"OMG Anderson. I need you to keep up here."

"How late? And how? Your pills sit on the counter; I can see that you've been taking them." I say, a bit shocked.

"I have no idea, but I'm in my second week of pills but haven't ever started. Can you stop by an out-of-the-way drugstore and get me a test or twenty?"

"Of course. I need to take Rab back to Sean's anyway, so I'll stop by one out that way. Try not to freak out too much until we know there is something to freak out about, okay?"

Fifteen minutes later, I'm standing in front of the largest, most confusing display of pregnancy tests I've ever seen. Hell, I've never looked for one before, so for all I know, this could be a small display. I pick up a couple and read the back; they seem straightforward enough, but do I get digital or not? The response time is pretty much the same. Rolling my eyes, I grab about 10 different ones and head to the candy aisle. This is definitely a time for therapeutic chocolate. The poor woman at the checkout must think I'm nuts because she asked me what I was hoping for, and I said a good night's sleep and toned thighs.

I'm still uncertain about driving here, so I don't speed on the way home, but I seriously considered it. The fates smiled at me, and I found a spot almost directly across from our building and didn't even have to parallel park! No sense in wasting precious minutes doing that when I could be bounding up the stairs to our third-floor flat.

I rush in, throw my purse in the direction of the couch and thrust the bag of tests at Jessica, "Here, there are about a dozen. Go pick one and take it now."

She starts laughing, and I get a good look at her for the first time since I left this morning. She's obviously over her freakout and has calmed considerably. I can't help but wonder if I've lost it or somehow entered a parallel universe.

"Ummm, did I miss something? Imagine that phone call?"

"No, the panic was real, but I've calmed down now," she says as she reaches into the bag.

"Ya think?!" I exclaim.

"You aren't kidding about buying a dozen. Did you buy one of every kind?"

"Have you ever looked at these before? There are almost hundreds of them. Ok, that's an exaggeration, but there are a lot more than I expected. I figured I would walk up, pick from one or two, grab a spare and come home. Nope. There are so many different kinds, and did you know they have test kits to know when you ovulate? How cool."

"I almost wish I could have seen your face," Jess says as she draws out one of the tests. "This one is as good as any, I suppose. Wish me luck."

Uh, yeah, luck." I collapse wearily on the small couch and replay my last half hour. I practically threw Rab out of the truck before heading to the drugstore. The poor dog probably thinks I'm mad at him. I'll make it up to him later. Rubbing my eyes, I hear my phone signal a text. I pull it out of my purse and see Sean telling me they are boarding the flight from London and he will see me tomorrow. I text back and drop my phone on the sofa as Jess comes out.

"One down, nine to go."

"And," I say with an impatient waving hand gesture, "what did it say? Am I going to be an Auntie?"

"You will," she says dramatically, "but not anytime soon. One negative and two more in the works. I'm going to save the rest for tomorrow; HCG levels are highest in the morning, so I'll feel more confident after those."

"Ok, so no, baby. Whew. You need to figure out what happened, or you need to have safer sex with Charlie. This took at least a year or two off my life."

"Your life? During my short period of panic, pun not intended, I think I lost a decade."

"Are you going to tell Charlie?"

"I already have. That's part of what calmed me down. He was so chill about it. I've never been in this situation before, but I really thought he would lose his shit and run for the highlands, so to speak."

"I'm glad he didn't. I like him; I'd hate to have to castrate him for being an asshole."

We both let out a relieved laugh and looked at each other. I stand and hug her tight, "It's good. You're good. We're good, and we would deal with whatever it was anyway. Just a bit glad we seem to have dodged it right now. It would explain your strange symptoms, but I say we go with what the pee sticks say."

"Time to check the last two." She ducks back into the bathroom and comes back waving two slim wands. "Two more negative results. I think we are good, but tomorrow morning is definite."

Chapter 33

While sitting around the living room and catching up over tea, I ask Franny about our parents. I spoke to them on Sunday, but they only told me so much. If I want the real state of things, I ask my sisters. The parents may keep things from me, but my sisters won't.

"Mother keeps having dreams and telling us it's your future wife. Siobhan has even said she's seen a woman lately, too, but has not connected her to anything yet. I'm wondering if it's your Anderson?"

"I told her about our family," I say, looking down at the cup in my hands. This sort of thing is not something we discuss in front of just anyone, so Franny knows it's a big deal.

"You have, have you? And what did she have to say about it?" she asks with an arched brow.

"Not really anything. She didn't laugh and tell me there weren't such things. Nor did she get strange and start asking for psychic readings or other such nonsense. She accepted it and then teased me. I'm still a bit surprised."

"How did you think she would take it? I mean, we're a strange lot anyway, but adding in this little twist and we border on the bizarre."

"That's the thing: before I opened my mouth, I had no intention of telling her and had not thought about how she would react."

"Well, I already like her, but the fact that she took it in stride and then teased you a bit tells me she is a good person."

I smile at the memory of what she said and the ensuing activity. "She asked me if I see dead people, the quote from."

"The Sixth Sense with Bruce Willis" chimes in Simon. "I loved that movie. Not as much as Die Hard, but good enough."

Franny laughs and nudges me with her leg, "See, I like her already."

Jessica has never been a morning person. She's learned to get around it just as she's learned to cat nap and work long shifts on little sleep. If she doesn't have to get up early, you cannot blast her out of bed before 10 a.m. This morning, she was motivated to be up with the sun and peeing on plastic wands. I was a bit put out by them all lined up on the ledge of the tiny tub, but I just decided to wait until later to shower.

I make the short walk to the kitchen to start coffee but decide I'll go with tea instead. I'm starting to see the lure of a good cup of tea instead of strong coffee. Don't get me wrong, when I need the jolt, I'm all about the java, but when I'm not in any hurry, I'll sip a cup of tea and enjoy a peaceful moment. I've also learned to like milk in my hot tea, something that I used to curl my lip and scoff at. Southern girls drink cold, sweet tea, not hot tea and good Lord, not with milk!

"Morning, sunshine," Jess says as she looks up from her phone. "What's on your agenda today? I've already got someone with a mysterious ailment who desperately needs to see me."

"Well, I'm light today—no filming, so no animals. I'm planning to drop by and see Detective McMillan and then go pick up my truck, hopefully. How much longer on the pee test row? I'm not showering next to those things." I tease her a bit, knowing she's in a good mood and not stressed out wondering.

Glancing at her phone, she says, "should be ready now," as the alarm she set goes off. Minutes later, I hear the sound of those tiny sticks hitting the trashcan, and she pops her head around the corner with a big grin. "All negative. I've emailed my GYN at home and asked if we can chat today. Hopefully, I can figure out why things are off."

"Good. You can help me pick out something to wear to dinner at Sean's tonight so I look good when I meet his sister and brother-in-law."

"Deal."

Chapter 34

"What's your schedule look like today, Sean? We've got a couple of appointments but should be back by tea time," Franny advises as she rinses out her tea cup and puts it in the dishwasher.

"No shooting today, just a script read-through which is only about three or so hours. I'll be back when you get here." Sean puts his own coffee cup to reach around and hug his sister. Hearing the chirp of the alarm indicating an exterior door opened, he glanced toward the mudroom as Maureen entered.

"Good morning, Maur. You're early today."

"Maureen! It's been ages! How are you? The children? Mom was saying the other day that you are overdue for a visit." Franny advances on Maureen with a wide smile and open arms. "More importantly, how do you like working for this tyrant?"

Maureen laughs and hugs Franny back, nodding and smiling at Simon. "Everyone is fine, right as rain. Mary Elizabeth is studying accounting, of all things, she's so like my Tom. Donald is enjoying his job at the mechanic shop. He's been made the second mechanic under the lead. I think he might be serious about the girl he's dating, too. As for working for your brother, it's a fabulous job that has me running around all over the place, and I love it! I'm grateful your mother thought of me when Sean's last assistant didn't work out."

Sean snorted, Simon laughed outright, and Franny just rolled her eyes. They all knew the story of the first assistant Sean hired, a young female who quickly became enamored with him and thought the position came with added benefits. After finding her naked in his bed, Sean decided to hire someone less inclined to behave that way led him to talk to his mother. She suggested he look at Maureen, her second cousin on his grandmother's side. She had been a homemaker until her children graduated then her husband abruptly passed away. She had been lost and not sure of what she would do to earn a living. Being family made her more trustworthy, and the extra few decades on him made her definitely unlikely to end up naked in his bed. Sean was convinced, and Maureen was hired.

"Maur is a treasure and keeps me on task and on time," Sean says with confidence and a bright smile.

"Is it time to head out?"

"Ah, no, actually. I have something I need to speak to you about." Her smile dimmed, and her expression changed to one of seriousness. She glanced at Franny and Simon, hesitated and didn't say more.

Franny took the hint, "We've got to run, or we will be late. Maur, I hope we can get together for a longer chat before we go back on Thursday. Let me know if you have an evening free, and we'll grab a bite out."

The pair left via the garage door, leaving Sean looking at Maureen with a slightly puzzled expression. It's not like her to refrain from speaking in front of his family. She knows how close they all are and that he is very open with them. Turning toward the coffee pot, he refills his and gets out the tea and a mug for Maureen.

"I've wondered if I should tell you this at all, but I slept on it and feel it's best."

"Maureen, you've got my full attention with that dire statement. What is it? You aren't quitting, are you? I'd be lost."

"No, no, not that at all. I love what I do to help you. It makes me feel young again," she says as she accepts the cup of tea from him. "What I have to tell you is about something I saw yesterday. It's not something I really want to get involved in, but I, well, you have to know sooner rather than later."

"Maur, out with it."

"I saw Anderson in the drugstore yesterday. She was very intent on choosing something; she spent several minutes comparing before taking several different ones." Pausing, she blushed, took a sip of tea and looked at Sean as if hoping he would guess what she was hinting at, but he remained clueless.

Wrinkled brow, he motioned with his hand to continue.

"After the mess with your last girlfriend, I thought you should know. She bought several pregnancy tests."

For a moment, Sean didn't really comprehend, but realization dawned slowly, and he stood straight. "You're sure?" he asked in a stony voice.

"Yes, I went to that exact spot to make sure. I was going to catch up and tease her a bit about having trouble choosing toothpaste or whatever, but then I saw what she was purchasing. Sean, I'm so sorry to have to tell you this. Was I right to tell you?" She was wringing her hands together in obvious discomfort with the topic, and her blush remained as bright as a flower.

Reaching over to lay a hand on hers, Sean forced a smile when he responded, "You were absolutely right to tell me. You've got my back and are my extra set of eyes when I need them. Don't worry about it. I'll deal with Anderson later. Let's get a head start on the day and the rest of the week."

Maureen visibly relaxed, and a genuine smile broke through. "Let's go then."

///

"Brother, you seem distracted. Is this not a good time for us to be here? We can take off if you prefer." Frances Catherine mentions casually as she eyes her brother over a glass of water. "You've barely said three words since we got back from our appointment."

258

"What?" Sean says, looking up. His mind was definitely on the news Maureen shared with him earlier. "No, I'm sorry. It's a fine time for you and Simon to visit."

"Then explain what's got you so far away?"

"Franny, let you brother alone. He's probably trying to wind down after a crazy week. You know how much the man works. Makes the rest of us look like lazy fat arses." Simon claps Sean on the back as he passes him, headed to where his wife is sitting on the patio. He detours as he hears the doorbell and an excited barking Rab. "I'll just go answer that since I'm up and about."

Moments later, a laughing Simon ushers in a smiling Anderson who is carrying a bottle of wine and a stunning bouquet of flowers. She looks amazing and so happy. Sean's temper immediately begins to simmer. She doesn't look like she's got a care in the world, which is at odds with someone who may be unexpectedly pregnant. Rising, he goes to where she is standing and still talking to Simon.

Sean takes the bottle of wine she offers and sarcastically says, "This is ironic."

"Good evening to you, too, Sean." With a raised brow at the unusual greeting, I turn to Sean's sister to introduce herself. "Hi, my name is Andi. I've got to tell you, your husband is already one of my favorite people, and I've only just met him."

Frances Catherine takes the offered hand, smiles at me, but shoots her brother a quizzical glance. "It's a pleasure to meet you, Andi. I'm Frances Catherine, but no one but my mum calls me that. Please call me Franny."

Releasing Andi's hand, she gestures to Simon and says, "As for that one, I'm partial to him, myself."

"I brought these flowers for you." I say as I hand the flowers to Franny, "I thought having some fresh flowers this week might help get past the gloomy forecast."

"They're lovely and very thoughtful. I must say, I love your accent. Sean said you grew up in Atlanta, Georgia, is that right?"

"Yes, I'm a Georgia native. I don't think I have an accent, but I'm outnumbered here. To me, your lovely accent is much nicer than mine."

Moving into the kitchen, Franny starts opening cabinets, looking for a suitable vase for the flowers, and Simon heads for the corkscrew to open the bottle Shiraz Andi brought. He opened the bottle expertly and set it out on the counter to breathe while helping Franny unwrap the flowers. All the while, Sean was noticeably silent, his expression as cloudy and stormy as the skies outside.

Franny continued the conversation with Andi, "Your speech is so smooth and rich with a touch of slowness. It's fascinating to a crisp, clipped British English speaker."

"That's a lovely description and makes me proud to be a Southerner." I glance over at Sean and give him a questioning brow raise. He's never been this quiet around me.

The doorbell rang unexpectedly, setting off a fit of barking from Rab. Sean muttered, "I'll get that."

Franny rolled her eyes and gave a laugh. "My brother has a stick up his bum tonight. No idea what, but he's in ill humor for sure."

"I noticed that. He's not normally so quiet."

Sean rejoins the group with several large insulated bags. Moving to the island, he begins unpacking what is obviously dinner for the four of them. Simon poured three glasses of the shiraz, handing one to Andi first.

"Do you think that's a good idea, Anderson?" Sean spoke in a clipped, controlled voice.

Wrinkling my forehead, I took the glass, thanked Simon and looked at Sean with a tilt of my head. "Why would this be a bad idea?

I took an Uber here and plan to take an Uber back to the flat, so it's not like I'm driving."

Sean reaches out and takes the wine glass, dumping the contents in the sink and clinks the glass down with more force than is necessary. "You'll have the flavored fizzy water you like; it's better for you, considering."

I am baffled at this point and really feel like I'm missing something important. "Ummm, ok. You're acting a bit testy tonight. Is everything ok?"

"Testy? That's rich. Is that how you plan to bring it up in conversation?" His tone has gone from clipped to cold and angry, which has been noticed by everyone.

I've never seen Sean act like this. The coldness in his eyes and his tone have my heart pounding and something akin to fear running through my veins. What is going on? Glancing at his sister and brother-in-law, I see matching expressions of surprise and bewilderment.

"Sean, what on earth is going on? I've obviously done something ditto annoy you. Care to enlighten me on what exactly that is?" I ask as I reach for the wine glass he just emptied and grab the bottle to refill it. Just as I go to take a drink, his words stop me cold.

"Should a pregnant woman drink wine, do you think?" the coldness in his voice radiates through me.

"Um, I imagine that would depend on the woman, the pregnancy and what her doctor recommends," I say with a shrug. Taking a sip, I look over the rim at him.

"Really? That's all you have to say? What does your doctor say? You live with her, so getting her opinion should be pretty easily available."

My expression must show my complete and utter confusion at the subject because he makes a frustrated sound, runs his hands through his hair and says, "How about this, will I be a good father, do you think?"

"What in the world are you talking about? I'm sure you will be if and when that day comes."

"When will it come, Anderson? I think I have a right to know."

At this point, his words and tone are starting to piss me off. "How the ever-loving hell do I know?"

"What did the bloody test result say, Andi? Positive or negative? Yes or no? God, I thought you were different."

Realization hit me like a glass of frigid water in the face. I blinked at him and stared for several seconds before I started laughing. The laugh is not one of humor but one of sheer, utter disbelief. Taking a gulp of the wine, I put the glass down, walk over to him and say, "Is that what this mood and shitty display is about? A pregnancy test, which, by the way, was not for me. I repeat it was not for me. Really mature way to discuss the possibility, Sean. Thanks for humiliating me in front of your family."

I brush past him, smiling tightly at Franny and Simon, "It was lovely to meet both of you, but I've reached my limit of being humiliated, so I'll be going." I continue into the foyer, where I grab my coat, bend down to pet Rab, who follows me and then walk out the front door and down the drive. My anger is growing in equal measure with my embarrassment. I just met his sister, and he's already making me sound like a tramp setting out to trap him—so much for communication and trust.

Long legs come in handy at moments like this because they carry you away at a brisk pace, putting nearly a mile between myself and Sean's house. The whole horrible scene replays over and over as I walk faster and faster. I reach the small restaurant that Sean and I have eaten at several times. I sit on the bench outside as I pull up the Uber app and request a car.

"Fucking idiot. Bat blind moron. Egotistical jackass." I'm muttering to myself as several couples walk by, obviously hearing me. I look and sound ridiculous, and I don't even care. I'm oblivious to my surroundings as I wait for my driver.

My phone pings with a text message from Sean. I don't even bother to read it. Seconds later, my phone rings, it's Sean. I declined the call. Another two calls and one more text before my Uber driver arrived. As I buckle in the car, I turn my phone off completely. I'm starting to slide into the hurt portion of this evening's emotional shitstorm. All I want to do is get back to the flat sooner rather than later.

Chapter 35

"You're a fecking idiot, you know that, right?" Franny said that while Andi was walking away from Sean's house. "You just opened your mouth and swallowed your entire damn leg, brother."

"Look at it this way, Fran; when he messes up, he does it epically," Simon says as he shakes his head, running his hand down the back of his neck.

Hands braced on the granite, Sean lifts his head and stares at his family. He's only just beginning to process how big of a fuck up he's made of things. He barely had time to process the idea of Andi being pregnant before he was faced with seeing her. He didn't think before he lashed out, and now that his mind is starting to function properly again, he's too late to stop the damage he's already done.

"I need to go get her and explain why I got so freaked out."

"Not a good idea, boy-o." Simon said. "That woman would as soon cut off your balls as look at you based on her expression as she left. I'd let her cool down before you see her. You're too pretty to be mangled."

"Call her, you git. I agree with Simon; you can't go after her now. There would be bloodshed."

I had calmed considerably on the Uber ride to my flat. I was still a bit angry, and my cheeks burned every time I thought of how I sounded to Sean's sister and brother-in-law. This was a side of Sean I've never seen and, frankly, didn't see it coming. Compared to my brisk stride leaving his house, I slowly walked up the stairs to my door. My thoughts swirling and spinning like a hurricane angrily churning off the coast. I walked in, turned to lock the door and leaned my head against it. Completely unaware I was not alone in the room, I stayed there for a moment, trying to settle my thoughts.

"Andi, hon, what's wrong? You look like you're trying to do complex trigonometry in your head while enduring water torture."

I sigh heavily and turn to see Jess sitting on Charlie's lap. Seeing his arms wrapped around her so securely makes me pause and brings a small smile to my lips. All is well on that front, at least. I didn't respond as I took my coat off and hung it on the hall tree near the door. Unwinding my scarf, I carefully hang it up before dropping my purse on the dinette.

"Anderson, you're startin' to scare me. What on Earth is wrong?"

"I'm trying to figure out where to start or even how to start. I'm not entirely sure what happened, but happened it did, and it was ugly."

"Did you and Sean have a fight?"

"I guess you could call it that. A fight typically means two people have the same information, but, in this case, I was in the dark." I sit in the armchair and share as much as I can remember of the disaster at Sean's place.

"Holy shit, how in the world did he find out about you buying me those tests?"

"Your guess is as good as mine. I'm guessing someone saw me and told him. If he'd seen me, I don't think he would have waited to confront me. It's all so surreal. We've only been together a few times, and we were both using contraceptives, so the likelihood is almost zero."

Charlie cleared his throat and looked uncomfortable enough that both Jess and I picked up on it. Jess shifted off his lap to sit next to him and asked him what he knew.

"I'm not at liberty to say, but I believe Sean has a strongly held reason why he reacted the way he did."

"That he's a bat-blind idiot who won't listen to reason and be rational?" I snap with more than a hint of temper.

Charlie winces and says, "I think you should talk to him. Ask him why he reacted that way, and he'll tell you. In all the years I've known him, he's never acted this crazy about a woman."

Rubbing my forehead wearily, feeling like I'm emotionally drained, I sigh again and say, "Well, I'm not talking to him tonight. I'm still too embarrassed and pissed off. I'm going to bed to forget it all."

Jess stands up and hugs me tight, "I'll bet he's here eating crow for breakfast first thing tomorrow."

I shake my head and walk to the bedroom. "Goodnight, Charlie, Jess. I'm sorry I barged in on your evening alone."

I was just getting out of the shower less than thirty minutes later when Jess pounded on the door. Wrapped in a towel with my hair dripping all over my shoulders, I open the door, expecting her to tell me Sean is in our tiny living room. Instead, she shoves her phone at me with wide eyes.

"It's Gretchen. There's an emergency."

I take the phone, "Gretchen, tell me."

Gretchen gives me the rundown of the severe storms that have littered the South with tornadoes and the meteorologist's forecast for at least two more days of similar weather patterns. The rescue agency I work with called her to ask about available help and Paws & Claws' availability to take animals. She told me both she and R^3 tried calling me, but went to voicemail.

"I'm at least 8 hours away, but I'll be there as soon as I can. I need to book a ticket…" pausing as Gretchen told me she was online now booking me a flight. "Ok, I'll leave here in 20 minutes. That should leave me plenty of time to get to the airport. I'll text you when I get off the plane. Call Tyler at R^3 and tell him I'll be ready to leave as soon we get to Paws & Claws."

Hanging up, I handed the phone back to Jess as I moved into the bedroom to grab jeans and a T-shirt. I reached under my bed for the smallest roller I had and started throwing some clothes and underwear in it while I heard Jess in the bathroom packing my toiletries. I braided my hair, grabbed my purse, jacket and phone charger, then headed out the door to the airport. Charlie was kind enough to drive me the half hour to the airport. I turned my phone back on as I buckled into Charlie's truck, wincing at the flood of incoming texts and missed calls. Ignoring the ones from Sean, I read Tyler and Gretchen's texts and then pulled up the local news app for Atlanta. Just seeing the first photos of the devastation made my stomach clench. Closing out the app, I looked out the window into the darkness and struggled to curb my impatience. I have a six-hour flight back to New York and then another 2 hours to Atlanta.

"Can I ask you a question?" Charlie says in his thick Scottish burr.

"Sure."

"You're across an ocean. Are there no other animal doctors who can help? It just seems like you'll arrive after the need has passed."

"Charlie, have you ever seen the aftermath of a tornado?"

"No. I've seen some pictures on the telly but never first-hand."

"I pray you never do. These types of storms leave complete chaos and destruction in their wake, and it is often years before these areas return to normal. I work with a non-profit called R3, which stands for Rescue, Reunite and Rebuild. We are basically first responders for animals after storms like these. We have a network of vets, shelters, etc., that we can transport rescued animals to who will coordinate their care. It's often weeks later when we can reunite them with their families. There are some cases where we have to rehome animals as well, but thankfully, those are few and far between. We also help the families rebuild their animal enclosures if necessary. The most critical time is right after these storms hit. The first 72 hours require as many hands as possible."

"Well, I hope you get there safely. Call us if there is anything we can do from here." Charlie pulls up to the departure area of the airport and gets out to open my door.

I hug him tightly, "Thanks, Charlie. You take care of Jessica for me, ok?"

Charlie gives me a big grin and assures me he will attend directly to that task.

The flight over the Atlantic is long. Extremely long when you are someone like me who does not sleep on planes. I usually work or read during flights, but this one is late at night based on when we left Scotland. The cabin is dark and comfortably cool, and the low hum of the engines seems to lend itself to sleep for almost all on board.

For me, it's a time of reflection and introspection. I spent a lot of time replaying what happened with Sean. What did I miss? How had our friendship not meant enough to him to talk to me privately? He's never acted like that before, almost bitter in his anger. I read his text messages, but they only asked me to call him back. I know I won't have the time we both need to unpack this mess when I'm heading into a literal disaster zone, and I would prefer to do it face-to-face. I opt to text him, which may seem the coward's way out, but right now, I'm too raw and have to focus on the situation before me.

> *I need some time to sort through things before*
> *we reconnect and talk about what happened.*

I know the text won't be sent until I'm back on the ground in New York, but writing it out gives me a small measure of peace and lets me dive into what is really bothering me. Am I making a mistake by allowing myself to get so close to Sean? This is the first time I've felt this way in a very long time, and I thought my feelings meant I was ready to move on, but what if I'm not? What if I'm rushing into this…whatever it is…a crazy hook-up? Friends with benefits? Casual relationship? I don't even know. Maybe this time away dealing with the tornado aftermath will be the space I need to figure out my next steps.

My time with Justin was so calm and comfortable. It was like being surrounded by a soft, warm blanket of security and stability. We seemed to understand each other from the first moment we met. He always made me feel safe. We had a lot of great times and many adventures when we were together, but we were apart more than we were together.

Am I looking back on my time with Justin with rose-colored glasses? There were few major disagreements and never coldness and icy disdain as I experienced tonight from Sean. Justin and I would argue, but we openly communicated with each other and talked through any disagreements. I know I shouldn't compare Justin and Sean, but how can I not? I don't have a deep well of expertise with men and relationships. Jessica is right; I am very green when it comes to being part of a couple.

Have I romanticized my time with Justin because I lost him? Am I overreacting to this situation in the same way Sean overreacted? In my head, I know Sean isn't a cold person, nor is he someone who strikes out in anger without just cause, but what could that cause be? Why wouldn't he talk to me before assuming I was hiding something from him? How would I feel if I found out he was potentially hiding something life-altering from me?

Rubbing my temples, I try to ease the headache that has taken root at the base of my skull and is slowly wrapping around my eyes. I'm thinking so much and going in circles. I need to distract myself, so I decide to listen to Michael Bublé on my phone. I have always enjoyed his music, and his ballads always soothe me. I close my eyes briefly, losing myself to my playlist, which calms my mind enough to let me drift into sleep.

///

A knock sounded at the door. Soft but with purpose. Walking to the door, Jessica looked out the peephole to see the distinctive form of Sean Miller standing at the threshold. Shaking her head, Jessica opened the door.

"She's not here."

Looking weary and a tiny bit wild, he grips the door frame and says, "Will you tell me where she is so I can talk to her? I know she told you how much of an asshole I was yesterday."

"Will I? Probably not. Can I? I could, but probably not." Jessica starts to shut the door when she hears Sean sigh.

"Please, Jess. I'll beg if you want me to. I need to see her and fix this before it's beyond repair. I know I fucked up. I know she didn't deserve the pile of shit I dumped on her. My sister and brother-in-law made me see just how much of a wanker I was to her. Please." Reaching out, he gently grips her arm. "Please. She means so much to me, and I need to fix what I fucked up."

Jessica softens at the genuine sorrow she sees in his eyes. His entire demeanor is dejected and just a bit desperate. This man knows how badly he messed up, and Jessica knows how much Andi has started to care for him, regardless of her assertion that they are just friends. "She's not here, Sean. She's on a plane to Atlanta."